THE LAST PRINCESS

ALSO BY
SHELLEY WILSON

The Phantom's Curse
Hood Academy

The Guardians Series

Guardians of the Dead
Book 1

Guardians of the Sky
Book 2

Guardians of the Lost Lands
Book 3

THE LAST PRINCESS

SHELLEY WILSON

Livonia, Michigan

Edited by Jamie Rich
Proofread by Hannah Ryder

THE LAST PRINCESS
Copyright © 2022 Shelley Wilson

Published by BHC Press

Library of Congress Control Number:
2020940649

ISBN: 978-1-64397-248-0 (Hardcover)
ISBN: 978-1-64397-249-7 (Softcover)
ISBN: 978-1-64397-250-3 (Ebook)

For information, write:
BHC Press
885 Penniman #5505
Plymouth, MI 48170

Visit the publisher:
www.bhcpress.com

For every young shield-maiden.

HISTORICAL NOTE

Although I've used historical figures and authentic names, phrases, and places, such as Bamburgh and Hedeby, which played their part in the Viking Age, the story and characters are entirely fictional. For ease of reading, I've opted to use the modern names of places rather than their medieval terms (for example, Hedeby instead of Haithabu and York instead of Eoferwic). I also use the word "Viking" throughout the novel, which was the term adopted by the Christian priests who wrote about their invasions and is what we are all familiar with today.

≫

GLOSSARY

Brullaup—A wedding game where the bride's family races the groom's family.

Churl—A churl refers to a man; however, in Anglo-Saxon England, it represented a peasant. Churls worked on the thane's land and looked after the animals.

Elderman—A high-ranking member of the king's council.

Freya—The pagan goddess of fertility.

Gothi—A chieftain (a pagan priest).

Jarl—A Viking ruler with land. Men swore fealty to them.

Odin—The high god of the pagans.

Thane—One who owned land granted by the king.

Witan—A council tasked with advising the king on all matters that concerned him, such as new laws, grants for churches, and how to deal with rebels.

THE LAST PRINCESS

'Better to fight and fall than
to live without hope.'

Volsunga Saga, Ch 12

PROLOGUE

Hundreds of bodies littered the grassland as their lifeblood soaked into the earth. Warriors in mid–battle cry lay facedown in muddy puddles, still clinging to their axe and shield, and the sound of conflict floated across the grey English sky like one of the king's banners.

In the eyes of the great warriors who had travelled across the sea, the king's army was outnumbered and weak. These foreigners didn't shy away from war; they embraced it with determination and passion.

Like a plague, they swept across all England taking what they wanted, killing, and plundering. Nobody was safe from their wrath. Kings and peasants were treated as equals as these warriors from the North defiled the land.

High up on the hilltop, a man sat on his horse watching the battle unfold. His eyes scanned the valley as he witnessed soldier after soldier cut down by the vicious army that advanced on his home. He'd sent all his best men to their deaths. No amount of manipulation, silver, or corruption could stop this curse upon his land.

The crown on his head weighed heavy as he glanced first left then right at the remainder of his army. Young men who stood on the brink of annihilation. The king knew all was lost, he knew the great warriors would never stop, and he knew why.

Deep within the battlefield, at the heart of the fighting, he had seen her. A sword in her hand, blood smeared across her tunic, and war paint decorating her face. It had been many moons, but he would have recognised her anywhere.

The end of their story was playing out in front of them, but the king wasn't quite ready to give up just yet. Failure had never been an option.

He sat a little straighter in his saddle and addressed the young army at his side.

'To the death!' he cried.

NORTHUMBRIA, ENGLAND
AD 866

'It's too far for them to travel without us,' my mother protested. There weren't many women who could admonish their king and get away with it, but Mother wasn't your usual woman. She was strong and capable, an equal match to my father's bravery and flair.

'Nonsense. Kings have been sending their children on pilgrimages for years without issue.'

'The girls aren't on a pilgrimage though, are they, my love? They're simply parading themselves for the good of our kingdom in the hope of snaring a suitable husband.'

Father dismissed her comment with a wave of his hand and snatched up his goblet of mead, draining the contents in one gigantic gulp. He threw his arm out and a servant jumped to attention, immediately filling the empty vessel.

'We'll be all right, Mother,' I said in a bid to quiet the unrest etched into the queen's brow. 'We've got Edmund and lots of soldiers with us.'

A trusted friend of my father's, Edmund was an elderman, and it landed on his shoulders to serve the king in any capacity. At the moment, it was my father's wish to send his three daughters across Northumbria on a "husband-grabbing rampage"—Mother's words.

'I'd feel much happier if one of us were accompanying them, that's all.'

My father rose from his elaborate throne and approached his wife, tucking a loose curl of her hair beneath her veil and kissing her gently on the forehead. My sisters always looked away when our parents were loving, but the exchange fascinated me. I hoped that our husband-grabbing rampage bore me a spouse as loyal, and handsome, as my father.

Although marriage at a young age wasn't what I'd hoped for myself, I understood the commitment we, as heirs to the crown, needed to make to secure the future of our realm. At seventeen, I should have been wed long ago, but Father had grumbled over every suitor who stepped through the doors of Bamburgh fortress and into his court. It was at Mother's insistence that we now embraced the task ahead.

'They're good girls, strong-willed like their mother.' Father chuckled and cupped Mother's chin in his hand, raising her head so they were looking into each other's eyes. 'They have Edmund and my best guard, but I doubt they'll need them. I saw Edith practising with a sword when she didn't know I was watching.'

Father winked at me as Mother rolled her eyes in dismay.

'When will you start to act like a lady, Edith?'

I shrugged and tried to look suitably mortified for my mother's sake, but I was elated that my father, the king of Northumbria, thought my skills with a sword were enough to keep us safe on the road. My private lessons with Edmund were paying off.

'Go. All of you, gather your things as you leave at first light.'

My sisters and I shot off in all directions, excited to get back to our chambers and start packing. As the eldest daughter, I could take the largest luggage chest, which meant at least two good dresses for the journey, whereas my siblings would have to entertain suitors in the same old dress. I could have cut back on the lavish jewels and slippers and let them pack more, but I wasn't that nice when it came to my sisters.

Being only two years apart in age from one another, my sisters had bonded so much that it was difficult for anyone to break through into their confidence. I'd tried over and over as they were growing up, but they always saw me as the older sister, able to come and go as she pleased. Over time it was easier to ignore, tease, or annoy them as I saw fit, something my father found amusing but our mother discouraged at every opportunity.

'Try to act like a princess, Edith,' she would tell me when I'd hidden their slippers or put a spider in their bed. *'One day you will be a queen, and a queen doesn't drop a leech into her siblings' bathwater.'*

It was unheard of for a daughter to succeed as heir, but as our father had only produced girls, it rested at my feet to take up the mantle of queen should something catastrophic happen to the king.

Father had spoken to me at length about it only recently, calling me into his private study, which contained hundreds of scrolls—or lessons, as Father liked to call them. He showed me a map of the kingdom and where our boundary lines met with Mercia, the centre of England.

'One day all this will belong to you, my daughter.'

I'd traced my finger along the map, outlining Northumbria from east coast to west, a sense of pride and passion rising through me. Losing my father was not something I wanted to contemplate—he was an amazing man and an even better king—but the thought of ruling our beautiful land was too tempting to push those wicked thoughts from my mind.

'I thought only sons could rule, Father.'

'Nonsense. If I will it, which I do, then you will succeed me when I die.'

'But the eldermen might object.'

'They wouldn't dare defy the ruling of their king.' The power in his voice thundered around the small room, and I knew he was right. Nobody would have the strength of character to argue with him, apart from my uncle.

Being the king's only brother, Aelle didn't cower like the other eldermen. He stood up to my father and tested him. Although Father always bellowed his dissatisfaction at being challenged in his court, I knew he secretly enjoyed sparring with his younger brother. They had a similar relationship to me and my sisters—they loved each other one minute and wanted to bury each other in the vegetable garden the next.

'What will your first act be when you become queen, Edith?'

I'd pondered his question for a moment as I studied the map on the table.

'I'd invade Mercia, then Wessex, and become queen of all England.'

He roared with laughter and swept me into a warm embrace that only a father can give.

'That's my girl,' he said. 'A warrior queen.'

❧

Edmund was waiting for us in the courtyard, dressed in his finest woollen tunic and riding cloak and receiving last-minute instructions from the king. Our mother sat on one of the carved wooden chairs that she and my father had received as a gift from the king of Wessex. Keeping up alliances with the neighbouring kings was all about lavish gifts, arranged marriages, and bloody battles—or so I was told.

'Here they are,' the king announced for everyone to hear. 'My beautiful daughters.'

I led the way with my chin high and my shoulders back, just like my father taught me. *A queen glides,*' he'd told me once, and I'd spent the next week practising my regal walk through the corridors of Bamburgh and out in the gardens. My younger siblings had giggled at me as I paraded through our home, but now, gliding toward the carriage to the cheers of our townsfolk, I felt more alive than ever.

My sisters climbed up into the carriage and proceeded to wave at the crowds who had gathered to see us off on our quest. It was beneficial to our kingdom for at least one of us to secure a marriage, as it meant acquiring much-needed funds, which would be passed along to build homes, provide farming equipment, and secure grain for the winter months. At fourteen and twelve, my sisters weren't as invested in our trip as our father desired, so it fell to me, as the eldest, to try to pacify our kingdom.

The townsfolk wanted our husband-grabbing mission to be fruitful even if Mother had her doubts about us going on this journey.

I studied her now and marvelled at how she could look so effortlessly beautiful. Her long dark hair was hidden beneath her veil—a purple velvet headdress that covered her head and draped around her shoulders. Her matching purple dress was edged in silver, which shimmered in the early morning sunshine. She sat on the wooden throne with her back straight and her chin high, smiling at anyone who called her name.

The people loved Queen Eadgifu, and I hoped that one day I would be just as loved, and just as impressive. Women struggled to be heard above the domineering presence of Anglo-Saxon men, but not my mother. When she spoke, everyone listened, and that made me swell with pride.

She caught my eye and gave me a warm smile. I knew she was concerned about us travelling across the kingdom without her or our father to chaperone, and I wanted so much to show her that I could look after myself, and my sisters. For me, this trip wasn't just about enticing a wealthy husband, it was about proving myself to the kingdom—and myself.

I gave my mother a small wave before moving off to find my horse. Edmund held the reins for me as I swung my leg up and over my mount. Mother had wanted me to ride in the carriage with Cynethryth and Ealhswith, but I knew if I had to listen to their whining and complaining about the bumpy road, their empty stomachs, or the length of time our journey was taking, I'd probably throw one of them out of the carriage window. It was safer for them and my own sanity if I followed them on horseback.

From a selfish point of view, it meant I could talk to Edmund uninterrupted, and I loved chatting with my father's elderman about politics, fighting strategies, and how the kingdoms fared. He never treated me like a child, or a weak-minded woman, and always engaged in debates with me. No doubt my father had a hand in making sure he never held back when I became inquisitive. Ever since I could talk, I'd bombarded Edmund with question after question and not once had he refrained from answering. He was honest with me, often brutally, but it helped me to shape my opinions and become a better person. As the heir of Northumbria, I needed to know who to trust, and Edmund was not only my father's number one, he was mine.

'Are you comfortable, Princess?' Edmund trotted up next to me as our procession prepared to leave.

'Yes, thank you, Edmund. I'm eager to get going.' I grinned up into his wise face, and the creases around his eyes deepened as he smiled back at me. He knew how much I loved being out in the wilderness and not confined to our home and the barricades that bordered our town. It was a necessary evil these days to enclose ourselves within high wooden walls with armed guards. Once upon a time, the threats to our home and kingdom had come from our neighbours in Mercia and Wessex, but for the past few decades, our lands had been plundered by another evil that swept across the land—Vikings.

I'd heard about their raids from travelling merchants and listened with morbid fascination to the stories of horrific massacres, vicious attacks, and looting. The invaders were ruthless warriors from the North who didn't stop to ask questions but simply wiped out entire villages and towns. The complete destruction of Lindisfarne and the murder of the holy men who resided within its walls was spoken of often within my father's court. It was only a matter of time before the Vikings attacked Bamburgh and our soldiers were forced to defend our home and realm.

We had been fortunate so far that our home had remained untouched. Bamburgh Fortress was an imposing structure built high atop volcanic rock, which guaranteed that our enemies gave serious consideration before invading, but my father was under no illusion that the peace would last. He had taken to stepping in with his generals and training with the army, proud to stand shoulder to shoulder with his men should the Vikings show themselves on our land.

Edmund had been secretly teaching me how to use my sword in defence, although I was beginning to realise that my father must have asked him to train me without alerting my mother. I enjoyed these sessions more than my needlework and reading classes. Sparring with Edmund was the highlight of my week, and I felt alive inside when I had a sword in my hand.

Mother would have turned green if she'd ever seen me wielding that sword, or if she'd noticed the bruises and grazes I'd covered up when I failed to protect my left flank or duck when Edmund swung the butt of his sword at me.

I chuckled at the thought.

'What's so funny?' Edmund asked as we set off on the slow trot toward the open gate.

'Just remembering when I managed to disarm you the other day, my old friend. It was a memorable moment for me.'

He straightened his back and shook his head, feigning embarrassment. 'I remember letting you win,' he said with a sly smile.

'You keep deluding yourself.' I laughed.

The king was waiting by the gate as our convoy moved forward. He caught hold of the reins of my horse and pulled me off to the side, allowing the rest of the guard to pass by.

'Take care of your sisters, Edith. Make sure they behave, and do what you need to do to keep them in check.'

I grinned, and he wagged his big finger at me.

'Without using violence or locking them up in small spaces,' he added.

'I will, Father.'

He studied me for a long moment before reaching up and enfolding me in his embrace.

'I love you so much, my daughter, and I hope you find what you seek.'

Tears sprang up in the corners of my eyes, and I blinked them away. Finding what I wanted outside of Bamburgh would be difficult, as I'd spent my entire life within the walls of this fortress. There was nothing out there in the world that I wanted more than my home and family around me.

'We'll be back soon, Father. Should only take me a couple of weeks to find a suitable husband and whip him into shape.'

His shoulders heaved as he laughed at my words. 'Oh, I've no doubt that the man you choose will be strong-willed and fierce, Edith. Just like you.'

I hugged him again and buried my face into his fur cloak, inhaling the musky scent of the one man I could never replace. My father was my world, and although this mission was all about finding a suitable match, I had no idea how I would ever find anyone who could live up to my father.

'Take care, Edith. Be watchful, be wise, be wary.'

I kicked the horse and moved off after the departing party. Be watchful, be wise, be wary. He had been saying that phrase to me all my life and yet it felt like I was hearing it for the first time.

I waved farewell to the gathered crowds as we passed through the gate and rode out across the rocky plateau high above the coastline. It was going to be a long few weeks without the loving support of my parents, but with Edmund by my side, I knew we would prevail, and hopefully I would show them, and the eldermen, what a suitable queen I could be.

Our procession made good time as we followed the coast road heading toward the Northumbria-Mercia border. There were several suitors making ready for our arrival in Mercia, but I secretly wished we could travel further, on to Wessex, and meet the sons of King Aethelwulf. I'd heard great things about Alfred and would delight in talking politics with such a bright young prince.

If I were being brutally honest, I'd prefer to fall in love the natural way than have it forced upon me because of a royal alliance. I understood it was my duty to the kingdom, and I was fully aware that girls were used as pawns to claim lands and win wars, but it didn't stop me longing for a bit of excitement.

Edmund always told me that my thirst for adventure would get me into trouble, but he never stopped me from sneaking out of our home to go on hunting trips, or from dressing up as a churl so I could go to the village festivals without anyone knowing who I was. If anything, Edmund had taught me a valuable lesson about survival.

We had travelled a fair distance from Bamburgh when a shrill screech filled the late-afternoon air, breaking into my thoughts. The guards at the front of the party swung around to investigate, but as the noise had come from the carriage, we could only begin to imagine what my sisters were doing to cause such a fuss. They may have been princesses in name, but they certainly didn't act like it most of the time.

I held my hand up to signal I had it under control, trotting my horse over to where the wagon had stopped. Edmund encouraged his horse forward so he could talk to the soldiers leading the way. I knew he wanted us to set up camp soon, and I was thankful for that as my stomach growled.

'What's going on?' I demanded, leaning down and pulling back the cloth curtain to peer inside.

Cynethryth's face had drained of all colour as she cowered in a tight ball on the floor of the carriage. It took me far too long to register the blood splatter across her cheek and along the wall. I often had to pull them apart when they started wrenching each other's hair, but this didn't feel like one of those moments.

I twisted my angle and examined the near side of the wagon, expecting to see our youngest sister in floods of tears; instead, she was deathly silent with an arrow protruding from her throat where it pinned her to the side of the carriage. Blood trickled from her small, perfectly formed mouth, and her lifeless eyes stared out of the window and across the tall grasses edging the road.

'Edmund!' I spun away from the scene, choking down my tears and the bile that rose up the back of my throat. 'We're under attack.'

2

Edmund whirled around, a deep frown lining his forehead. I knew he couldn't see the carnage inside the carriage, but one look at my face should tell him everything he needed to know.

No sooner had the words left my mouth than a deluge of arrows flew through the air, taking out half of our guards. Our attackers were smart and kept their location hidden within the tall grass and woodland that bordered the main road.

'Come with me.' I reached inside the wagon, holding my hand out to my sister. 'Quickly.'

She turned her pale face up to look at me, and that simple action unlocked the shock she was in. The screaming and sobbing startled me even though I'd seen her in a similar state when her dog died. Comparing our little sister's murder to the death of an animal was clearly not on the same level, but her hysteria was identical. I leaned forward and slapped her hard across the face, shocking her into movement.

'Climb up,' I urged, helping her swing up behind me on my horse. She flung her arms around my waist and clung on, her sobs vibrating through her chest.

I scanned the road for Edmund and saw him break off with a small group of soldiers. They tore across the grassland with their swords drawn. Bloody bodies lay strewn across the road, and riderless horses reared up in alarm. The first of the attackers emerged from their hiding place and engaged with Edmund and his group. The sound of metal on metal filled the air. I felt torn. Part of me wanted to charge after Edmund and kill the men who had murdered Ealhswith, but the sensible me, the one who my father knew would do the right thing, had to get Cynethryth to safety.

With one last lingering look at Edmund, I heaved the horse in the opposite direction and drove him into a gallop. We sped off back down the main road toward Bamburgh. It would be nightfall when we arrived at our destination, and that gave me some time to think about how I was going to break the news of Ealhswith's death to my parents.

'They're coming!' Cynethryth's panicked cry in my ear punctured my thoughts as the sound of hooves on the hard ground surrounded us. The men in the grass had jumped on the stray horses and given chase.

Sweat coated my steed as I pushed him harder and harder to outrun the enemy. Cynethryth's bawling was distracting, and for the briefest of moments I wanted to yell at her to shut up, but I knew it wasn't her fault. None of this was her fault. We were victims of a vicious attack by bandits, and I had to keep my head if I was going to get us out of this.

The first blow landed on my right shoulder as the man tried to knock us from the horse. I twisted us to the left and we thundered into the woods, leaving him behind, but he was replaced by another who slashed out with his sword. The sting of his blade cut into my arm, and I twisted the horse back to the right. Blood soaked my arm and trickled onto the reins, making them slippery to the touch. Tightening my grip on the leather strap, I dug my knees in more firmly to my horse and powered him forward, willing this magnificent beast to help save us from harm.

The bandit lunged forward again, swinging his sword in a wide arc as we rushed past him. My sister's screams bounced off the trees as she slid away from me.

'No, Cyn.' I tried to reach for her, but it all happened so fast. Glancing back, I saw her body fall to the ground, her blood coating the pale blue dress she wore and soaking into the earth. A rider jumped from his horse by her side, nudging her with his foot. She didn't move or cry out. Her dead eyes followed my departure as I pushed ahead.

Why was this happening? I tried to get a good look at the men following me. They didn't look like the Vikings all the merchants were talking about; they were thin and wiry, whereas the invaders were supposed to be as wide as houses, with long blond hair and axes.

Skirmishes had been breaking out across the land as more and more churls became disgruntled with their lords. The thanes were supposed to support their workers, but some had begun to grasp for titles and land at the expense of their village. Were these men discontented farm labourers? It didn't seem that way. They were heavily armed and knew how to use a sword and bow. My chest tightened. I was up against pirates.

I had two options ahead of me—die or become a slave. Neither appealed to me, so I chose to carve out a third option, which would mean my survival. At least that way I could avenge the death of my sisters.

I wiped at my face as the sweat dripped into my eyes. My headdress had come loose and trailed behind me like a flag, and there was blood coating my left arm, mixed with Cynethryth's from when she was cut down. What a frightening sight I must have been. As I spotted a way through the woods back to the main road, one of the attackers caught hold of my headdress and pulled.

I barrelled off the back of my horse and slammed into the compacted earth, knocking the wind out of me. Everything hurt, and I struggled to inhale as the impact consumed my body. It took me a few moments to gather my thoughts and start breathing normally again, but by the time I was ready to act, the men had surrounded me.

'Got a fighter 'ere,' said a toothless man with a scar along his arm.

'She'll be worth a fair bit o' silver,' said another with a dirty rag tied around his forehead like a headband. 'Her hair's unbound too, so she's not been claimed by a husband yet.'

A third man stepped forward and appraised me. 'She's too headstrong for a slave. I doubt I could even sell her to the Vikings.'

The three men laughed at his words as I sat dazed on the floor. I'd tucked my sword into a leather carrier attached to my horse, which was probably halfway home by now.

I lifted my chin and awaited sentence. If they thought they were going to take me, Princess Edith of Northumbria, quietly, then they were mistaken.

The third man drew his sword from its sheath and handed it to the toothless man by his side.

'Kill her.'

I scrambled to my feet and readied myself for a fight, clenching my fists and holding them out like I'd seen the soldiers do in training. The men watched me with bemused expressions dancing across their dirty faces.

'Aw, she thinks she can fight us off.'

'Maybe we should let her try.'

'Yeah, maybe we should. It'll be fun.'

The leader of the three men took his sword back and stepped toward me.

'We're wasting time. She needs to die so we can finish this.'

'Aw, there's plenty of 'em attacking the fortress. They won't miss us.'

My heart lurched at the mention of Bamburgh. I'd ridden hard and fast and knew the nearest place they spoke of had to be my home. Was my father under attack from these pirates too?

'I have jewellery,' I said, thinking of ways to delay my death and find out more about the attacks. 'You can have it if you let me go.'

Toothless grabbed at my wrist and eyed the silver bracelet littered with engravings. My mother had given it to me as a gift after she returned from a trip to Wessex. According to my father, the king of Wessex had taken a shine to our mother and furnished her with a chest of jewels and silk, much to my father's amusement. *She could get any man to part with his last coin,* my father had told me, pride shining in his eyes.

Toothless and Headband pulled at my arm as they toyed with my bracelet.

'What else you got?'

I dragged the amulet from around my neck, another gift from my mother, who had acquired it from a foreign merchant. The amber stone glinted in the sun as I held it out for my captors to look at.

'I've got more, but it's in a leather pouch on my horse. I can take you to him. Then the treasure is all yours.'

Greed flashed across their faces. It was a look I recognised from sitting in my father's court when thieves were brought in for trial. Their spoils would be displayed at the king's feet, and without fail, the accused wouldn't be able to tear their gaze from the silver and jewels.

'*Classic sign of guilt,*' my father had told me once. '*If you come across a drooling churl, then you're justified in cutting off his thieving hands.*'

Toothless snatched at the amulet as Headband tugged the bracelet from my arm.

'I'd say this was a good day's work,' said Toothless, slipping the chain over his dirty head. 'You can go on yer way.'

I blinked. Could it really be that easy?

I edged away from them, not wanting to make sudden movements that might make them change their minds. I'd only taken four steps when I bumped into the third pirate, who was standing behind me.

'You think we're going to let you go?' he said.

He towered over me with his chest to my back, but in my peripheral vision, I saw his sword drawn and primed to my right.

The time had come to fight or die, perhaps both, but I wasn't going to disappoint my father or Edmund by making it easy for these villains.

I stomped my heel down on the pirate's foot as hard as I could, and he yelped and stumbled backwards. Kicking out with my leg, I hit his arm, making him drop his sword, which I scrambled to collect.

The pirate roared and launched himself at me, but I steadied my stance, and, using his forward momentum against him, I drove the sword into his belly. He gave a surprised gurgle, dropping to the ground with blood bubbling out of his mouth.

Toothless cried out in anger and pitched forward, pulling a dagger from his belt. I passed the sword into my left hand and swung in a wide arc, slicing through his throat as he advanced.

'Two down,' I said as Headband flung my bracelet on the ground and drew his sword. 'One to go.'

We circled one another in the clearing, our eyes connecting us across the moss-covered floor. My hands were shaking, and my heart was beating so loudly all I could hear was the rush of my blood as it charged through my veins. Sweat trickled down the man's face from beneath his headband as he crept to the side. I matched his steps, holding his friend's sword out in front of me. Two steps to the left. Two steps to the right. Was he going to dance all day? Somewhere in the distance, I heard horses' hooves and briefly hoped that it was Edmund and not more of the marauding pirates. I had to believe that some of our guards had survived the attack.

'Sounds like your time has run out,' I said, silently praying that it was indeed Edmund. 'Tell me why you attacked us and I'll let you live.'

Headband sneered at me, but I didn't miss his sidelong glance into the woods. He was plainly as clueless as I was about who was thundering toward us.

'Nowt to tell. We got our orders, and we carried 'em out.'

'Orders from who?'

'Dunno. We weren't privy to the elderman's conversation.'

'An elderman hired you to kill us?'

He grinned at me, showing his blackened teeth. 'You got a traitor in your house, miss.'

Who? If it was an elderman who had hired these thugs to murder the king's daughters and attack the king himself, then the plot ran deep. It was no easy task to usurp a throne. Who wanted the crown badly enough that they'd slaughter innocent people?

'Go!' I shouted. 'But remember that I spared your life and you owe me.'

He hesitated for a second and then gave a half bow. I watched him disappear into the trees. I wasn't sure why I'd let him go if I was honest, but part of me believed that if I could show leniency to a pirate, it might make me a better leader in the long term.

I gathered up my bracelet and unhooked the amulet from the dead man's neck as two of my father's guards burst into view. Their tunics were torn and covered in blood, and their faces were pale, but when they saw me, relief washed over them.

'Are you all right, my lady?' The first guard leapt from his horse and ran to my side, visibly checking me over for injuries.

'I'm fine, Baldred, not all of it is my blood.' I remembered my sister's body out on the road and swallowed down the tears. 'Cynethryth and Ealhswith are dead.'

'Yes, my lady, we recovered Cynethryth's body,' he said. 'Edmund has her.'

My heart soared at the mention of my friend and mentor. 'Edmund's alive?'

'He is, my lady. It was a tough fight, and we sustained many losses, but a few of us survived.'

Relief flooded through me at his words. After hearing about the attack on the fortress, I didn't know what we would find upon returning home, and I needed my friend with me.

Baldred shared his horse with me as we left the woodland and made our way back to the main road. His companion rounded up a few of the riderless horses on our way to meet up with the depleted convoy. My heart broke at the bedraggled sight. We'd lost three quarters of our men as well as my sisters. The soldiers had placed the girls carefully within the carriage side by side and were escorting them home with as much honour as they could.

I spotted Edmund near the back of the party and jumped from Baldred's horse to greet him. He limped to my side, scooping me up into a warm embrace.

'You're hurt,' I said, disentangling myself and looking at the tourniquet tied around his thigh.

'Just a flesh wound,' he said, unhooking an empty horse and helping me onto its back.

'Who were those men?' I asked, waiting to hear if he had any further information before telling him what I'd learnt.

'Hired thugs,' he said. 'Baldred secured a prisoner, so we'll get some answers out of him once we're home.'

'What if there's no home to go back to?'

'What do you mean?'

'Three pirates attacked me, and one of them told me an elderman hired them.'

'Are you all right? How did you get away?'

I waved my hand in the air dismissively, as if fighting off assailants was an everyday occurrence. 'I killed two of them, and the third… ran away.' Best not to tell him I let the man go.

'You killed them?'

There was a strange tone to Edmund's voice, and I squinted across to see my friend studying me, pride and fear flashing in his eyes.

'You really are a warrior princess, aren't you?' he said.

I chuckled at his words but squared my shoulders. Killing a man was a sin, but surely dying a horrible death at the hands of pirates allowed me some leniency with our God. Father Bertram, my father's Christian priest, might argue that point with me, but I wasn't exactly going to tell him.

I was certain that my killing spree would remain a secret between Edmund and me so that my mother wouldn't find out. A silent pact between friends.

My thoughts shifted to my parents, and I became anxious to get home. Following the bodies of my sisters as we trundled down the main road wasn't how this journey was meant to turn out. Only a few hours ago, we were contemplating marriage, eager to find suitable husbands, and now they were dead, and I was a murderer.

3

Darkness had taken hold as our exhausted party neared the town, and a sprinkling of stars blanketed the sky, leading us home. In the distance, the warm glow of the torches upon the battlements surrounded the houses and barns, but as my eyes adjusted, I noticed the ferocity of the flames. It wasn't the torches that were burning—it was the houses.

'Edmund!'

'I see it, my lady. Stay with the carriage.'

Edmund tore off ahead of the rest of the party, drawing his sword as he dashed toward Bamburgh. Baldred and a handful of the guard went with him.

I dropped from the back of my horse and led it up to the carriage, which doubled as a funeral cart for my sisters. Never taking my eyes off the orange glow in the night sky, I tied my horse to the carriage and paced back and forth.

My patience wore thin, and I continued up the road in the direction of the fortress.

'We need to stay with the carriage, my lady,' one of the guards called after me with a quiver to his voice.

'It's all right. I just need to see it for myself.'

'Please, my lady, stay with the horses.'

I held my hand up to silence him and progressed a few more steps along the road. Any moment now I would step out of the trees and onto the open expanse of land that rose up to the home where I was born and had grown up, the safest place in the entire world. Until now.

One more step. Two more steps. I crumbled to my knees with an audible sob as I took in the scene that lay ahead of me. Dead bodies littered the slight incline to the wooden fence that circled the town, most of them my father's guard. The gates that we had exited through only that morning stood open, inviting any onlooker to witness the burning buildings within.

From where I sat on the road, I could see the stables ablaze and the horses running wild through the carnage. Edmund stood illuminated against the fiery sky as he barked orders at anyone left alive. Baldred rushed through the gates with a piercing cry, and I flinched at the sound. Swords clashed as some of the pirates tried to flee the scene only to be hacked down by a single brave soldier whose heart was clearly as broken as mine.

Jumping up from the damp earth, I raced back to the carriage and swung myself up onto my horse.

'Follow me,' I snapped. 'We need to help them.'

Our small unit raced over the grassland toward the open gate, the carriage lurching from left to right and the rumble of the ocean below filling the night air. For the briefest of moments, I worried what my sisters might say about being tossed around in the back of the wagon, but then I remembered, and anger fuelled my actions.

'Go left,' I called to the two guards who were riding closest to me, hoping they'd spotted the pirate running for the cover of the trees. Within moments, they'd buried their swords in his back and were turning back toward the gate.

'Fetch water,' I screamed as the rest of us barrelled through the gate and into the courtyard. Everything was on fire no matter which way I turned. The thatched roof of the king's house, my home, collapsed in on itself, and a great swirl of orange flames burst into the darkening sky.

I screamed at the sight and turned my horse to face the front door. Were my parents inside or had they escaped the fire?

Edmund must have sensed my desire to ride my horse straight into the flames in search of my family and grabbed for the reins before I could kick the animal into action.

'There's nothing we can do, my lady,' he yelled above the roar of the flames and the cry of the soldiers who were desperately trying to tackle the blaze.

'Where's the king?' I cried.

Edmund shook his head, but his eyes darted across the court-yard, searching every opening, every corner, and every dead body.

'He must have escaped and made it to the safe house,' he said, wiping the sweat from his brow. The shadows under his eyes seemed darker somehow, and I glanced down to look at his leg. Blood soaked through the bandage he'd administered and coated his trousers.

'Edmund, you're losing too much blood,' I said. 'We need to get you to the healer.'

'No, we must find the king.'

I shook my head in annoyance as he turned our horses, and we galloped back out of the gate. We circled the outside of the town's protective walls, seeing firsthand the devastation. Iron hooks attached to ropes had breached the fences, and the soldiers on guard would have had no warning as the enemy sneaked over the top of our defences.

The broken bodies of the guards were impaled on fence posts or lay at the foot of the wall, flung from their station by the invaders. Great plumes of smoke choked the night air as the fire raged on in this part of the fortress.

Whoever had orchestrated the attack was clever and knew the town well. I thought once more about what the dirty pirate in the woods had said. If it was an elderman who had brought about the downfall of the king and murdered his family, then I vowed to find him and kill him in return.

Men and women from the outlying villages ran past us as we rode for the farms bordering the fortress. Men dashed toward the burning buildings with their buckets at the ready, hoping to save what they could of the one structure that represented everything that my father had built in his kingdom. Children clung to their mothers' legs as fear danced in their eyes.

Edmund dropped from his horse, landing unsteadily on his injured leg, to direct the churls into action. He spoke firmly but kindly, making sure every man knew the seriousness of the situation.

'Control the blaze, collect the dead, save the livestock.' Easy instructions for the villagers to follow as he urged them up the hill to carry out their tasks.

I followed his example and made my way to a group of women who were watching the bewildering sight with panic and terror wrinkling their brows.

'Help your men,' I said, trying to keep the alarm I felt out of my voice. 'Please, we must work together to save Bamburgh and our people.'

'Don't worry, my lady,' said a young boy no older than my youngest sister. 'We'll do all we can.'

The women grasped at my hands or touched my shoulders as they rushed off to do whatever they could to help, and an enormous sense of love and loyalty surged through me. The burning of Bamburgh affected them just as much as it did me.

Edmund was back in his saddle and readying himself to return to our search for the king and queen. Within seconds, I was on my horse and galloping after him.

∽

After a short ride from the main town, we reached a farmhouse, which to any unsuspecting traveller looked like any other house in the kingdom, but the king's trusted advisors knew its real purpose as a safe house for the royal family in times of trouble.

I'd say the obliteration of our home qualified as a troubled time, and as Edmund manoeuvred our horses to a halt outside, I prayed that my parents were safe inside.

'Stay behind me,' Edmund said, dragging his sword from its sheath and limping to the front door.

I did as he said but snatched a dagger from the harness on the horse as I went. The house was in darkness, which wasn't unusual. If my parents were inside, they wouldn't want to draw attention to themselves.

The door squealed when Edmund pushed it open, and we both froze, but there were no sounds of movement or signs of loitering pirates, so Edmund took a step inside.

He sucked in a sharp breath, spinning toward me and pushing me back outside. His grip on my arms was strong and painful, and I winced as he almost knocked me off my feet.

'Edmund, you're hurting me.' I ripped my arms from his grasp and shoved him in the chest to stop him.

His eyes shone with tears, and he appeared even paler than he had a few moments before.

'What is it?' I asked in a whisper. Somewhere in the back of my mind, I knew. I knew he'd seen something so terrible that his first instinct was to get me away from it no matter how much force he had to use. 'What did you see?'

He shook his head as he tumbled to the side, and I got the impression that he had expended all his remaining energy in those last few seconds. He pitched to his knees, and I grabbed hold of him.

'Steady, my old friend,' I said, helping him to sit on the floor outside the farmhouse. 'Rest a while. Let me take over.'

He clutched at my arm before I could rise from the floor beside him.

'No, don't go in there,' he said, his glassy eyes pleading with me.

'Why not?'

He didn't answer; instead, he grasped my hands in his own.

'There is so much I wanted to teach you,' he whispered. 'You have been my finest student.'

'Stop it,' I snapped. 'You're talking like you're leaving me, and I won't let you do that.'

'I'm so sorry, Edith,' he whispered.

My brow knitted together as he released my hands, and I watched him slump to the floor. He only called me by my name when things were bad and he didn't have time for royal formalities.

'No, Edmund, please try to hold on. We'll get some help.' I stared around at the emptiness that surrounded us. Any soldiers left alive were trying to save what was left of my home. We were alone.

'You can't leave me, Edmund,' I pleaded. Tears flowed down my cheeks. 'I need your help to sort this mess out. Who's going to train with me if you're not around?'

He reached for my hand, and I took his, holding on to him as tightly as I could. Blood soaked into the grass around us from the wound in his leg.

'I don't think that's a flesh wound, Edmund,' I said with a shake of my head.

My friend chuckled and then coughed, blood gathering in the corner of his mouth.

'Do whatever you can to protect yourself, my lady,' he said. 'Heed your father's words and be watchful, be wise, be...' His hand slipped from mine as he breathed his last.

'Be wary,' I finished for him as I laid his head gently on the ground and closed his eyes. Tears streamed down my face as I kissed the top of his head. My dearest friend was dead, my home destroyed, and my sisters assassinated. I wasn't sure how much more I could take, but there was one thing left that I had to see for myself.

Edmund was no longer here to protect me, and if I was going to help rebuild the kingdom, I had to witness what I feared most.

The wooden door to the farmhouse squealed when I swung it open again, and I took a deep breath. Whatever was in here had made a grown man turn and run, so I braced myself.

A large open grate dominated the far wall, and in front of it sat two wooden chairs. At first glance, it looked like my parents had fallen asleep in front of the fire and let it go out, but as my eyes adjusted to the darkness, I saw the jagged scars across their throats and the blood covering their clothes. My mother's dress was torn to shreds, exposing her breasts, which were littered with bruises and knife marks. Both had had their stomachs sliced open, revealing their insides, which had slithered out to sit on their laps. My parents' hands were bound, and my father's face was bruised and bloody where he had clearly been beaten.

I wanted to scream and cry, but no tears came. The scene in front of me would be forever burned into my memory, and my heart ached as I stretched forward and closed first my mother's and then my father's eyes. In the distance, soldiers were calling my name.

Baldred was kneeling over Edmund's body when I emerged from the building. 'Are you all right, my lady?' He jumped up to greet me. 'What happened?'

I looked into his eyes, seeing only confusion and fear, and it tore my heart apart. Life had changed beyond all recognition in the space of a few hours for all of us. This young soldier was set to enjoy a tour of the countryside, escorting the three princesses of Northumbria, and I was meant to return home with the guarantee of a new husband. Life could be so cruel.

'They're gone, Baldred,' I whispered. 'They're all dead.'

4

By the time the sun rose the next morning, there was nothing left but the charred remains of a once-thriving settlement. Baldred and a couple of the king's guards had carried the bodies of my father, mother, and friend into the town, where they now lay bound in winding sheets side by side with my sisters.

Seeing my entire family laid out in front of me was like a nightmare I was unable to wake from. I'd ripped the cloth from inside the carriage and used it to wrap the bodies of my sisters the best I could. Father Bertram had survived the onslaught from the previous night and was on hand to perform the burial, but the assembled mourners were few. He had sent a messenger by horse to my uncle to inform him of the devastation wreaked upon Bamburgh, but as yet, Aelle had not come to our aid.

A handful of farmers, a couple of servants, a blacksmith, and the healer had lasted the night along with twenty or so soldiers, the rest of the villagers who had helped contain the fires returning to their homes defeated at the break of dawn. Baldred had stayed by my side as we moved my family and Edmund and tended to their bodies, and refused to leave me when I wept long into the night.

'Are you ready, my lady?' he asked as the priest signalled his impatience to begin.

'Proceed,' I said, rolling my shoulders back so I was standing tall, just like my father had shown me.

The priest launched into his sermon, but the sound of horses on the road beyond the burnt remains of the gate interrupted him.

'Wait.' I recognised my uncle's voice immediately, and even though I had never warmed to the man, I was relieved to have at least one surviving relative. Circling to watch him approach, I gasped at the sight of my father's crown on his head. I whirled to look across at Father Bertram, who avoided my gaze. He had clearly sent more than a note to Aelle. Seeing that crown on my uncle's head unravelled my carefully constructed restraint and ripped a hole so deep and infinite in my chest that I feared I would never recover.

The soldiers took a knee as their new king rode into town, but my shock at such a sight halted my movements. What gave him the right to wear the king's crown? I was supposed to be crowned heir of Northumbria just as my father had wished. Of course, his wishes were discussed with eldermen who had died in the fire and written about on scrolls that had perished along with the hands that crafted them.

I had no legal claim to the throne aside from a dead man's wishes.

Aelle cast a stony glare across the assembled party until his eyes found mine. His posture stiffened for the briefest of moments, but he recovered himself enough to nod in greeting.

'My dearest Edith,' he said, trotting his horse up alongside me. 'I'm thrilled to see you're alive. It broke my heart to hear about my brother's death.'

'Thank you, my lord.' I bowed my head. 'Do you have any idea who carried out these atrocious acts?'

My uncle studied me for a long moment before shaking his head. 'I can only assume that the Vikings who have been plundering the lands for many months finally arrived at my brother's door. You must be prepared for the fact that we may never catch them.'

'I don't believe it was the Vikings that did this, Uncle. The devastation you see was the handiwork of pirates. Hired thugs.'

'Hired by whom?'

His eyes narrowed as he waited for me to answer.

'I don't know, my lord. We have a prisoner who has yet to die from his injuries, and I intend to question him.'

'Don't you worry your pretty young head about that. My guards will interrogate the prisoner.'

I kept my back straight and my gaze steady, but the roar of anger that swirled through my body at his words threatened to overwhelm me. By refusing me the right to perform a simple interrogation, he was announcing to everyone present that I was a nobody.

'Well, my dear niece,' he continued, 'it's with a heavy heart that I must bear the burden of my brother's crown. I'm sure you understand that under the circumstances the kingdom cannot be placed under the protection of a young girl.'

My blood boiled beneath my skin at his treasonous words. He was fully aware of my father's wishes to crown me as queen should he die, but he had chosen to snatch my legacy for himself.

'Perhaps we could discuss your reign in a few years when you're more experienced and have a husband to support you,' he said. 'It's imperative that we find you a match as soon as possible.'

'My lord, I would much prefer to live my life as a spinster so that I can serve the people of Northumbria.' The excruciating pain in my heart that overwhelmed me was a constant reminder that love and loss were too much to cope with, and I was prepared to live a life of solitude rather than open my heart to such agony again.

'Nonsense,' he said with a dismissive shake of his head. 'You're the last bargaining tool we have, and I'll use you in whatever way pleases me.'

I swallowed down the scream that threatened to erupt as Aelle added 'and for the good of the kingdom' as an afterthought.

It took every ounce of strength I had not to drag Aelle's sword from his belt and bury it in his deceitful chest.

'Of course, my lord,' I said instead, bowing my head like a dutiful servant. 'Whatever you think is best.'

'Excellent. Now, let's lay my brother to rest and rebuild this town.'

He rode away with his guard, leaving me, Baldred, and a smattering of soldiers to grieve for our departed king and queen. The service was swift, and as the cart trundled out of the gates toward the burial site, I thought once again about my uncle and his rapid succession to the throne.

In all the years I'd listened in on the witan and observed the men of the court, I'd never recognised my uncle as a serious contender for the throne. Had he always coveted the crown? Had what I'd seen as harmless sibling rivalry been hiding something darker? Had I missed that vested interest in succeeding his brother as king of Northumbria? There was no denying that he was a ruthless elderman, and yet he despised council meetings and argued with all of my father's advisors. The only person he ever enjoyed discussing politics with was his brother, and I was sure that was only because he got to shout and curse at the king.

Now that he held the crown of Northumbria, would he be truly invested in uncovering the plot against his family? I believed that his guard would interrogate the prisoner, but I feared that the answers I longed for would never arrive.

I felt Baldred's eyes on the back of my neck as we followed the funeral procession.

'Baldred, do you trust Aelle?'

The young soldier quickened his pace until he walked beside me and gave me a sidelong glance, looking over his shoulder to see if anyone was listening.

'Honestly, my lady, I would trust the Vikings more than your uncle.'

Direct and to the point. Just what I asked for, and yet Baldred's words only echoed my own thoughts. I didn't trust that Aelle was the right person for the kingdom, but I was in no position to fight his authority. The small band of soldiers whom I'd bonded with over the previous day and night's events would probably stand with me, but Aelle could muster an army far greater and stronger. He had links with eldermen across the kingdom—and the rest of England, if the rumours were to be believed. He was devious, yet effective, as my father had pointed out to me once.

'Your uncle is an expert in getting eldermen to part with great swathes of land and yet never realise they've been swindled.'

I'd always thought he would make a great ally when I ruled these lands, but now I was forced to bend the knee to him.

❦

The building work was strenuous, and with limited men and resources, it would take many moons to rebuild the defences surrounding the settlement, but we all carried out our duties in silence.

Baldred and I found the prisoner dead when we went to see if the guards had questioned him about the plot to usurp the throne. I'd hoped to discover if it was supported by the Vikings or someone closer to home, but finding the man's corpse meant we remained in the dark about the attack on Bamburgh and the convoy.

Aelle had left me in charge of clearing out the kitchen and dining hall, giving me plenty of work to occupy my days. Thankfully, he had allowed Baldred to work alongside a few surviving churls and me. The young soldier felt like the only friend I had left in the world.

'It still tastes a bit sooty, my lady,' Baldred announced, his hair flopping into his eyes as he took his role of chosen taster seriously.

I giggled as he screwed up his handsome face and glanced around for somewhere to spit the mouthful of soup he'd just taken.

'We've scrubbed that pot out a hundred times, so I think you'll have to get used to the taste of soot.'

His shoulders jiggled up and down as he laughed at me, and I reminded myself of how grateful I was that we'd found something to smile about in this harsh reality.

'Once the farmers can replenish our vegetable stocks, we'll be able to add some flavour to this slop,' I said, lifting the ladle and smelling the soup. 'At least it's wet and warm. What more do you want?'

Baldred laughed out loud as he dragged the last of the burnt beams out of the kitchen door and into the courtyard.

'A bit like our summer weather then, my lady.'

I grinned as I watched him step outside into the summer rain. If anything, I was glad of the rains as they washed so much of the grime and dirt off the buildings. Father Bertram said it was like washing away the sins of the old. Part of me wanted to slap him for associating my father's reign with sin, but I understood his meaning.

We needed something to look forward to, and if that meant embracing the English weather and all its rainfall, then so be it.

Baldred burst back into the kitchen with such speed he startled me, making me drop the ladle into the soup.

'Baldred, whatever is the matter?'

'My lady, we have visitors.'

From the dark storm clouds that rolled across his face, I half feared that the pirates had returned to finish what they started.

'You're scaring me, Baldred. Who is it?'

'Elderman Wood, my lady. King Aelle is greeting him in the courtyard.'

I cast my mind back to the days of my father's court when all the eldermen of Northumbria would gather for great feasts. I'd been a child then, able to sneak in and out of the hall undetected. Over the years, I had grown fond of only one or two of my father's council, and Elderman Wood was not one of them.

He was a wrinkly old man with wisps of grey hair and a fat belly. His cheeks bore a constant red flush from drinking too much wine, and he smelt of pickled herring.

'What on earth is Elderman Wood doing here?'

I thought back to the pirate's comment about an elderman being responsible for the murders of my family, but Elderman Wood didn't have the brains nor the brawn to carry out such a feat. My uncle had never liked the man either, so I couldn't imagine it was a meeting of minds between the two men.

Dread pooled in my stomach. I shooed Baldred back outside into the rain. 'Be my eyes and ears, my friend. Find out what he's doing here. Elderman Wood has a sizeable estate, and my uncle may wish to ally himself with a wealthy lord.'

Baldred gave a short bow and disappeared into the charred remains of the hall. The fire damage was so great that all council meetings were now being held in the guard house at the other end of the fortress. Baldred could easily slip inside without drawing attention, unlike me.

I waited, absent-mindedly stirring the soup, my eyes never leaving the doorway. It felt like hours before Baldred returned, and from the creases across his brow, I wasn't sure I wanted to hear his report.

'Aelle summoned the elderman,' he said, shaking the rain from his cloak. 'You were right. He hopes to make an ally of Elderman Wood and call upon him should he need men for his army.'

'Why does my uncle need an army?'

'I'm not sure, my lady. Perhaps to stand against the Vikings that test the borders of Northumbria with every new moon, or maybe he desires to invade Mercia.'

I was almost impressed. Invading Mercia and Wessex to become queen of England had been an ambition of mine once—albeit fleetingly—and an idea that my father had found amusement in, but the thought of Aelle becoming king of all England filled me with trepidation.

'What does my uncle offer Elderman Wood in return for his allegiance?'

Baldred lowered his eyes and studied the floor for a long while. My hands trembled as I waited for him to answer. Deep in my bones, a chill arose. I didn't need my friend to tell me what Aelle had offered because in my heart I knew exactly what my uncle could and would give to the old man. He'd been quite clear on the matter.

'I'm so sorry, Princess,' Baldred whispered. 'King Aelle offered him a suitable marriage. He offered you.'

⌇

There was no denying that the silver dress laid out across my bed was beautiful. Elderman Wood had excelled himself when it came to providing the princess of Northumbria with a wedding gown. The fire had wiped out my home and taken all my worldly possessions with it. I owned a couple of dresses, each one torn at the hem or sleeve, bloodstained or, as with the one I wore most days, sewn together where a blade had sliced through the fabric along with my sister's throat.

'I'm not wearing it,' I snapped at the young servant who had travelled with Wood to assist me on our wedding day.

Aelle had not consulted me about the marriage before announcing it to the witan. He was using the occasion as propaganda to demonstrate his devotion to Northumbria and its last princess, but I knew the truth behind his actions. He was eliminating the threat of a true heir to the Northumbrian throne and buying himself an army with my life. Although I could see through the facade, the people bought it and celebrated the joining of two houses that held a promise of more soldiers, food, and sanctuary.

Elderman Wood had travelled to Bamburgh with a large group of servants, advisors, and guards, and was welcomed into the bosom of the fort with pomp and ceremony.

'My lady, you must wear it. My lord had it made especially for you.'

The serving girl appeared to be no more than fourteen years old and yet she had been tasked with dressing me, binding my hair, and making sure I arrived at the chapel on time.

I slumped to the floor, resting my head on the cool flagstones.

'I can't wear it,' I mumbled. 'I can't bear to marry that foul old man.'

Cold fingers pressed against mine as the young girl took my hands in hers.

'I understand, my lady, I do, but it'll do neither of us any good if we disobey Lord Wood and King Aelle.'

Her wide eyes told me everything I needed to know. If she couldn't get me into this dress and up that aisle, then she would be beaten and possibly killed. Servants' lives meant nothing to the eldermen.

'What's your name?' I asked.

'It's Meg, my lady.'

'Well, Meg, if you promise to stay with me throughout this ordeal, I'll promise to do my best and play the dutiful wife.'

Tears pooled in the young girl's eyes, and I wrapped my arms around her shoulders. The servants might be invisible to their owners, but they were the backbone of the realm. My father had always taken pride in knowing the names of all his servants and asking after their well-being. It was why he was the most beloved of all the kings. For decades, Northumbria had been plagued with instability as king after king was expelled from rule or chose to follow the holy orders. When King Osberht, my father, rose to power, the realm rejoiced, and even though I was nothing more than a pawn in my uncle's game, I vowed to reclaim my throne one day and make my father proud.

Meg helped me up and slipped the dress over my head. Its long folds fell to the floor, covering my bare feet and clinging to every curve of my body. Tiny pearls decorated the collar, which shimmered in the candlelight, and the long sleeves ruffled at the shoulders, then fit snugly to my arms. An embroidered veil cascaded down my back, acting like a cloak as it skimmed the floor. On any other occasion, I would have relished wearing such splendour, but as Meg fiddled with my train and adjusted the hem, I swallowed down the desire to scream.

A tap on the door attracted my attention, and a wave of nausea washed over me. It was time.

Baldred entered the room dressed in a bright new uniform, King Aelle's crest emblazoned across the breastplate. He stopped in the doorway, and his eyes took in every inch of me.

'My lady,' he gasped, 'you look beautiful.'

His cheeks coloured, but I chuckled and moved forward to grasp his arm.

'Thank you, Baldred,' I said. 'I only wish it was a day for celebration rather than duty.'

He lowered his gaze and, as if realising that Aelle's crest might offend me, used his red cloak to cover his tunic.

'My dear friend, don't be ashamed of your duties. You're one of my father's and Edmund's most treasured soldiers, and my uncle should be delighted that you're now in his service.'

His smile didn't reach his eyes as he took my hand and linked it through his arm.

'If only my first duty weren't to escort you into the arms of an old man not worthy of such a beautiful and brave princess.'

I blinked away the tears that threatened to fall and laid my head on Baldred's shoulder.

'Try and visit me whenever you're in the area.'

'Of course, my lady.'

'And promise you'll care for my family's tomb.' The thought of leaving my entire family behind hurt me more than I could say. I'd found great comfort sitting in the mausoleum over the past few months. Even though I sat amongst the bones of my ancestors, I could feel their spirits were close, and I knew my father was watching over me.

'I will keep their memory alive in every way I can, my lady.'

Baldred leaned forward and kissed my forehead. It was a simple act of friendship: an act that would have caused my sisters to giggle, my mother to roll her eyes, and the eldermen of the court to gasp in horror and raise a fuss. The idea of a princess and a soldier would never be accepted, and yet at that precise moment, I would have happily run away with Baldred by my side, fled the realm and my duties to the new king, fled the arranged marriage to a wrinkled old fart of a man, fled my responsibilities, and never looked back.

Instead, I held my chin high, just as my father taught me, and, on Baldred's arm, I glided through the damaged corridors of Bamburgh, past the remaining eldermen of the witan, and up the aisle to an uncertain and loveless future.

5

The sun rose over the treetops, and I sat back on my horse to breathe in the sights and sounds around us. The wedding ceremony had been short and to the point, Aelle hurrying us out of the fortress with the assurance of a guard escort.

For the first time in memory, I was grateful for my uncle's decision, as his eagerness to expel us from Bamburgh meant that my wedding night with the disgusting, fat old man was postponed until we arrived at Wood's estate. Holding on to my precious virginity for one more day seemed like a gift from the heavens, and I was happy to embrace the delay.

The sea crashed against the rocks far below the road we travelled along as I contemplated throwing myself from the animal to avoid a wedding night altogether.

My father would be rolling in his grave to think his eldest daughter, and heir to Northumbria, was considering such horrors, and it jolted me back to the present moment.

'Are you all right, my lady?' Meg asked as she trotted alongside me.

'I'm fine, thank you, Meg. Just admiring the view.'

'The sea's wild, isn't it, my lady? Where do you suppose it ends?'

'It doesn't end, Meg. I remember reading my father's scrolls about the many oceans that lead to new worlds. I've heard it said that the Vikings have explored many of these seas and plundered countless lands.'

Her face paled as she stared out across the blue ocean.

'I hope they stay away from us,' she whispered. 'They sound terrifying. The stories say that when they first landed on our shores, they murdered anyone that crossed their path: men, women, children, and priests. All of them. God's chosen men hacked to pieces.'

Recalling the tales that had filtered through the towns, I shuddered. In addition to the massacres, the accounts told of how the Vikings stripped the churches of England bare of all their gold, silver, and precious metals, of which there was plenty. None of the sacred texts were taken, which led me to believe the invaders were not only heathens but probably couldn't read.

'They kill for sport; that's what Elderman Wood says, but he'll protect us all. He's added another lock to the gate as well as the barns.'

Meg's face lit up as she shared the news of her lord's attempts to keep his people safe, and I didn't have the heart to tell her that no lock or gate had been able to stop the men from the North so far.

'I'm sure we'll be fine with Elderman Wood,' I said instead, hoping my voice didn't give away the sarcasm I intended.

Meg lowered her voice to a whisper as she looked around to see who might be listening. 'I know you don't like Elderman Wood, my lady, but you're his wife now, and that means he'll protect you above anything else.'

I laughed, and poor Meg's cheeks flushed.

'I'm sorry, Meg, but no man, especially an elderman, would look after the needs of a woman above themselves. We're pawns in their stupid games, and we only matter when they want something.' I breathed in the sea air and released the anger that had descended like a brick in my chest. 'We're both slaves now, Meg.'

We followed the convoy of horses in silence, Meg looking sorrowful as she no doubt pondered my words. I took the opportunity to watch the rolling waves and wished I could be anywhere but here.

The clouds on the horizon swept toward the shore in great swathes of grey and white as the sun rose higher in the sky, illuminating the lands. The summer rains had ceased for a time, and the heat from the sun held the potential for long, pleasant days. From this vantage point, I could see far out across the ocean, and as my gaze carried along the twinkling sea, a large ship crept into view.

'Pirates,' I cried.

Meg bolted upright next to me with a little cry of alarm as the guards rallied round to get a better look.

'Damn cutthroats,' Elderman Wood bellowed, turning his horse back up the lane. 'Leave them to their plunder, and let's hope they come face-to-face with the damn Vikings. Then maybe they can all kill each other. That'll save us a job.'

We hadn't travelled far from Bamburgh, and although there were no real ties left there for me, I still felt responsible for the people, and for Baldred. Should the pirates come ashore on the beach below us, the first town they would discover would be my old home.

'My Lord Wood, surely we should offer some assistance to my uncle against these invaders, or at the very least warn them of their arrival?' I said.

Elderman Wood glared at me with contempt. Clearly a woman had never spoken to him in this manner. Instead of embracing this new and exciting advancement in relations, he chose to gallop off down the track, increasing the gap between Bamburgh and us.

'I'll take that as a no then,' I mumbled as I urged my horse to follow the departing soldiers.

I raced after the convoy, tossing a curious look over my shoulder in time to see the pirate ship casting off their rowing boats, heading for the shore. I hoped that Aelle was up to the challenge of protecting the town and Northumbria from these men.

Elderman Wood's estate was lacking in every way; although Meg tried to cheer me up with the promise of a great feast in my honour, it was hard not to compare this draughty and unwelcoming place to the opulence of Bamburgh. Before being destroyed in the fire, Bamburgh had been the envy of every earl and king in the realm. My mother's touches had been evident in every corner of the fortress, and as my gaze travelled over the barren walls, the empty hearth, and the dirty floors of my new home, I couldn't imagine ever being able to replicate the homemaking talents of Queen Eadgifu.

'Your rooms are this way, my lady,' Meg said with a smile far too wide for my liking. She seemed quite at home in this uninviting environment, and I wondered if maybe the young servant was more suited to life as Elderman Wood's wife than I was.

'How long have you been here, Meg?'

'All my life, my lady. I was born in one of the houses bordering the estate. My parents worked for Elderman Wood's father and his father and grandfather too.'

Her dedication to this desolate land made more sense now, and I tried to rouse a warm smile for her, but my heart wasn't in it. I didn't belong here. I belonged in Bamburgh, taking over the duties left to me by my father, the king.

My father's face danced into my memories, and my throat tightened as I remembered his grin and booming laugh. Mother's face drifted into my mind next as she rolled her eyes at something Father had said. Somewhere in the deepest recesses of my brain, I heard the constant babble and giggle of Cynethryth and Ealhswith and the rousing praise of Edmund as I worked on my sword skills. My entire family had been taken from me in a heartbeat, and I didn't think I would ever feel whole again.

Fighting the overwhelming desire to cry, I jumped as two of Wood's guards burst into the hall, their swords drawn.

'My lady, we've been sent to escort you to your room.'

From the deep wrinkles stretching across their brows, I thought there might be something more serious going on than me finding my way around the estate.

'What's happened?' I asked.

They looked at one another as if weighing up whether to tell me or not, but eventually the man who had spoken took a step forward.

'There is a sizeable force of pirates outside the gates, my lady. Elderman Wood has asked that we make sure you are secure and guarded.'

Meg gave me a satisfied smirk as if this guard had confirmed everything she'd said to me out on the road about her master's desire to protect me.

'Well, I'm grateful to my lord for his concern,' I said. 'I would, however, feel much safer if you could provide me with a weapon so that I can protect myself if the need arises.'

Again they exchanged looks.

'I'm…I'm not sure my lord would be agreeable to that.'

Rounding my shoulders, I set my jaw and pressed my lips together, the look that Edmund told me could turn milk sour and make men tremble on any battlefield. It appeared to work, as the second guard handed over his sword without another word.

'Thank you,' I said. 'Now, where does Elderman Wood need us to go?'

I might be willing to fight if necessary, but I wasn't stupid. *Don't go looking for trouble, my lady,* Edmund used to say.

The two soldiers ushered us across the courtyard and into an annexe building at the far side of the estate. I could hear the cries of the men beyond the walls and the clash of metal as Elderman Wood's forces defended their home.

How strange that these pirates hadn't ventured to Bamburgh, the nearest town available to raid, and instead had followed a different path bringing them straight to my door. I pondered once again on which elderman had aligned himself with these pirates as the men in the forest had told me. What was their goal? They wiped out my entire family, but I had managed to escape.

It hit me like a bolt of lightning. There was only one reason why these pirates had come to this estate and not invaded Bamburgh: me. The king and queen were dead, along with two of their daughters. I was the last princess of Northumbria. Their goal was to destroy my bloodline.

∽

Meg cowered beside me, her small frame trembling. I slung my heavy woollen riding cloak around her shoulders, hoping to provide the support and comfort she needed. The soldiers had bundled us into what I now realised were my private chambers and blocked the door. It was their duty to be the last line of defence between the pirates and me. Personally, I hoped to see these two young men again and not have to use the sword they'd given me, but from the noises beyond the walls, I doubted that anyone would survive this day.

'Are we going to die?' Meg asked, her voice so quiet I had to strain to hear her.

'Not at all,' I said, patting her hand as my mother used to do with me when I was upset. 'Elderman Wood's men will protect us.'

I took in our surroundings and inwardly groaned. Perhaps being captured by pirates would be better than living in this desolate hole. The room was square, wooden, and cold—so cold I could see my breath in the air when I spoke. No fire had warmed the grate in many years, and the layers of grime, cobwebs, and moth-eaten bedding added to my suspicions that my new room hadn't been in use since the lord's first wife was alive. Having known Elderman Wood all my life through my father's court, I was aware that the old man had been a widower for over five years.

My mind wandered to the prospect of life as a slave. I'd seen many servants during my time in Bamburgh, some of them bought from merchants passing through the kingdom, but it was only now that I wondered where these people had come from. Were they highborn children snatched from their beds by bandits, or orphans who had lost everything dear to them only to be thrown into service, never allowed to grieve?

A gasp caught in my throat, and I struggled to hold back my tears. Was I going to be stripped of my title in more ways than one? Would these pirates consider the fact that I was a princess? Perhaps they would get more money for me, or maybe I'd be more trouble than I was worth and they'd slit my throat.

I jumped to my feet, startling poor Meg as I did, and rushed to the main door. Turning the handle, I pulled, but it didn't budge.

'Hello?' I pressed my ear to the wood and listened for the sounds of breathing or moving soldiers beyond my prison. 'Are you there?'

'What are you doing?' Meg hissed, her eyes wide with fear.

'I can't stay locked in this room. We need to leave the estate and ride back to my uncle. He'll be able to help.'

It wasn't a plan as such but more of a desire to suppress the burgeoning claustrophobia that threatened to consume me. I *had* to get out of this room.

A scraping sound from beyond the door made us both jump, and I sent up a silent prayer. All we had to do was slip past the soldiers, steal two horses, and ride past a raging battle.

I moved to the side of the door to give the soldiers room to open it, readying myself to use all the resources I had to outwit them. It wasn't fair to use them in this way, as Elderman Wood would probably punish them for disobeying his orders and letting us out, but if it came down to them or me, then it was no contest.

The door sprang open and Meg, who was standing facing the opening, let out a scream so piercing I had to slap my hands over my ears. A metal axe sailed across the space and embedded itself in her skull, silencing her forever. Her tiny body lifted from the floor and crashed into the wooden wall behind her. Blood spread around her lifeless body as it crumpled to the floor.

Bile rose up my throat, and I pitched forward, steadying myself on a carved blanket box. How many people was I going to have to watch die? My mind tore through every possible scenario about the predicament I now found myself in. Who were they? Why the hell did I have to alert them to our presence? Meg was dead because of me, because of my need for freedom, and now I was either going to join her or have that freedom ripped away.

'Can't do with wailing women,' said the dirty man who had thrown the axe. 'It makes my teeth itch.'

Another man walked into the room behind him, assessing the now silent form of Meg.

'She was a young'un; we could have sold her for a good price.'

'Nobody wants a slave that screams that loud,' the man with the axe replied.

The two men hadn't spotted me as I clung to the wall behind the door. They stood over Meg's body, discussing the pros and cons of murder over the possibility of making money, and I took the opportunity to make a run for it.

Curling my hands into fists to stop them from shaking, I pushed away from the wall and took a tentative step forward, then another, and another. The men were oblivious as I backed out of the open door and into the corridor. The two soldiers assigned to protect us lay on the floor, blood surrounding their dead bodies. I swallowed more bile and stepped over the one who had given me his sword.

I'd made it to the end of the corridor when I heard boots and raised voices heading my way. A tall wooden cabinet stood at the end of the hall, and, as silently as possible, I climbed inside, pushing aside the linen and pulling the door closed behind me. Through the intricately carved slots in the wood, I could make out the dark corridor.

'We've got our orders, old man, and keeping you and your new bride alive ain't one of them.'

I flinched. A large man dressed in a hooded cloak was dragging a bloody and beaten Elderman Wood down the hallway.

Five men followed behind with their swords drawn. Blood dripped from their blades, and a sheen of sweat covered their foreheads. There was no doubt in my mind that these pirates had been sent to wipe out Elderman Wood's estate, but by whom?

They stopped outside the room I'd just escaped from and pushed Wood to his knees.

'Is that her?' the big man asked. 'Is that Princess Edith?'

I pressed my hand over my mouth as Elderman Wood raised his head and stared into the room. His face was swollen and disfigured, but I still saw the tear that rolled down his cheek. I held my breath and waited.

'Yes, that's my wife,' he said.

The big man drew his sword and sliced Elderman Wood's head clean off. It clattered to the floor, disappearing inside the room and out of my view. The lord's body slumped to the side, twitching as the blood poured across the corridor.

The pirates jammed their swords back into their sheaths and turned back toward where I hid trembling in the linen closet. Elderman Wood had lied. He had told them that Meg was me. He didn't know if I was dead or alive, but he must have known his own fate was sealed. I had to survive this to avenge him and Meg, not to mention my entire family.

The men marched past my hiding place, and I closed my eyes, willing them to keep walking. The sound of their boots faded into the distance, and I allowed myself a tiny sob.

What Elderman Wood had done for me was an act of kindness even though it was totally out of character. Did he know who these men worked for? Was that his final act of defiance toward the elderman who had hired these men?

My joints felt stiff from being cramped inside such a small space. Slowly, I pushed the closet door open. It creaked before coming to a stop, and I winced, holding my breath again and listening. Silence. Perhaps the pirates had left already.

I lowered myself out of the cupboard and into the corridor as quietly as I could. A bundle of linen fell to the floor behind me, and I scooped up a plain grey woollen dress from the pile. In the middle of the hallway, I stripped off the fine green dress edged in silver that was another gift from Elderman Wood and wrestled the servant's dress over my head. Sewn into the lining was a small pocket, into which I put my mother's bracelet and amulet. Having such fine jewellery would give me away as a highborn Anglo-Saxon, and I couldn't risk discovery until I was safely away from Elderman Wood's estate and back in Bamburgh. I unbound my hair to give the impression of being an unmarried servant, although, in truth, I was now a widow.

I stepped away from the closet, then grimaced at the sharp pain that coursed through me as something struck my head and I slumped forward onto all fours.

'Where do you think you're going, girl?'

The man's voice was the last thing I heard as the world spun away from me and everything went black.

6

THREE MONTHS LATER

The only reminder that I was still alive came from the spray off the sea and the nauseous feeling as we battled the swells of the ocean. Remembering that I was a princess of Northumbria was hard. There were times when I felt like I was living another person's life, like a dream that pulled me beneath the waves and cocooned me in a suffocating embrace. Then I'd kick and fight to the surface and remember. I recalled the bloodshed, the murder and betrayal, and the fact that I was kidnapped, stolen from my homeland, and brought here.

Dragged from one strange land to another and back to the pirate ship and the open sea, I'd been paraded alongside the other slaves for leering merchants to haggle over. In some cruel twist of fate, nobody wanted me, and I was returned to the bowels of my wooden prison.

What was so wrong with me that the sneering merchants overlooked me time and time again? I realised that life wouldn't be any better if a wealthy merchant had bought me. I'd heard terrible stories from the slaves passing through during our voyage. Serving the pirate lord, scrubbing the decks, and cooking for the men wasn't so bad when I heard of slaves being killed when their captors grew tired of them.

I needed to do my job and keep my head down, as this was something the pirate captain respected. The men would watch me going about my duties with a quiet hatred smouldering behind their sharp eyes. They didn't understand the Anglo-Saxon ways; my beliefs and customs made them wary. Given a chance, or with a single word from the captain, I was certain my throat would be cut and my body dumped overboard. They only kept their distance out of duty to their captain.

Keeping my wits about me and staying focused had been my only goal these past few months. The men aboard the ship were dangerous, and if I wanted any chance of escape, I needed to stay one step ahead of them.

It still seemed strange that my daily thoughts were flooded with strategy, planning, and violence and my actions from one moment to the next were all about staying alive. Not so long ago, all I had to worry about was if the colour of my dress matched my eyes.

The beauty of being a nobody on a ship full of bandits was their ability to overlook me when they were engrossed in eating, fighting, or torturing the slaves. It was during these times when I learnt more about the ship's next destination, who would be meeting with the captain, and the value of the slaves held in the bowels of the floating prison.

At breakfast, I'd overheard the men talking of our next stop: a trading station to the east. If I was clever, I could slip my bonds and make a run for it. The lack of food had helped my already petite frame waste away even further, and I could easily wriggle free of my shackles, something my captors hadn't yet noticed.

I was prepared to wait. Wait for my moment to escape. If I didn't break free, then there was a strong possibility I would die on this ship, and that was not an option.

⌒

Shouting overhead enticed me from my slumber. The ship had stopped moving. Over the past few months, I'd managed to find my sea legs and stop being sick long enough to be calmed by the rocking motion of the boat on the waves. It always took a while for my head to clear once the ship was in the harbour.

The other slaves in the cell huddled close to one another, but I didn't have the heart to tell them it would do no good. Their lives were about to change forever—again.

'*Ut! Ut!*' One of the pirates opened the cell door and started yelling at the prisoners. They exchanged confused glances as the man yelled once more. '*Ut! Ut!*'

I stepped to the front of the line and straightened my bony shoulders.

'He's saying "out,"' I told them. 'He needs us to leave the ship now. Just follow me.'

The pirate nodded as I walked past like the pied piper, leading the other slaves to a life of servitude, abuse, or possibly death. It was a game I'd played for many moons now, offering the slaves a friendly face to keep them calm and then handing them over to whatever fate had in store. Survival sucked.

'*Biddu.*' The captain held up a hand as we emerged on the ship's deck.

The slaves all turned to me as one, and I had to push down the urge to laugh. How had I suddenly become the translator for a group of bandits when only months ago I was studying Latin texts and practising needlepoint?

'He wants us to wait,' I said.

A sizeable harbour with crowds of people jostling for space along the dock was visible beyond the rigging. The selling of slaves attracted an impressive assembly, as this was often the first time people saw men and women from other lands. The ports we visited on our journey would erect special tents and lay out sumptuous feasts for the pirates, who brought with them such treasures as gold, silver, and spices. The slaves were a bonus for anyone wealthy enough.

Looking along the line of captives, I noticed that this time they were all girls. Only a couple of boys had passed through the ship during my time on board, and they had been sold as sacrifices to the pagan gods.

My stomach churned at the memory of it. Dragged to the ship's deck, I was made to watch as a boy my age was hanged between two trees and sliced open, his insides spilling into the street for the dogs to feast on. I'd thrown up over the side of the ship as my pirate kidnappers laughed and drank ale.

Girls at least stood a better chance of survival out here, which was almost laughable when I thought about all the times I'd tried to be heard in my father's court. A woman was nothing more than decoration or a bargaining tool to the Anglo-Saxon men, but here, across the sea, women were prized possessions and often equal to the men. Granted, a slave girl wasn't treated as equal, but if you worked hard and kept your head down, then you could at least keep your life.

'Dear God, they're Vikings,' said one of the English slaves with a quiver to her voice.

'Are we going to die?' a young girl with filthy blonde hair and wide, expressive eyes whispered in my ear as we waited for the captain to herd us off the ship. My mind flicked back to another young girl asking me the same question. Meg's lifeless face floated across my vision.

'Probably,' I said in all honesty. 'Show them you're strong and they may buy you as a worker, but any sign of weakness will get you killed.'

The girl tensed next to me, but she stood a little taller, and that made me smile. If all women stood up for themselves maybe there wouldn't be such a thriving slave trade. 'Be watchful, be wise, be wary,' I added as the captain called us forward, 'and you may just survive this ordeal.'

They took us to a barn on the outskirts of the town where a stage was erected so the traders could get a better look at the slaves on offer. The air buzzed with excitement, and the captain's eyes shone with greed and corruption. He stood with his chin up and his inked hand over the pommel of his sword, exuding influence over the waiting crowds.

'There is wealth in the air, my little Anglo-Saxon slave,' the captain said to me as I took up my position in the lineup.

I stared out at the fierce faces in the crowd and swallowed down my unease. The stories of Vikings invading England were still fresh in my mind. They lived by their own set of rules, and slaves were used for physical enjoyment as well as chores, something I didn't want to think about. As the last princess of Northumbria, it was vital that my virginity stay intact, ensuring I could attract a husband when the time came to take the throne and produce a pure bloodline of heirs. A familiar face walked across the crowd, interrupting my thoughts as he whispered into the captain's ear. I struggled to place where I'd seen him before, but whatever he said related to me as they both turned to focus their attention on me.

The captain's eyes sparkled with greed as he strode over to the line of slaves and took me away from the lineup with a firm hand.

'You'll stay close to me,' he said with a sly smile.

I did as commanded and scrutinised the assembled Vikings as they prodded and poked the rest of the girls. I didn't know why the captain had chosen to take me out of the lineup, but I had the strangest feeling I was now his personal property.

I'd resigned myself to the fact that I was a servant to these pirates until I could make my escape, but as I studied the harsh faces in the crowd, I was secretly pleased not to be up for sale in this place.

The stories I'd heard about the Vikings didn't do them justice. Seeing them up close was terrifying. They were each as wide as a house, with painted faces and braided hair, axes and swords secured to their bodies with leather straps, and I wondered if they slept with their weapons too.

The Vikings were far more ferocious than the pirates who stood off to the rear of the room, and as my gaze swept across the assembled group, it struck me where I remembered the man from. I realized allowing him to walk away might not have been my best idea as I recalled the dirty headband, crooked teeth, and grubby outfit. With horror, I realised the man who had attacked me in the woods the night my family died had just told my captor who I was. To the captain, I was the most valuable asset he now owned.

A huge man with long dark hair and a matching beard climbed to the front of the stage, and the crowds fell silent.

He spoke in their dialect, and the slaves' faces drained of all colour with every syllable. I knew what they thought because I'd had the same thoughts. This wasn't how they hoped life would turn out. Being sold into slavery was one thing, but to be unable to understand the people you would serve meant more misunderstandings—more beatings.

The big man handed the crowd's attention over to the captain, who initiated the bidding. In the frenzy that followed, seven girls were wrenched from the stage by their new owners. Some appeared to genuinely need a slave to help with the chores, but one or two had a glint in their eye that would only mean pain and suffering for the young women.

I closed my eyes and tried to steady my breathing. There was nothing I could do to help. I was one girl.

'How much for you?'

A deep, rumbling voice startled me, and I opened my eyes to see a large man with long, wild hair and a bushy beard staring at me.

'Er, you'll need to speak to the owner, my lord,' I said as my eyes darted across the room looking for the ship's captain.

He lifted my chin with his big hand and grunted in what I took to be approval. Letting go of my face, he then took my hands in his and turned them over.

'You haven't been a slave for long, have you, girl?'

I resisted the urge to snatch my hands back out of his grip. 'Long enough.'

'Where have you come from?'

'England, my lord. Northumbria, to be exact.'

The big man released my hands with another grunt.

'What is the name of your king?'

I sucked in a breath and drew on every ounce of inner strength to stop myself from wailing for my lost family.

'I believe it's Aelle, my lord. They crowned him just as I was taken from my home.'

'Do you miss your home, girl?'

I resisted the urge to laugh. If only he knew the truth.

'I miss the smell of the ground after the summer rain, I miss the sound of the ocean as it crashes against the beach, and I miss my family, my lord, so yes, I do miss my home.'

He seemed satisfied with my answer, as the corners of his mouth twitched into a smile.

'I've been watching you, and you don't act like a slave,' he said, crossing his massive arms over his chest.

'I'm sorry, my lord. I'll try to do better.'

The big man laughed, instantly transporting me back to Bamburgh and my father chuckling at something I'd done. The pain in my chest crushed me like a rock pressing down on me.

'Who sells this slave?' he bellowed across the barn.

The captain raised his head in our direction, and panic flitted across his features. He hurried to the stage and addressed the Viking with an unfamiliar flourish.

'Jarl Aaric, what an honour to see you again.'

A jarl. This man was important.

'I want to buy this slave girl,' Aaric said, pointing a massive finger at me.

Beads of sweat gathered on the captain's forehead as he looked between the jarl and me.

'This slave is no good,' he said, placing a hand on the Viking's arm and herding him away from me and to the leftover girls on stage.

'I do have a fine specimen that will meet the needs of you and your fine sons.'

Jarl Aaric detached himself easily from the pirate and pointed once again in my direction.

'She is the slave I want, not these weaklings. Name your price.'

The captain fidgeted, and I understood why he was so reluctant to sell me on. I knew my cooking and cleaning skills weren't any good, so he certainly couldn't use that as an excuse to keep me. He knew I wasn't a true slave. He knew I was a princess, and he was keeping me for himself. The ultimate bargaining chip should the need arise in the future. The captain was a smart man, and having me at his side meant he could trade entire armies for the simple knowledge that I lived. There was no way he was going to sell me to anyone.

'Name your price,' the Viking boomed again.

'She is not for sale, Jarl Aaric.' The captain placed a hand over the hilt of his sword as he spoke. His posture was one of servitude rather than dominance, and for the first time since meeting the pirate, I saw him for what he was: a pawn in a much larger game. I'd given the captain too much of my attention, thinking him to be a powerful man, but seeing him cowering beneath the glassy stare of the Viking, I understood how small and insignificant he was.

'I am not leaving without that slave girl, so you either name your price or I take your head as a trophy.'

I knew I shouldn't be feeling so elated that two men were fighting over me. There was every possibility that I was about to become this jarl's whore or worse, a sacrifice, but on first impression, he didn't appear to be an evil man. His touch had been warm and gentle, and I couldn't shake the similarities between him and my father. True leaders had a certain manner about them, and Jarl Aaric possessed those qualities.

The captain shuffled on the spot and wiped the sweat from his eyes. The entire barn had fallen silent and was watching the exchange.

'You are a slave trader, and you have a slave I want to buy. Why do you refuse my offer?'

I leaned forward, eager to hear what he was about to say. Would he tell everyone in the room that I was the last princess of Northumbria? Could he risk anyone else discovering my secret?

'She is my slave, Jarl Aaric. Simple as that. My slave and my whore.'

I flinched backwards, wrinkling my nose in disgust. The thought of sleeping in the same room let alone the same bed as the pirate captain made me sick to my stomach.

The Viking glanced at me as the wave of disgust rearranged my features.

'She doesn't seem to agree with you, so I say again, for the last time, how much for the slave?'

He drew his sword before I registered what was happening. The captain lunged at me with a loud cry, but before his blade could connect with my throat, his head detached from his body and bounced harmlessly across the stage.

I clamped my hands over my mouth as the Viking wiped the blade of his sword on his highly embroidered mantle.

He turned to me and smiled. 'Looks like you belong to me now, girl.'

I followed him out of the barn, stepping over the decapitated corpse of my former owner, and glided past the remaining pirates, who had drawn their weapons but were too afraid to use them.

For all his faults, the captain had become familiar to me, the ship had become home, and this way of life had settled into a normal routine. It startled me how easily I'd allowed myself to adapt to slavery. Nobody liked change, even when there was a possibility of a better existence. It was human nature to settle for what fate handed you, even though that's not what my father had taught me. Still, fear pooled in my belly as I climbed on the back of a grey horse and trotted out of town after the huge Viking. I peeked over my shoulder to see the ship fade into the distance as my stomach churned with nerves over the future.

I'd made a pledge to myself that I would escape and return to Bamburgh to avenge my family, but that dream was now getting further and further away. I was in a new land, far from England with no way of finding my way home. With the hills and the port disappearing, I made myself a new vow. If I remained watchful, I might be able to find my way back to the harbour and steal away on one of the ships destined for England. It was a plan full of holes, but it was something I could cling to over the coming months.

7

'What's your name, girl?'

The big Viking jolted me back to reality as he spoke to me. He had stilled his horse, allowing me to catch up, and we now travelled side by side along the track.

'It's Edith, my lord.'

'I'm Jarl Aaric. I rule the lands to the south of here. Is there a skill you are well known for, Edith?'

Edmund's voice swirled through my head as I thought about my skills with a sword, but I didn't think the jarl would appreciate a slave who could fight back. I pondered all the things I couldn't do well against those I enjoyed.

'I'm not a decent cook, my lord, but I can sew. Lack of food over the past few months means I'm not as physically strong as I would like, so dealing with heavy manual work might be a trial.'

The big man chuckled. 'Heavy manual work? Do you think I'm going to set you to work on building my walls or digging my ditches?'

I wasn't sure what to say in response. The servants in Bamburgh had done anything my father asked of them, so I believed that I was to do the same if I didn't want my new lord to discover my secret and have me hanged.

'I'm yours to command, my lord. If you've got a ditch that needs digging, then I'll dig it for you.'

His booming laugh made me jump and my horse skitter. I grabbed for the reins and ran my hand along its shoulder to calm the creature.

'There are no ditches for you to dig, Edith,' he said as his shoulders continued to shake with laughter. 'Cooking, helping my wife around the great hall, and tending to the animals will do for now.'

I was relieved that my list of chores didn't include being thrashed, sacrificed, or married off to another old man.

'As you command, my lord,' I said with a nod.

We rode on in strangely companionable silence for many miles as the sky darkened. Jarl Aaric pulled on the reins of his horse and dismounted next to a winding stream.

'We will make camp here,' he said, tying his horse to a tree branch alongside the water. 'Find some firewood, Edith.'

I slid from my horse and tied it next to the jarl's, watching it drink from the stream. Fallen twigs littered the floor, and I started to collect as many as I could carry.

Darkness blanketed us, and for a moment I could barely see my hand in front of my face. I clung to the firewood and thought how easy it would be to melt into the blackness enveloping us and disappear. No sooner had the thought entered my head than Jarl Aaric was by my side and taking the wood from my arms.

'It's a warm night, but a fire will help us see what we are doing, don't you agree, Edith?'

I nodded and fell to my knees sorting the pile of logs into a point and striking rocks to get the fire going. It only took two goes before the wood caught and the flames crackled. Jarl Aaric fumbled in the bag on his horse and took out a pouch.

'Here,' he said, handing me the leather container. 'Eat.'

I yanked open the strings, and the smell of roasted chicken filled my senses. I looked up at the jarl, thinking it must be a trick.

'It's all right, Edith. Eat your fill. There's plenty.'

He produced a second pouch and began chomping on the contents. I didn't need telling twice and stuffed a large piece of moist chicken breast into my mouth. Never had I tasted anything so good. Memories of the great feasts we'd had back at Bamburgh rolled through my mind. Pheasant and duck with plums and ale had covered my father's table, and everyone ate their fill with a smile and a story.

'What does it mean that you are a jarl?' I asked between mouth-fuls, the food in my belly giving me confidence that I'd forgotten I possessed.

The Viking laughed again and cleared his throat. 'A jarl is a sign of nobility in my world.'

'So, you're like a king of the Vikings?'

'We have kings who reside over great lands, but jarls deal with their own lands and trading routes. I am proud of what I've achieved, and when I go to Valhalla, my sons will inherit Hedeby and all its glory.'

'What's Valhalla?'

The Viking lowered his huge frame onto the ground beside me and nudged a burning log with his foot, making sparks spit high into the dark sky.

'Valhalla is where all the bravest Viking warriors go when they die. It's a gigantic hall where we drink, fight, and celebrate our success with Odin.'

I'd heard my father's Christian priest talk about the pagan gods and recalled that Odin was the god of gods.

'In my people's faith, they believe you ascend to heaven when you die, but only if you are free of sin.'

Jarl Aaric glanced across at me as the flames from the fire reflected in his eyes.

'Are you free of sin, Edith?'

I shrugged and thought about the pirates I'd killed in the forest and all the ill thoughts I'd had about my sisters, Aelle, and Elderman Wood.

'I don't think any of us are free of sin, my lord, but I do believe that some sins are more forgivable than others.'

'Like murdering a pirate who refuses to sell me a slave?'

I giggled. 'Yes, my lord, that sin is definitely forgivable.'

∽

With the breaking dawn came my first sighting of Hedeby far off in the distance. Jarl Aaric had talked at length about his home as we warmed ourselves by the fire. The pride he felt flowed through his words, and it lightened my heart to be a part of his world, even if only for a short time until I made my escape.

Even though he owned me, I didn't feel like a true slave. He spoke to me as an equal, talking easily about the differences in our two cultures. He was interested in what I had to say and allowed me to speak without reproach. Our conversations reminded me of all the times I'd quizzed Edmund about life beyond the walls of Bamburgh.

Jarl Aaric was easy to talk to, and we had chatted long into the night about the pagan gods, the Christian God, and the kings of England. He was intrigued by our Anglo-Saxon ways, and I was equally fascinated by the laws of the Vikings. I was aware that I'd let my guard down around the big warrior, but I didn't feel a sense of alarm. *I'm not being very wary,* I thought to myself as we rode over the grassland in the direction of a hill fort. Edmund would have scolded me for being so familiar with the enemy, but I saw it as tactical. If Jarl Aaric trusted me, then it would make my escape easier. As such, I needed to show the jarl my worth and prove he could rely on me.

'My lord, I don't want to alarm you, but I think we're being followed.'

The Viking adjusted himself in the saddle to look back at me, an amused smile dancing across his face.

'Really?' he said.

'Yes. I felt eyes on us in our camp last night but thought I was just unnerved from sleeping outside, but now I'm certain of it. There are men in the tree line to our left and right.'

He jumped from his horse and drew his axe from the leather sheath across his shoulder. I scrambled off my own horse and rushed to his side.

'My lord, I don't think you can fight them all on your own. If you have a spare blade, maybe I can help.'

He raised his eyebrows, but I chose to ignore the mocking gesture, as we faced an uncertain situation. I took a moment to marvel at the beauty of the intricate decoration of the dagger he handed me from his belt. The handle was made of bone and embedded with jewels, and the blade glinted as the early morning sun caught its surface. I also respected the jarl for trusting me with such a dangerous weapon. There was no way I could take on the mighty jarl in combat, and we both knew it, but he was within his rights to be cautious of his new prize. Instead, he chose to place his trust in me.

I planted my feet wide and held a defensive stance, just as Edmund taught me. My dagger might be short, but I could still inflict some injury upon the attackers. Part of me was angry that I might die today when I had so much more to accomplish, but if I got to expel some of the rage that sat like a boulder in my chest, I would be thankful.

From the seclusion of the trees, a line of Vikings stepped forward. There must have been forty men, all armed with circular shields painted bright blue and an assortment of swords and axes. We didn't stand a chance, and my heart sank as they approached.

I scanned behind me to see if Jarl Aaric was ready for battle and was surprised to see the big man leaning on his axe, watching me with a wide grin.

'You are like no slave I have ever met, Edith,' he said with a laugh. 'Perhaps I didn't buy a slave at all. Maybe I bought an English warrior.'

He roared with laughter as the Viking men advanced on us.

Two men broke away and walked toward Jarl Aaric.

'Everything all right, Father?'

Father. The men embraced, and I noted the resemblance between them. They all had the same hard jawline, strong features, and long blond hair.

'My sons,' Aaric said with humour in his tone, 'I want to introduce my Anglo-Saxon bodyguard, Edith.'

I was still clutching the dagger and brandishing it at the army of men who now stood in a semicircle around us. I let my arm fall to my side.

'Very funny,' I said, handing the dagger back to Jarl Aaric. 'Why didn't you tell me they were there?'

'I don't know how it works in Northumbria, but in my country, our jarls never travel anywhere without their army.'

'They've been behind us the entire time?'

Aaric laughed again and slapped a big hand on my shoulder. 'Yes, Edith, they've been with us all the way home, but I'm impressed that you managed to sniff them out.'

The taller of the two sons dug his brother in the ribs. 'I said you needed to wash in the river, Torin. The slave girl could smell you.'

'I think it's your odour that gave us away, Harmod,' Torin replied with a laugh. 'It was all that spicy fish you ate at the harbour.'

The boys pushed and shoved one another playfully as the heat crept up my neck and along my cheeks. I'd made a fool of myself by being too relaxed. I needed to remember that these men were my captors, and ferocious Vikings.

❧

Aaric's great hall was like nothing I'd ever seen. Unlike my father's hall in Bamburgh, this one was made entirely of wood with straw across the floor and a vast raging firepit in the centre of the room. Separate rooms were sectioned off for the jarl and his family at the back of the hall, and to the left of the main door, goats and chickens occupied animal pens.

Antlers and animal skulls decorated the high ceiling, and all around the room, large wooden tables and benches had been placed for visitors. Every inch of space was alive with laughter and conversation. My father's hall was only ever occupied when he called the council or there was a celebration, but here it seemed the Vikings could drop in and make themselves at home whenever they chose.

'Allow me to introduce my wife, Ingrid,' said Aaric as we approached a raised platform with two large carved seats covered in animal furs. 'You work for her now.'

I nodded and gave a little bow to Ingrid. She was beautiful and exactly the kind of woman I would have expected Jarl Aaric to be with. Her hair was like honey with two braids trimmed with cream ribbon running from either side of her temple down her back. She wore a linen dress with a fur collar, and an assortment of bracelets adorned her slim arms.

She held one of her arms aloft and waggled it around, making the silver bracelets sing.

'I hope you're not thinking of stealing my jewellery, girl.'

'Forgive me, my lady. My moth—old mistress wore similar bangles, and for a moment it reminded me of home.'

Ingrid stood up and stepped toward me, lifting my face with her delicate fingers.

'Never apologise for thinking fondly of your home, Edith. But if I see you coveting my belongings again, I'll have your head removed and fed to the pigs. Are we clear?'

'Yes, my lady.'

She studied me for a moment longer before leaning in to whisper in my ear. 'I see why my husband was drawn to you, Edith. You aren't like the other slaves he has bought, but only time will tell if you are worthy of us.'

I wasn't sure of her meaning. Did she believe I wouldn't survive my duties, or life in a Viking town? So far, my dealings with the Vikings had been reasonably pleasant and in no way reflected the horrific stories that swept through England, but was that about to change? After all, in their eyes I was nothing but a slave girl. I was dispensable.

'You'll find clean clothes and a fresh bed of straw in the barn. Eric will show you where to go. Your duties begin at dawn, so take this day to acquaint yourself with the town.'

Ingrid nodded at a young boy sitting by the fire and then disappeared into the back behind a heavy curtain. Watching her glide through the great hall, I understood everything my father had been trying to teach me. Ingrid was a noblewoman, a queen in every sense of the word, and once again, I found comparisons between Aaric, Ingrid and my parents.

'I'm Eric,' said the young boy who seemed to me no older than ten. 'Follow me.'

He shot out of the hall, and I struggled to keep up with him, his bright mop of blond hair acting as a beacon through the streets of Hedeby as I splashed through puddles and manoeuvred around the crowds. Stopping outside a single-storey thatched barn at the outskirts of town, I managed to catch my breath.

'You're fast,' I said.

Eric beamed at me. 'Nobody can catch me,' he said. 'My brothers might be bigger and stronger, but they'll never be as fast as me.'

I giggled. 'Who are your brothers?'

'Harmod, Torin, and Leif,' he said.

'You're Jarl Aaric's son?'

'I am.' He grinned up at me with pride shining in his eyes. I recognised that look, as my eyes used to shine similarly when I talked about my father.

'It's an honour to meet you, Eric,' I said, giving the boy a short bow. 'Thank you for escorting me to my sleeping quarters.'

He chuckled, then sprinted into the crowds, his blond head darting in and out of the men and women going about their daily business.

The women in the streets wore long woollen dresses and carried woven baskets laden with bread, fish, and an assortment of other goods. The men hurried to and from the harbour with rope and provisions. It resembled any thriving settlement in Northumbria, and yet I was surrounded by Vikings. Were these the fierce creatures the Christian priests wrote about?

My heart felt heavy as I thought about home and all the people I'd lost or left behind. These Vikings were no different from us. Yes, they worshipped a variety of gods and fought for entry into Valhalla, but they loved and laughed and worked hard as a community to succeed in putting food in their bellies, the same as any farmer would in England.

A strange sensation washed over me as I watched these people work. It was a sense of peace, something I hadn't experienced for quite some time, but I couldn't afford to let my guard down. If I could survive long enough to build my strength, I could become indispensable, and then I could escape.

I stepped into my sleeping quarters and found a clean woollen dress on my cot. The tattered dress I was wearing had been stolen from a linen closet many moons ago as I hid my identity from the pirates. It seemed like an entire lifetime had passed by, and yet suddenly I was reluctant to take it off. The grubby dress was my final link to home, but it also reminded me every single day of poor, sweet Meg and Elderman Wood's final sacrifice. I stripped off the old and climbed into the new, hiding my mother's jewels in a small pouch that hung from my belt.

I shook my head and reprimanded myself for being a sentimental fool. I was alive, and that was all that mattered. Alive was one step closer to returning home and finding out who murdered my family. Alive was better than the alternative.

8

The days turned into weeks as I built my strength back up. My duties were varied and strangely therapeutic. There was something quite calming about digging in the gardens, cooking over a raging fire, and sweeping out the animal pens.

If Edmund were here, he would have told me it was a worthwhile life lesson, whereas my sisters would have giggled at my attempts to wrangle the pigs and goats.

The similarities I found between my family and the jarl's continued to surprise and confuse me. I observed them each night as I served ale to the many Vikings who visited them, and marvelled at the loyalty and friendship that filled the great hall. To an insider, it was the safest place to be, but for an outsider like me, it was a daily reminder of what I'd lost.

Ingrid remained indifferent to me, but it was nothing I wasn't used to. The men in my father's court had been the same. The only difference was Ingrid's generosity in providing me with a woollen dress to keep me clean and presentable.

'Good morning, Edith.' Young Eric plonked himself down on an upturned bucket, interrupting my musings as I poured water into the feeding troughs for the pigs.

'Good morning to you, my lord.' I smiled at the boy, who had taken to seeking me out every morning. It had become one of the highlights of my day, but I wasn't yet sure if it was the curious chatter of a child or whether he had been sent to spy on me. 'What are you doing today?'

'It could be a busy day,' he announced. 'Father wants to take me hunting, but Mother says I'm too young. I'm letting them fight it out.' He rambled on at great length about the tug-of-war between Jarl Aaric and Ingrid, and I couldn't suppress the chuckle that erupted at his words.

'My mother and father used to have the same conversations about me when I was a young girl,' I told him, remembering the last time I'd seen my parents and the disapproval my mother felt about our mission.

'What did you do?'

I curled my finger to beckon him closer, and when his pale face was level with mine, I whispered, 'My father took me hunting, but we didn't tell my mother.'

Eric squealed with laughter, and the sound melted something inside me. I'd never had a brother, but if I had, then Eric was exactly how I imagined he would have been. He was bright, funny, and competitive, and reminded me of myself the more I got to know him.

'Leif returns to Hedeby today too,' he added with a little puff of his chest and a sparkle in his eyes. Eric doted on his older brothers, but he held a soft spot for the only one of Jarl Aaric's sons that I was yet to meet.

'How exciting,' I said, securing the gate on the animal pen as I joined him. 'I'm sure your brother has missed you just as much as you have longed to see him again.'

There was no time for Eric to respond before an arrow fell from the sky and slammed into the boy's thigh. Screaming, he dropped to the ground, clutching at the bleeding wound in his leg. I spun around, looking for the attacker, and spotted a rake outside the grain store. Without thinking, I seized the wooden pole and brandished the prongs at our invisible enemy.

The arrow had sailed over the perimeter fence, and as I stepped forward to investigate, two burly, long-haired Vikings charged through the open gate. I thrust the rake forward and caught the first man in the throat, the sharpened teeth of the rake puncturing his neck and silencing his cries, spraying blood over me in the process.

The second man advanced with more care, his sword drawn and pointed toward Eric. The boy had pulled himself up from the floor and stood holding his own sword with the arrow still protruding from his leg. Blood coated the ground around him as he clenched his teeth, and I couldn't decide if it was due to the pain he must be in or if it was a universal expression of all Vikings, young and old.

Pulling the bloody rake from the fallen man's throat, I swung myself around until I stood between the Viking and Eric.

'Leave him alone!' I yelled. 'He's just a boy.'

The man snarled at me and slashed at the rake, jarring my fingers and causing me to drop the makeshift weapon. I snatched it up from the ground and held it out in front of me, poking the air in a bid to deter the man's attack.

'I said leave him alone!' I shouted again.

My cries had aroused attention; yells and commands carried through the town. Jarl Aaric would soon hear of the disturbance, and I wouldn't want to be in this Viking's shoes when the jarl arrived.

'Stand aside, girl. I want the boy.'

I widened my stance and held my ground. There was no way I was letting this man get to Eric. I don't know why it mattered to me so much. I was a lowly servant and he was a Viking jarl's son, but something deep in my gut bubbled with repressed anger and a desire to defend.

My sisters' faces tore across my mind: the arrow protruding from Ealhswith's throat and Cynethryth's lifeless form on the dirt road. Something inside me snapped. I charged forward with a savage scream and embedded the prongs of my rake in the Viking's side. Stunned, he stumbled backwards and landed heavily on his back. Eric was beside me in a heartbeat, holding the tip of his sword against the man's gullet.

I glanced at the boy to see if he appeared capable of killing but only saw a mask of calm contemplation. For such a young age, Eric showed great restraint. Something I didn't think I could do if the roles were reversed.

Jarl Aaric, Harmod, and Torin pushed through the gathered crowd until they stood alongside us, Aaric's eyes darting around the scene, taking in the dead Viking, the arrow in his son's leg, and the prisoner bleeding into the compacted earth with a rake in his side and a sword at his throat.

'Take him away,' Aaric boomed as two burly men stepped forward to drag the attacker to his fate.

'He's one of Ozur's men,' said Torin, collecting the man's axe from the floor. The intricately carved handle bore what I could only assume was his people's crest.

Aaric nodded in confirmation, his brow wrinkling as if deep in thought. It took a few moments for his deliberations to pass before he swung toward Eric.

'Let me see,' he said, kneeling on the ground by his son. He examined the arrow and, without warning, yanked it from the flesh. A wave of nausea washed over me as Eric yelped and blood spurted over Aaric's big hands.

'Just a scratch,' he said with a flicker of pride in his eyes. 'You acted like a true Viking leader today.'

Eric squared his shoulders, and his little chest puffed out in delight at the jarl's words. Harmod and Torin slapped their meaty hands on their brother's shoulders in support, and the youngster laughed.

'See your mother; she'll clean you up.'

Torin scooped his brother up and flung him over his shoulder, making him laugh even more. They strode off to the great hall, leaving me with Jarl Aaric and a couple of farmers.

Aaric spoke to the man nearest to the gate. 'What happened here?'

'It was fast, Jarl. Two attackers went straight for young Eric, but the slave girl stood in their path. Cut the big fella down and then stabbed the other.'

Aaric's eyebrows raised.

'You really are a warrior slave, aren't you, girl?' he said with a chuckle. 'I'm indebted to you for saving my son.'

'Does that mean I don't have to do any chores?' I said, wiping my bloody hands down my dress.

He laughed again, shaking his massive head. 'Ingrid would have me flayed if I freed all the slaves, but I do think you're more valuable than I first assumed. Let me think about it for a while. In the meantime, continue to do as my wife asks: cook and tend to the animals.'

'Yes, my lord,' I replied.

'I'll have food and a clean dress sent to your room,' he added.

He strode off through the town, following the path his sons had taken, and I marvelled once again at how I'd ended up in his employ. What made this big, hefty Viking jarl pick me out of a crowd of wretched slave girls? It was something I hoped would become clearer as time progressed.

By the time I returned to my sleeping quarters, there was a clean woollen dress and apron waiting for me on my bed. I hugged the outfit close like it was my most precious possession. It was strange how something so simple now gave me such joy.

At the end of my bed was a bowl of water and a jug. I needed to wash away the bloodstains that still coated my skin following the brief altercation with the Vikings.

Slipping the old dress over my head, I dropped it to the floor and stood naked in the small enclosure that was now my home for the foreseeable future. The water was cold but refreshing as it touched my skin, and my body erupted in tiny goose bumps as I scrubbed at the grime and dried blood.

I was so engrossed in cleaning that I didn't hear the boy enter until he coughed. Whirling around, I knocked into the bowl and sent it flying across the floor as I scrambled for something to cover up with. I pressed the new dress to my front and backed up to the far wall until my heels hit the wood.

He didn't seem embarrassed about seeing me naked; in fact, he seemed quite pleased with himself. If I hadn't been using my hands to cover my modesty, I might have slapped his amused face. I assumed from the light blond hair and cropped blond beard that this was the only one of Aaric's sons whom I had yet to meet.

'I'm Leif,' he said, taking a step forward into the small room.

I pressed my back harder against the wall and clutched the cloth even tighter to my naked body. My neck and cheeks burned with humiliation.

He placed a small plate of bread and meat on the bed and a mug of ale on the table, gathering up the fallen water bowl as he went.

'My father sent me with food,' he said. 'But I was also intrigued to meet the warrior slave girl who's the talk of Hedeby.'

Why the town was talking about me I couldn't fathom. They were Vikings for goodness' sake. They butchered their enemies, murdered entire monasteries full of priests, laid waste to every land they plundered, and did it with a song in their heart. I stabbed one bad guy, and suddenly I was interesting. Edmund had always told me that my thirst for adventure would get me into trouble. Well, I thought the adventure I was living at this moment was dangerous enough without drawing additional attention to myself.

Words failed me as I stared at this handsome boy who leaned against the doorframe of my room, oblivious to my mortification. He was tall with muscular arms and shoulders, and when he smiled, a tiny dimple sank into his cheek. All the years I'd spent in my father's court surrounded by Anglo-Saxon men, and I'd never seen anyone as handsome as Leif. I'd met Harmod and Torin out on the road with Jarl Aaric and had marvelled at their good looks—even young Eric was going to be a fine and attractive man when he grew up—but Leif was something different. If the pagan gods did indeed exist, then I imagined that Leif was who they'd modelled themselves on.

'It's an honour to meet you too, Leif. I wonder if you might allow me to dress.'

'Sure,' he said.

He still didn't make any move to leave, and my temper started to give.

'Alone,' I said. 'In private.'

'Ah, of course.' He grinned at me and slowly turned around but not before dragging his gaze along the curves of my body. My toes curled as I flattened the dress against me. I couldn't imagine Elderman Wood would have had this effect on me if we'd made it to our wedding night.

'Come and find me at the water's edge when you're ready,' he added.

Leif finally left me alone, and I flung the linen dress over my head and attached the apron over the top. Soft leather shoes sat in the doorway, and I slipped my feet into them, stuffing the contents of my plate into my mouth and heading out into the afternoon sun.

It felt strange to be a slave and yet be able to come and go as I pleased around the town. Thanks to my earlier actions, the farmers and merchants greeted me with warm smiles. If I wasn't careful, I'd end up in the same position I'd been in on the ship, and my life as a slave would slip into normality.

Making my way to the harbour in search of Leif, I stood a little taller and raised my chin. I might have looked like a slave girl, but I was the last princess of Northumbria. There was no way I was going to let my legacy die along with my family.

9

Leif was sitting on the wooden jetty at the harbour with his long legs swinging over the edge.

'Thank you for the food,' I said, stopping just behind him.

'Father sent it,' he said, absentmindedly skimming stones across the water. 'He thought you needed fattening up.' He paused to look up at me. 'I agree with him.'

'I'll have you know I've managed to put some of my weight back on since your father freed me from the pirates. We didn't get much to eat on that ship,' I said in defence of my scrawny frame. 'I could have killed the rats, but I hear they taste just like chicken.'

Leif laughed, and something shifted inside me. Edmund had laughed at my jokes, but never like that, and poor Baldred had suffered my humour through our darkest days, but I still wasn't sure he hadn't done so out of duty.

'Sit with me for a while.' He patted the jetty beside him, and I sat a respectable distance away with my legs tucked under me.

'I've heard many stories about you, Edith, and yet you've only been in Hedeby a short time.'

'What stories have you heard?' A fluttering panic rose in my chest as I worried that my secret was out. If the Vikings found out I was a princess, they could use me to invade England by holding me to ransom. I wasn't convinced that Aelle would deliver on their terms, which would mean certain death for me and possible invasion and destruction for the people of Northumbria.

Leif continued. 'My father told me you were willing to take on the entire Viking army to defend him.' His eyes twinkled as he spoke, and I realised he was making fun of me.

'I didn't know that Jarl Aaric's men were following us that day,' I said with a slight huff. 'But if they hadn't been the jarl's army, then nobody would be laughing at me now.'

'Do you know how to use a sword?'

I clamped down on the desire to boast. Edmund had been an amazing teacher, and he often told me how proud he was of my ability to take what he showed me and use it in a fighting scenario. Even Baldred had struggled to keep up with me at times.

'I can handle myself,' I said instead.

'That's good to hear, warrior slave girl. Maybe one day you'll show me what you're made of.' He jumped up from the jetty and held a hand out for me. 'For now, let me show you around.'

My stomach lurched as I slipped my palm into his.

We wandered through the town, and I tried to ignore the stares and hushed conversations that surrounded us as we passed the merchant stalls. The usual warm smiles I received had gone, and now there was a sense of disapproval in the air.

'Why is everyone looking at us?'

Leif glanced around at the many faces watching our movements.

'My brother Harmod is married, and Torin has an arrangement with a woman in a neighbouring town, and as one of Aaric's sons, I'm supposed to have a similar bargain in place, but I haven't found anyone I want to marry. The people stare because I'd prefer to spend my time with a slave than a suitor.'

My cheeks coloured at his words. It was nice to hear him say that he preferred my company over anyone else's, however inappropriate it might be.

Thinking about my friendship with Baldred, I understood what Leif meant. Expectations were always higher for those in power, and love didn't seem to count for anything.

'In England, the princesses are bought and sold between kingdoms to avoid war or build alliances. Or so I've heard.'

He raised his eyebrows at my words.

'The more I hear about your England, the more I dislike the place. You allow Christian priests to hoard your treasure in their holy buildings, and your kings squabble over land and titles but don't protect their borders. I'm sure you know nothing of this, being a slave, but surely even the servants are afraid for the future.'

I wished my father was here to listen to Leif's words. He spoke about matters that were brought up in the witan all the time and appeared to hate a country he'd never seen, purely because of the reputations of its leaders.

Swallowing down the lump in my throat, I jumped to my country's defence.

'It's not all bad. In Northumbria, we had a great king who was loved by everyone. He ruled fairly and wisely and cared for the people in his realm.' I was aware of the softness in my voice and hoped that Leif took this as simple patriotism.

'What happened to him?'

I stayed silent for a long while until I felt Leif's eyes studying my profile.

'He was murdered,' I said. 'His crown usurped by an elderman.'

'See what I mean,' Leif said, throwing his hands in the air. 'All they do is squabble over titles.'

We continued out of Hedeby through the southern gate until we arrived at the earthen wall that stretched across the peninsula. The earth was dry out here, and we made clouds of dust with our footsteps. Leif took me further away from the settlement until we were able to look back at it from a distance. It was the first time I had seen the town in its entirety.

The nine-foot-high semicircular earthen wall stretched along the north, west, and south sides of Hedeby. To the east was the inlet and harbour, where many trading ships docked.

Hedeby was a sizable fortress in a defensive position on the top of a hill. I must have looked impressed, as Leif began pointing out various landmarks to me.

'It's magnificent,' I said, meaning every word and wishing I could see Bamburgh one more time. 'There's a fortress in Northumbria that's just as beautiful and sits overlooking the coast. You can hear the roar of the ocean on a calm day as it batters the rocks below.'

Lost in my memories, my eyes misted over. Hedeby disappeared, and in its place stood my home with its high turrets and tiny chapel. My mother's voice drifted through the corridors, and Edmund's sword sang in the courtyard as he trained with the guards.

'Edith?' Leif pushed into my thoughts as he nudged my arm. 'Are you all right?'

I swiped at the tears that spilled down my cheeks.

'I'm fine,' I said, quickly changing the subject. 'Tell me more about your home.'

He didn't say anything else for a long moment, and I wondered if I'd been too sentimental and given myself away, but as the sun sank lower in the sky, he started talking again. I was happy to sit back and bask in the view, listening to his tales.

'It was my father's idea to add the jetties,' he said. 'We sit on a direct route into the North Sea and the opportunity for trade was too good to ignore. Ships pass through from all over the world with strange spices, animals, and, of course, slaves.'

He looked almost embarrassed to say the word, and I giggled at his reaction.

'I'm sure I'm not the first slave your family has bought, Leif. I'm no different from the other girls you've had in your town.'

'But you are,' he replied, looking at me in a way no lord should ever look at the servants.

Heat flushed my cheeks, but I chose to brush off his comment, and his look.

'Slaves come and go; it's their way of life. Just a few weeks ago, I was a slave on a pirate ship, and today I'm the slave of a Viking jarl. Tomorrow might bring something different for me. Who knows?'

'Who owned you when you lived in England?'

I bristled at his question and had to bite down the desire to shout 'Nobody owned me!' Instead, I smiled and lied through my teeth.

'I was a servant in the king's court, but when Aelle took the crown, he sold me to a wrinkly old elderman. It was when I arrived at his fort that the pirates came.'

Leif laughed again, and my stomach flipped at the sound.

'A wrinkly old elderman.'

'He was,' I said with mock horror. 'And he smelt of pickled fish.'

Leif doubled over, and my mouth tugged into a grin at his delight. It felt good to be laughing again. I was just about to tell him how wrinkly Elderman Wood was when I spotted a row of shadows moving at speed in the distance.

Grabbing Leif's arm, I pointed after the figures.

'There are men in the tree line,' I said. 'Have you fetched your own army with you too?'

Leif's expression changed as he surveyed the line of men threading their way along the earthen wall toward Hedeby. The shrubbery secluded us from view, but it wouldn't be long until they cleared the bushes and saw us.

'Ozur's men,' he whispered.

'Torin said the men who attacked Eric were Ozur's men too. What do they want?'

'They want to murder my father and take Hedeby.'

Was it possible that I'd left behind one murdered family in England to then become involved in another attempted massacre, this time of a Viking family? Surely my luck wasn't that bad.

'We need to warn my father,' Leif said.

We scrambled to our feet and started running along the length of the grass mound in the direction of the marsh. I followed Leif, keeping a wary eye out for Ozur's warriors.

Once on the border, with the town in view, Leif stopped beside a huge hollowed-out tree stump and pulled out a bow and arrow hidden within the carcass.

'I'm going to signal the men on watch, but I need you to find my father and make sure my family gets to safety. Can you do that for me, Edith?'

There was total trust in his eyes as he asked me to help him, and I didn't falter with my answer.

'Of course,' I said, a quiver of alarm in my voice. 'What do I tell Jarl Aaric?'

'Tell him they've surrounded the town; he'll know what to do.'

I nodded and sprinted off toward the southern gate. The sun had dipped below the horizon, and as I ran, my heart pounded at the possibility of being in the thick of a battle. Not a single part of me wanted to run and hide. Instead, I hoped the jarl would throw me a sword and let me stand by his side. Exhilaration powered my muscles as I barrelled through the gate and along the darkening streets toward the great hall.

'Jarl Aaric,' I cried upon bursting through the huge doors to the hall. 'You're under attack. Ozur's men have you surrounded, and Leif is outside the gate.'

The jarl and fifty Vikings leapt to their feet and rushed for the door, grabbing their axes and shields as they went. Harmod and Torin raced after their father, and only the strict hand of his mother stopped young Eric from joining them.

'My lady, what can I do to help?'

Ingrid took a moment to look around the hall before pointing at a woman dressed in a black leather tunic and matching trousers. Her hair was braided tight to her scalp, decorated with metal rings, and her face was painted black in a strip around her eyes. She held a spear in one hand and a sword in the other.

'Solveig, take the girl and protect the great hall.'

Solveig marched forward, handing me the sword and herding me back outside into the street. She slammed the wooden doors shut and spun to face the courtyard beyond the hall.

'We wait,' she said. 'Enemies who break through our walls will make their way here, and it falls at our feet to protect Ingrid.'

The tales that travelled across England about the raiders from the North talked about the women who fought alongside their men. At the time, I'd listened with fascination but believed them to be only stories, nothing more.

'You are thinking too loudly,' Solveig said, never once taking her eyes off the streets.

'Sorry, I…I've never met a female warrior.'

'I'm a shield-maiden,' she huffed as if that explained everything.

'What's a shield-maiden?'

Solveig dragged her watchful gaze in my direction for the briefest of seconds, and I wilted under the intensity of her stare.

'*I'm* a shield-maiden.'

She left it at that, and I had to admire her confidence. Every inch of her screamed warrior and what I assumed was at the core of any shield-maiden: the pursuit of battle.

'Be ready,' she added, dropping her spear so it pointed out into the darkness.

Three of Ozur's men rushed forward with their swords drawn and bore down on us, bellowing a war cry as they moved.

Solveig flung her spear into the chest of the middle man, who was catapulted backwards, leaving two men—one each.

Remembering my training, I gripped the hilt of the sword in two hands and braced myself for the attack. The Viking was about a foot taller than me and as wide as a door. Blood speckled his face, and his tunic had torn where a blade or axe had already penetrated the leather.

He lunged forward with his sword, and I managed to block his strike, using my leg to kick him in the groin and push him away. For a second, he lowered his guard, and I swiped the blade along his forearm. He swung his sword at my head, and I ducked below the knife-edge. I hurled myself at the man's torso, sending us both flying. We hit the floor with a grunt, and I sprang to my feet, plunging my sword into his chest.

My heart pounded in my ears as I pushed down on the hilt, watching the life leach out of the man's eyes. There was no time to contemplate my actions before another assailant burst into the courtyard and ran at me.

His axe caught the top of my arm as he whirled it in an arc, and the metal stung as it tore open the skin. Blood poured from the wound. The momentum of his swing carried him off-balance, and I used the falter in his step to my advantage. I smashed my elbow into his nose, and he lurched forward, allowing me space to run my sword along his throat. A spray of blood arced across the air, covering my face and hair. The beautiful apron I'd only just received was drenched in blood and sweat, but I'd never felt more alive in my life.

Somewhere in the deepest recess of my brain, I imagined doing this to the elderman who helped usurp my father's throne and had my family murdered. I pictured the look on his face as I buried my blade in his chest and reminded him of who I was when he took a final breath. The feeling of satisfaction was like a drug, and I raised my face to the heavens and hollered like a wild animal standing over its fresh kill.

'Edith?'

I blinked and wiped at the blood dripping into my eyes, trying to focus on who was calling my name. Solveig was cleaning the blade of a sword on the edge of her tunic with a pile of bodies at her feet.

Jarl Aaric shoved his way to the front of the rapidly assembling crowd, holding a man's severed head in his hands, and Torin was helping Harmod sit on the ground to tend to a wound.

'Edith.' The voice came from behind me, and I spun to see Leif studying me with a mixture of wonder and surprise on his handsome face. 'Are you all right?'

'I'm fine,' I said, but no sooner had I uttered the words than the world tilted. I remembered the axe biting into my arm and peered down to see the blood-soaked sleeve of my dress. 'I think I might be hurt.'

Twenty feet away, Ingrid opened the doors to the great hall, and the Vikings flooded inside to tend to their injuries and drink ale. They had secured a victory over Ozur's men and slaughtered the entire band sent to destroy Hedeby. Aaric was holding on to the head of their best warrior and boasting about his eagerness to dispatch it back to Ozur with a warning.

Leif helped me inside and ripped the sleeve of my dress open. I gagged at the gash on my arm where the skin was jagged and raw. He soaked strips of cloth and washed away the blood. It didn't look quite so bad once cleaned.

'I need to sew the skin together,' he said, handing me a piece of wood.

'What's that for?'

'Bite down on it.'

A wave of nausea rose up in my throat as he readied the hook and thread in his hand. I was about to get a real-life battle scar, but it didn't quash the sudden desire I had to throw up.

Leif seemed to sense my wobble and handed me a large jug of ale, which I drained in one go. A couple of the Vikings sitting at our table clapped their hands on my shoulder in admiration as I hiccupped.

'All right,' I said. 'Do it.'

With the ale sloshing in my belly and muting my thoughts, I bit down on the wood as hard as I could as Leif pushed the hook into my skin and started sewing my arm back together. The pain was horrific, but with the discomfort came the realisation that I was *feeling* something. Over the past three months, I'd numbed myself to everything. I'd become an emotionless slave with no identity and no drive. As I rotted in the cells of the ship, my brain was full of plots and escape plans, and my heart was full of hatred, but as the days stretched into weeks, and then months, I began to exist instead of live, and I almost forgot who I was. I'd kept telling myself I was the last princess of Northumbria, but saying it and believing it were two very different things.

With each stitch, I was getting closer and closer to the light, and I knew that I needed help if I was ever to get revenge for my family. I knew I couldn't tell Jarl Aaric, or Leif, the truth about who I was, but I could use my time here with them to build my strength and become the warrior queen of England I'd promised my father I would be one day.

10

The summer months faded fast, and the winds and rain of autumn descended almost overnight to batter Hedeby and drive everyone indoors to the comfort and warmth of the raging fires.

The great hall was full every evening as I attended to the jarl's needs. Pouring ale and serving food to the hungry Vikings seemed to be an endless task. I'd never seen men eat so much in my life. In my father's court, we had used crockery and delicate knives to eat our meals, but here it was like serving the cattle that lived in the pens.

Night after night, I served up great bowls of roasted meat, which were torn apart by impatient hands. The ale slopped over everything, leaving a pungent smell in the air that penetrated my clothes and hair.

Ingrid had kindly gifted me another dress and apron after I ruined mine in the battle with Ozur's men, but I'd almost washed them away trying to get the smell of food and mead out of the garments.

'More ale for me, warrior slave girl,' called Harmod above the buzz of laughter and swapped stories.

I pushed my way through the beefy arms and wide shoulders to pour more ale into Harmod's horn and smiled in greeting to Leif, who sat opposite his brother.

I hadn't had a chance to speak to Leif since Ozur's men attacked Hedeby. Our one stolen moment out on the earthen wall looked to be a singular occurrence as Jarl Aaric sent him out across the lands to rally allies against the future threat of invasion.

Leif held his drinking horn toward me, and I filled it to the brim.

'How's your arm?' he asked me as I topped up more cups.

'Much better, thank you. It's healed well.'

He nodded and took a long swallow of his drink.

'You fought well that night,' he said softly.

The Viking to his left, an immense man called Magnus, slapped a meaty hand on Leif's back and roared with laughter. 'Does the son of Jarl Aaric have a soft spot for our warrior slave girl?'

Leif shrugged Magnus's hand from his back and dropped his head to pick at the chicken on his plate.

Everyone around us laughed and teased us, but I ignored their jibes and carried on with my duties, a warm sensation pooling in my gut. I'd learnt the art of becoming invisible in the great hall, as it allowed me time to listen to what was being said and find out who was coming and going from the harbour, but I couldn't deny that any moment spent in Leif's company was always welcome.

With the winter months rolling in, it meant the inlet would freeze over and no more boats would arrive until the spring. In a way, I was pleased with this discovery, as it gave me more time to watch and learn the Viking warrior ways.

I trailed after Solveig at every opportunity, much to her annoyance, but she tolerated my presence so long as I kept quiet.

'Maybe you could meet our Leif in the pigsty after dark,' Magnus hollered to another round of laughter. 'Isn't that where the slaves sleep?'

A pink flush crept across Leif's cheeks, and anger bubbled up beneath my skin as I eyeballed the brawny Viking.

'That would be ideal,' I said loud enough for everyone to hear. 'For the pigs have left the sty, preferring the stench in your house.'

A blanket of silence settled over the great hall as the words left my mouth, and I feared I'd crossed a line, but the big Viking's shoulders started to tremble, and then he was laughing and slapping the table with his hands.

'I like you, warrior slave girl,' he boomed across the hall, and everyone cheered.

As I made my way back to the jarl's table to replenish my jug, the warriors patted and congratulated me. I was still grinning when I arrived at Ingrid's side, but her cold stare wiped the smile from my face, and I mumbled an apology for being inappropriate.

'You are a constant source of surprise, Edith,' she said. 'But I can't fail to admire your courage.'

Jarl Aaric clapped his hands, silencing the good-humoured murmurings until all eyes were on him. I stepped back into the shadows and watched.

'I know we are preparing for the winter months ahead, but I can't help but think about the future. Ozur is keen to win Hedeby, and with that threat hanging over us, I fear it will force my hand once the spring raids are upon us. I intend to invade his lands and end the feud as soon as possible. Who's with me?'

Every man was on their feet and punching the air with either fist or axe. The jarl's people loved him, and I wondered if they'd do anything he asked of them. My father used to evoke the same reaction, albeit a slightly more reserved one, when he needed to rally the soldiers of Northumbria. The sign of a good leader was in how they used the power entrusted to them by the people. Cruelty and fear might keep men in line, but loyalty and passion meant they would cross oceans for you.

'Where will we raid when the time comes?' asked one of the men sitting at the front of the hall.

Jarl Aaric's eyes searched the room until he met my gaze.

'We invade England,' he said.

My heart lurched at his words, and the jug I was holding fell from my grasp and clattered to the ground. A great cheer went up from the assembled warriors, and their excited chatter invaded my head, making it spin.

England. My England. Why did Jarl Aaric want to invade my homeland? He'd stayed away from the raids on my country, choosing to maintain his trade route and build the reputation of Hedeby. I couldn't understand why he was now following in the footsteps of some of the most notorious Viking warriors who had swept across Europe.

Aaric held his hand in the air to silence the men and then pointed at me. My limbs grew heavy as he beckoned me to approach. I was a shadow. I was a slave. I wasn't a symbol of invasion.

'You all know our warrior slave girl,' he said, at which Magnus slapped Leif on the back again. 'She can tell us about England, about its riches—and its weaknesses.'

No, no, no. The words screamed through my brain as I walked to the raised platform where Aaric and Ingrid sat on their thrones. I couldn't betray my home. I couldn't help a Viking army cross the sea and invade Bamburgh. I could, however, use this to my advantage. My goal had always been to learn what I could by watching the Vikings, to build my strength, and to escape.

The idea jumped into my head fully formed—convince Aaric to take me with him as a guide. Once back on English soil, I could run away and return to Bamburgh and my uncle. He was the king of Northumbria now and would want to know that his niece was safe. Although there was no real affection between us, I hoped he would want to find out who murdered his brother and extended family, as that plot might run deep enough to threaten his own life. I was also sure he would have amassed a large army by now, and that they would be able to defend Northumbria from the enemy I was about to unleash on its shores.

I could give away small fragments of secrets, just enough to entice the Vikings to make the trip, but as I studied the sea of expectant faces, I fought to sort through my jumbled emotions. England was my home and I loved it dearly, yet as I glanced out toward Leif, I realised I'd formed bonds here too, and I felt torn between two worlds.

My head and heart were divided. The princess of Northumbria was eager to return home and work hard to show the people how much she deserved the crown, but the warrior slave girl had opened her heart to the Vikings, and they had provided trust and friendship.

'Tell us,' shouted one of the men, 'what is England like?'

I glided across the stage, standing front and centre. All the warriors in the room were looking at me, and I felt the power beneath my skin like an itch. Is this what my father experienced when he spoke at the witan or addressed the people of Northumbria? It was good practice for me to talk like this if I was going to claim my crown one day.

'England is a rich and fertile land full of treasures beyond your wildest dreams,' I said. 'She is ruled by many kings who fight amongst themselves. They divide the kingdom instead of uniting it, and that's where her greatest weakness is.'

The Vikings cheered again, and I stepped back to let Jarl Aaric take the stage and build on the buoyant mood.

'That was quite the speech, Edith,' Ingrid said over my shoulder. 'Worthy of a leader perhaps.'

I shook my head and slouched in the hope that I appeared more subservient than superior.

'Not at all, my lady. I watched King Osberht give many speeches during my time in his service, and I suppose you could say he inspired me.'

'Your king must have been a great teacher,' she said. 'But maybe it's time you had another great teacher to guide you through the rest of your journey.'

I didn't understand her words until Solveig emerged from behind the black curtain. Then I understood her meaning, and it was everything I'd hoped for but had not dared to voice.

'You have defended my home, protected my son, and proved yourself to be a trustworthy slave. Although you are not a free woman, I no longer require you to work for me. Instead, I want you to train with Solveig to become a shield-maiden. If you prove yourself worthy as a true warrior, then you may yet win your freedom.'

The magnitude of what she was saying crushed me like a rock. If I worked hard, I could be free. Free to fight, free to return home, free to marry. Leif's face floated into view, but I pushed it aside. Was it possible to live in both worlds? I bowed to Ingrid and Solveig to show my appreciation for the gift they had given me. This was no time to think about chores or relationships; it was time for archery, sword skills, and learning the ways of the Vikings.

Whoever murdered my family was oblivious to the horrors heading their way.

~

'Are you born a shield-maiden or do you have to be made one by a jarl?'

Solveig and I had been training hard all morning, and as the rest of Hedeby was waking for breakfast, we were taking our first break.

'I was born a shield-maiden, as were my mother and grandmother. My father was a great warrior too, and my brother, but they were killed in battle a few years ago.'

'I'm sorry to hear that,' I said. 'My family was killed too, but not in battle.'

Solveig slid her piercing eyes in my direction, which over time I'd learnt meant she was semi-interested in what you were saying.

'Bandits murdered my parents and two sisters. I was the only one to survive, although my escape meant I ended up as a slave on a pirate ship.'

'Would you rather have died with your family?'

I stopped to think about her question, having never thought about it until now. 'No, at the time I would have happily followed them to heaven, but now I'm on a different path.'

'This heaven you speak about, it's a Christian belief, isn't it?'

'Yes, a bit like your Valhalla, but without the ale and fighting.' I chuckled.

'There are many differences between our peoples, and yet I see many similarities too. We farm the fields and work hard to provide for our families, and this is the same all over the new lands.'

'Family and community are so important to the Vikings, but I can tell you it's the same in England. When we get to the shores, you'll see it for yourself.'

'Jarl Aaric has said you can come then?'

I slumped a little in my seat. 'I haven't asked him yet,' I said.

'Your training is progressing well, but the decision to take you to England or leave you here to defend Hedeby is his. Perhaps the seer will help him decide.'

The blood in my veins ran cold at her words. The seers were revered in this part of the world. They predicted good crops, battles, and interpreted portents which would help guide a jarl to make good judgements, but they could also see behind the dark veil of secrecy, and I lived within that veil.

'There's a seer in Hedeby?' I tried to keep my tone normal and hoped Solveig wouldn't recognise the spike of alarm in my voice.

Solveig nodded and bit into an apple, oblivious to my growing unease. Would the seer know who I was? Would they be able to sense that I was planning to escape once the boats landed on the English shore? I made a vow to avoid the great hall for a time and stay out of the way of any newcomers to Hedeby.

I changed the subject, hoping Solveig wouldn't pick up on my agitation, and started chatting about the stories I'd heard about shield-maidens.

'The merchants and wanderers who pass through Hedeby always have a story to tell, Edith. You need to learn which ones are tales spun for entertainment and which are true.'

'So tell me the true story of a shield-maiden,' I pressed, enthusiastic to learn more about the incredible warrior women.

Solveig threw the core of her apple into the nearby animal trough and cleared her throat. 'The only shield-maiden you need to know about is Hervor,' she said. 'She was the daughter of a great warrior called Angantry who was killed in battle overseas. When he died, he was buried with the cursed sword, Tyrfing. Hervor wanted the sword for herself and claimed it was her birthright.'

I could relate to Hervor's need to retrieve what was rightfully hers and prompted Solveig to continue with the story.

'She sailed to the place where her father died and his body was buried with the sword and called out to him until his ghost appeared to her. She asked for the sword, but her father told her of its curse. He told Hervor that anyone who wielded it but was unable to kill once the blade was out of its sheath would be driven mad. Hervor told her father she was capable of wielding the sword, and eventually he gave it up.'

'What happened to her?' I asked.

'She wielded the sword easily until her death, but when it passed to her sons, they couldn't control the curse and were driven mad.'

'That's incredible,' I said. 'Why was she able to wield it but not her own flesh and blood?'

'Because, my dear Edith, the sword could only be commanded by a shield-maiden.'

I mulled the story over and over in my mind as Solveig continued my training with a bow and arrow. Could I be like Hervor and wield a sword to change England forever? More and more I'd been thinking about my plans to kill whoever helped usurp my father's throne, to kill the elderman whose actions had helped my uncle Aelle steal my title, but I also couldn't shake the desire to unite all England under one crown. I'd said it as a joke to make my father laugh all those moons ago, yet why couldn't it become a reality? Being young had its flaws, yes, but there were also a great number of advantages to me being a young queen. My brain leapt to the possibility of uniting the Anglo-Saxons and the Vikings through marriage. It was only what my uncle had done with Elderman Wood and me, but at least if I got my way, I'd marry a handsome Viking instead of a smelly old man.

A pebble hit me on the side of the head, and I snapped back to the present moment.

'I hope I'm not interrupting your daydreams with our training, girl.'

I giggled. There was a time and a place for daydreaming, but now it was time to become a shield-maiden. I could fantasise about Leif later.

'If you ever want to be worthy of Hervor's respect, then you need to concentrate,' she snapped. 'Being a shield-maiden means dedicating yourself to the protection and defence of Hedeby for so long as you have breath in your body. Can you commit to that, girl?'

Picking up another arrow from the ground, I readied it on the bow. The target danced in the breeze as the shield we used for practice swung on the end of a rope. I focused on the movement, channelling all my power and thought on the object ahead of me, and steadied my breathing until all I could see was the arrow tip and the target.

I'd protect Hedeby and its people, I'd defend the Viking family who had brought me into their home and allowed me to live, but my last breath would be taken on English soil as I avenged my family.

I let loose the arrow, and it struck the centre of the shield with a satisfying thud.

If I could stay away from the seer and remain an invisible slave until the raids, there was every chance I could be back home in Bamburgh and resuming my life as a princess before the spring equinox. I wouldn't need to earn Hervor's respect then because I'd have the regard of the people of Northumbria. I just hoped that my actions and dealings with the Vikings wouldn't bring about the destruction of my home. Guiding Aaric's raiding party to a remote coastal beach far from Bamburgh should ensure the safety of some of my kinsmen, but I knew that many would die in battle regardless of how hard I tried to send the Vikings the wrong way.

Protect and defend. That's what Solveig wanted me to do, but all I wanted was revenge and death.

11

It had proved more difficult to avoid the great hall than I'd hoped. My duties to serve the ale to the men might have ended, but Jarl Aaric still requested my presence, and he was one man I couldn't ignore.

I walked through the doors, and the vibrant energy in the room hit me. The warriors were on their feet thrusting their swords in the air, and their excited chatter bounced off the walls.

Solveig was at the back of the hall with her arms crossed over her chest and her expression slightly darker and stormier than usual. I made my way to where she stood.

'What's going on?'

She slid her gaze over me and shook her head. 'When will you start dressing like a shield-maiden, girl? You're embarrassing me.'

I peered down at my woollen dress and apron: the uniform of a slave. Solveig had gifted me with tight-fighting trousers, a linen tunic, and an outer garment made of leather and metal rings. It was a warrior's outfit, and I didn't yet feel like a warrior.

'I'll wear it when Jarl Aaric tells me I can,' I said, lifting my chin as I spoke. I needed to continue the ruse of being a slave, and slaves asked for permission from their lords before doing anything.

Solveig huffed and adjusted her stance so she was leaning more toward me.

'I get the impression you'll be getting his blessing very soon.' She nodded toward the raised platform as Aaric and Ingrid glided into view. The Viking warriors erupted in great cheers, and the hairs on my arms prickled with the sound.

'We have fought off skirmish after skirmish over the past few moons,' Aaric said, his voice carrying across the great hall. 'Ozur continues to send his men to prod and poke at our defences, looking for weaknesses, but time and again we send the bloodied remains of his army back to him.'

More cheers from the warriors.

'Preparations are going well for our spring raids, and so I want us to turn our attention to Hedeby and the threat that hangs over her. When we sail for England, we will be taking our best warriors and leaving her exposed, and that is unacceptable.'

I watched the Vikings as they listened to their jarl's speech. Respect and loyalty oozed from every pore, and it reminded me of my father's last witan. The king of Mercia had appealed for allies to help him beat back the threat of his own cousin, who had raised a small army and was causing upset for the eldermen of Mercia. My father had stood at the front of the hall to address the men of the witan just like the jarl stood in front of his men now. I was hidden in the shadows, watching and listening as the council debated the idea of sending aid or letting the king fall.

'*The kingdom of Northumbria is my first concern,*' my father had said, silencing the witan with authority in his voice. '*Leaving our borders unprotected while we rush to help our neighbour is a foolish act. I will not leave this land exposed.*'

'*We must do something to help them, my lord king,*' added Elderman Proctor, a small, wiry man with jet-black hair. '*We may need their help in the future should the Vikings invade.*'

My father had mulled this over for a short time before making his decision. '*We can spare fifty men, but that's all.*'

The witan was pacified, the king of Mercia received assistance, and our home remained intact and protected.

Listening to Jarl Aaric's speech, I began to understand how great leaders thought. Both my father and the jarl's first instinct was to protect their home. Nothing else mattered beyond that task.

The jarl continued. 'No longer can we stay behind these walls and fend off attacks. It's time to take the fight to Ozur. In two nights, we march for our neighbour's fortress and put a stop to Ozur and his campaign for good. Are you with me?'

The cheers nearly lifted the roof this time.

It was easy to get caught up in the elation and potential of a battle. Training with Solveig had prepared me well, and with my experience with a sword, I felt ready to march with Jarl Aaric.

Nudging Solveig with my elbow, I leaned forward to whisper in her ear.

'Will we both be going into battle?'

She almost smiled at me, but the twitch of her lip vanished within a second.

'That's not for me to say, girl.'

I didn't notice the jarl working his way through the crowds until he stood towering over Solveig and me.

'Is she ready?' he asked Solveig, ignoring me altogether.

'She's ready,' Solveig said with a nod. 'But not dressed like that.'

Jarl Aaric laughed that hearty laugh I'd come to love hearing so much and slapped a big hand on my shoulder.

'My warrior slave girl is fit for battle,' he said with a smile. 'You will join us when we march on Ozur's fortress, and you will wear something more appropriate, as Solveig suggests. Does this sound acceptable to you, girl?'

Rolling my shoulders back so I stood a little taller, I grinned up at Jarl Aaric. 'It would be an honour to fight at your side.'

'That's settled then. You travel with Solveig and Leif.'

He left us then, melting into the throng of warriors impatient to talk battle plans with their lord, and I savoured the thought of fighting alongside a real Viking army. I wondered what Edmund would say if he could see me now.

'You're in great demand this evening, girl,' said Solveig, stepping aside so I could see straight across the hall.

Ingrid was beckoning me to join her, but my feet remained rooted to the spot as my gaze landed upon her companion.

'Who's that?' I asked Solveig, although I already knew the answer.

'That's the seer,' she said. 'Good luck, warrior slave girl.'

Everything inside me screamed at me to run. Run from the building, run from Hedeby, and keep running until I hit the ocean, but to ignore Ingrid was to sign your own death warrant.

My feet grew heavier with every step I took across the hall. The seer was a wizened old woman dressed in black. A heavy cloak hung from her thin frame, and wisps of white hair escaped the hood that masked her face from view. She carried a twisted walking stick engraved with rune symbols with a mixture of feathers and bones attached to the tip.

'I hear you will be fighting alongside my son in the upcoming battle,' Ingrid said as I arrived at her side. 'Solveig tells me you are an impressive student.'

I wanted to laugh at her words. Solveig was incapable of showing any emotion other than a simmering annoyance over anything and anyone. To hear that she thought I was worthy made my heart sing.

'Thank you, my lady. I hope to make her proud.'

Ingrid nodded but remained straight-faced. Ever since my arrival in Hedeby, she had refused to let down her defences and allow me in. She seemed to prefer keeping me at a safe distance, but I couldn't understand why. The other slave girls were often invited to bed down in the great hall at night to avoid travelling through the town in bad weather, but Ingrid had yet to extend the same courtesy to me.

'I have someone who wants to meet you,' she said, standing aside so I could focus on the seer, who hovered behind her.

The blood in my veins turned to ice as I shifted my gaze and turned to the figure in black.

'It's an honour to meet you,' I said, not forgetting my upbringing despite my growing fears.

The seer stepped forward, lowering her hood. Although her face was deeply wrinkled and her hair as white as snow, her eyes were sharp and the clearest blue I'd ever seen.

She balanced her walking stick against Ingrid's throne and took both my hands in hers. I was surprised at how soft and warm they were and at the sense of peace that flooded through me.

'I see great suffering,' she said. 'Great loss.'

I tried to tug my hands free, but she had them in a tight grip.

'You've lost everything that was dear to you,' she continued. 'Yet your heart is not as hard as I would expect. There's a small flame that burns within you still.'

A trickle of sweat crawled down my temple. I felt like I was rooted to the spot, frozen in time and space, unable to move. Ingrid remained at our side, and I prayed that the seer wouldn't break through my mask and reveal my secrets.

'She is the one I foresaw,' she said, turning to Ingrid. 'The girl from my dreams.'

I wrenched my hands free and took a step backwards, my head spinning like I'd just drunk a gallon of ale. What did she mean by the girl from her dreams?

Ingrid took a deep breath, and I half expected her to call for an axe, but instead she turned to the black curtain and swept it aside.

'Come with me, Edith,' she said, pointing through the curtain into the jarl's private chambers.

I followed her into a spacious room with a large bed and a long table with benches on either side. Animal furs covered the bed and woven blankets stretched across the seats; the entire room was warm and inviting, unlike my draughty barn. I'd never seen the inside of my parents' rooms, and so it felt wrong to be standing in such a private space.

'Sit,' Ingrid instructed.

I balanced myself on the edge of the nearest bench to the door, hoping I wouldn't need to make a run for it. Whatever the seer had said clearly meant something to Ingrid. Fine wrinkles lined her usually smooth brow.

'What do you remember about the day my husband bought you at the slave market?'

Her question threw me. That had been many moons ago and surely couldn't have any relevance on what the seer must have predicted, but I answered her just the same.

'Jarl Aaric wanted to buy me from the lineup of girls on display, but the captain refused him. The jarl was upset by this, and there was a…difference of opinion.'

'He killed the captain.' It was a statement rather than a question. I assumed Jarl Aaric had told Ingrid what happened at the harbour.

Ingrid turned to the seer, who had followed behind us into the chamber.

'You saw a single girl, seer, a lone slave. Are you sure she's the one?'

The seer shuffled forward, and I squirmed on the seat.

'You weren't part of the sale, were you?' she asked, leaning on her walking stick.

I swallowed down the discomfort that threatened to unhinge me and addressed Ingrid once more.

'I was at the market with the other slaves, but at the last minute, the captain kept me separate. I got the impression he no longer wanted to sell me.'

Ingrid paced the floor, and my pulse raced beneath my skin. Why was it so important how the jarl had come by me?

'I saw you in my dreams,' the seer said again. 'A single slave touched by death and deceit. A slave who is not a slave but has the power to unite or destroy a kingdom.'

My heart hammered.

'Edith, I'm going to ask you this once, and I need you to be honest with me,' Ingrid said, taking a step forward.

Her sincerity shocked me, and I chewed at my lip as I waited for the question she was about to ask.

'Are you truly a slave?'

I was holding my breath. My answer was obviously important to both Ingrid and the seer, although I had no idea why. I could tell them the whole truth, or I could offer half-truths, but I feared the seer would know if I was lying. My brain battled with my heart as I deliberated on what to do next.

'No,' I finally heard myself say. 'I'm a princess.'

⁓

I guided my sword into its sheath and secured the buckle to my belt. It nestled at my waist. The leather tunic Solveig had given me fitted perfectly and hugged my curves. I wore leather shoes, woollen trousers, and straps along my forearms to protect the skin from our enemies' blades.

'You look every inch the warrior slave girl,' Leif said with a laugh as he entered my room.

I giggled and took a small bow. 'Ready and willing to serve you, my lord.'

Hearing him call me by my adopted nickname meant that Ingrid must have kept my revelation a secret. My meeting with the seer had ended soon after I'd owned up to who I was, but Ingrid had insisted that I return to her chambers should I survive the battle.

For a fleeting moment, I prayed that I wouldn't make it back at all and my secret would remain just that, but then I thought about my parents, Edmund, and even Baldred, and I knew that I would fight well and survive this day. Ingrid now knew I was a princess, and the time had come to piece together how she knew, and why it was so important, and what the seer's prophecy meant. I'd expected her to call for the jarl, but she hadn't. She'd just sat on the bed and clasped her hands together as if in prayer. The seer had shooed me out at that point, and I'd run through the hall and back to the sanctuary of my barn.

'Stay close to me,' Leif said, and his soft voice pulled me from my thoughts. 'Keep both Solveig and me in sight at all times.'

'Of course,' I said. 'Don't worry about me. Solveig has taught me well.'

His jaw set in a hard line as his piercing eyes studied me.

'I know I'm a jarl's son, and I have responsibilities, but I care deeply about you, Edith, and I don't want any harm to come to you.'

My skin tingled at his words, and a warm sensation flooded through me. I'd never met a man like Leif. None of the Saxon men I'd met over the years stirred such emotion in me, and I wondered if this was what love felt like.

'I understand the duties you have to Hedeby,' I said. 'But nothing can ever happen between us, Leif. I'm a slave first and foremost, and your parents would want better for you.'

I pushed down the desire to tell him I was more than worthy of his love, that I was his equal. We might be the same, but we lived in very different worlds.

He stepped up to me so we were inches apart and cupped my face in his hands. His eyes were full of compassion as he lowered his mouth and kissed me. My stomach flipped over, and my heart hammered beneath my rib cage. It was a perfect kiss: soft and gentle.

'I'm in love with you, Edith,' he whispered into my hair. 'Nothing can change that, not my father, not my mother, not the people of Hedeby. I know my own heart.'

Words bubbled up in my throat, but I had to stuff them back down as Solveig strode into the barn with two long spears.

'Ah, my apologies for the interruption,' she said, coming to a halt in the doorway. 'It's time to leave.'

Leif removed his hands from my face and nodded at Solveig as he left the room. My face burned, and I wondered if there were flames leaping from my skin. Solveig raised an eyebrow as she watched me adjust my belt and turn to the door.

'What?' I said.

A wide grin spread across my mentor's face, and it changed her entire look. She had a beautiful smile, and her eyes twinkled with mischief. It was a side of Solveig I'd never seen. In truth, it was a side of Solveig I don't think anyone had ever seen.

'You two make a lovely couple,' she said with a chuckle. 'That's if the jarl keeps you alive long enough for it to work out.'

She laughed loudly, and I laughed along with her. My predicament amused her, and I revelled in this bond we shared.

'If you survive the day, girl, I think the winter months will be highly entertaining.'

'Thanks for your support, my friend,' I said. 'I truly don't know what I'd do without you.'

She laughed again and shoved me through the door into the street, where crowds had begun to gather and make their way to the great hall.

'I'll always be at your side, warrior slave girl—always.'

She marched off after the Vikings, and I faltered at her words. They had been sincere, heartfelt even. For all her icy exterior and moody temperament, Solveig had become as important to me as Edmund had been in my other life.

Shaking off my thoughts, I sprinted after my mentor and fell into step beside her. The early morning air was cold, making our breath settle in tiny clouds that danced around us. Viking warriors milled around us dressed in leathers and furs, and the sounds of sharpening blades and the exchange of war stories carried on the breeze. Children scurried between legs and spears in a frenzy as everyone painted their shields and faces.

Upon reaching the hall, Solveig ushered me to a woman who was handing out pots of crushed berries. I took an earthenware bowl from her and started applying a band of the blue paint across my eyes to match the black band that Solveig always wore.

The men around us painted runes and symbols on their skin, and I wondered what they all meant as I surveyed the hundreds of assembled fighters.

We looked terrifying, and I finally saw what the villagers of England must have seen when the Vikings landed on their shores for the first time. Huge men with arms the size of ale barrels brandished their axes. Female warriors covered in war paint with their hair tightly braided smashed the pommel of their swords against their shields. It was a sensory overload as the Viking army prepared for battle, and a sliver of icy panic trickled down my spine. I stared down at my warrior outfit and the paint staining my hands. I glanced at the spear in my hand and the sword at my belt. I was every inch a Viking.

I'd stepped into their world with ease and embraced their way of life as my own. Many moons ago, I'd told myself I'd use the Vikings to teach me how to defend myself until I could escape and avenge my family, but as I stood in the centre of Jarl Aaric's warriors, I could only see what I'd become.

If I survived this day, I would be forever immortalised as a shield-maiden, the silk dresses and jewellery from my days as a princess fading into distant memory. The time was growing nearer for me to decide which life I wanted to pursue—that of a princess or that of a Viking.

12

The ground was crisp with the first smattering of frost as we marched out of the southern gate and headed up the Jutland peninsula. Ozur's fortress was a couple of hours away, but the warriors were in high spirits as we snaked through the grasslands.

I'd seen my father's soldiers head off to battle only once, when I was much younger, and the mood of the men had been stoic yet apprehensive. The Vikings, however, were a different breed of men. They enjoyed battle; they saw it as a noble pursuit and a doorway into Valhalla where they could drink and fight with the gods.

'What are you thinking about, girl?' Solveig asked, handing me an apple.

'I never saw a battle when I was in England,' I said. 'I watched the soldiers marching off to war, and I witnessed the aftermath when they returned to the fortress, but I never got to see the fighting.'

'Are you eager to plunge your sword into another man's belly?'

I pondered Solveig's question. In such a short time, I'd killed three men: two pirates back in England and one Viking since arriving in Hedeby. None of these acts filled me with the glory I heard in the other Vikings' tales.

'I'm not eager to do it, but I'm not afraid.'

It was the truth. When Edmund had started teaching me how to handle a sword, my hands shook with fear and anxiety. It took me many months before I could pick up the weapon and hold it steady. Over time, I'd developed the skill to strike, block, and swing a blade with ease. But you couldn't compare sparring with my mentor in a secluded courtyard within the safety of my father's fortress and fighting for my life on a field in the middle of winter.

'I'm not afraid,' I whispered again.

'Are you trying to convince yourself or me?'

I glanced across at Solveig and smiled. She was like a demon, dressed in black from head to foot with matching war paint across her eyes. The spear she carried rested against her shoulder and wobbled in the air with every stride. At the end of her braids, she'd tied chicken bones and metal rings. *'To my enemies, it looks like I wear the bones of their children,'* she'd told me as she fastened them to her black hair. She was a ferocious sight, and I was glad to be fighting alongside her rather than against her.

'How many battles have you fought in, Solveig?'

'More than I care to remember,' she said with a sidelong glance. 'My father would take me with him when I was a youngster and leave me in the trees to observe and learn. I used to watch him plough through his enemies, hacking them down and screaming to Odin of his success.'

'When did you stop watching and start fighting?'

She sucked in a deep breath, and I thought for a moment she was growing weary of my questions.

'It was a clear winter's day, very similar to this one, and my father and brother were marching to aid a jarl on the west coast. They took me along as always, and I found a sturdy tree to hide in which looked out over the battlefield. There was a strange taste in the air that day, and I begged my father not to leave me, but he didn't listen. He fell in battle, and I watched three men bring him down with swords and axes.'

The men around us had fallen silent as they listened in on Solveig's story. She raised her spear and moved it to her other shoulder before continuing.

'He was a strong man, and even with an axe buried in his back and men hanging from his arms, he still managed to lift himself from the ground. My brother rushed to his side to help, but he never made it. The enemy was upon them, sliding their swords into their bellies and leaving them to bleed out on the cold ground.'

I shivered at the thought of a young Solveig watching the murder of her family and not being able to do anything.

'What happened?'

'I was discovered by the jarl's men and dragged from the tree. I thought they were going to kill me, but instead they kept me as a slave. They passed me around their camp like a jug of ale and then tossed me aside when they'd had their fun.'

Icy tendrils chased over my skin, but it had nothing to do with the weather. No wonder Solveig was so guarded and cold. What she had experienced at their hands was what I'd feared the most about slavery.

'How did you escape?' I asked, my voice barely more than a whisper.

'Jarl Aaric took me from them when he invaded their lands and killed them all. He saved me, just like he saved you.'

She looked at me, and unshed tears shone in her eyes. My heart split in two at the pain I saw there.

'Yes,' I said. 'He saved us both.'

We marched on in silence, lost in thought. Had Jarl Aaric saved me from a similar fate? Would the pirate captain have grown tired of keeping me fed and watered and eventually thrown me to the crew? I shivered at the thought.

I may have been saved from pirates, but I was still a slave, and still far from home, and yet no matter how much I tried to remember my roots, I couldn't help but feel that those days were slipping further away. Maybe Jarl Aaric had saved me after all, and I was looking at it the wrong way. I'd been married off to a wrinkly old elderman by my uncle after he stole my crown, been kidnapped by pirates, and then claimed by a jarl. He'd saved me from an uncertain future and possibly from myself. Did Ingrid and her seer believe that too?

The men in front of me came to a standstill. We'd arrived at our destination. On orders from Jarl Aaric, the army split into four. Two branches circled left and right around the open field while Leif headed the third group, who sat back and prepared the bows and arrows.

Through the clusters of men, I could just make out Ozur and his men across the field, their yellow shields gleaming in the early morning sunshine. Our army roared and laughed as they hammered their weapons against their shields. Bellows carried across the frosty land, and for the first time in a while, I felt sick with nerves.

'We stand at the rear and wait for orders to advance,' Leif shouted to our group. Harmod and Torin addressed the assigned groups at their positions around the field as Jarl Aaric sat on his grey horse at the front of his warriors.

Battle cries raised the hairs on my arms and caused the skin to tingle at the base of my neck. It was like the ground itself was moaning and even the skies were shouting down their disapproval.

'For Valhalla!' Jarl Aaric's voice boomed out above the din, and as one, the warriors in front of me drew their swords and charged across the field.

'Hold,' Leif reminded us.

The explosion of iron, bone, and blood covered the open land as Viking fought Viking. I watched in horror at the brutality of it. There was no way I could fight like a Viking; there was no way I would survive this day. What the hell was I thinking?

I took a step backwards just as Leif called for us to advance, and then I was running. Not in the opposite direction like my mind was telling me to, but hurtling across the field toward the fight.

My blade sliced through a large man wearing nothing but trousers and a leather belt, and he crumpled to the grass beside the man he was trying to kill. Jarl Aaric's man nodded at me as he leapt from the ground, unharmed, and threw himself back into battle.

I swung my sword with ease until it found another belly, another throat, and another victim. Blood coated my leather tunic and dripped from my face. Flying swords cut me as I ducked and weaved across the ground, but my mind refused to register the pain. It only allowed me to focus on the enemy, the men with the yellow shields who wanted to harm Jarl Aaric and his family. The enemy who had tried to invade Hedeby, attempted to harm young Eric, and who now represented the elderman responsible for murdering my parents.

The feral cry that erupted from my mouth surprised me, but my chest felt lighter, freer. I sucked in a great lungful of air and searched for my next kill.

Solveig had a deep gash above her eye and was swinging her sword toward a hairy man on my left. Leif's beautiful blond hair and beard had been smeared red with blood as he cut down his enemy to my right. Just beyond the ring of Vikings within my reach, Torin buried his axe in a man's head, and further on still, Harmod grappled with two men. He faltered and then stumbled to the ground, rolling to his left to reach for his sword as he went, but he wasn't quick enough. The Viking closest to him pushed his sword into Harmod's belly, and a spray of blood exploded from his mouth.

'No!' I screamed, charging through the crowds as I tried to reach him. Leif called my name as I ran, but I didn't stop to hear what he said. I couldn't stop. Anger fuelled my actions as I barrelled into the man standing over Harmod, knocking him to the ground. Within seconds, Torin and Leif were by my side and bearing down on Harmod's attackers without mercy.

I dropped to my knees and cradled their brother's head in my lap.

'Stay still,' I said, trying to assess his injuries. Blood coated his tunic and soaked the frosty ground he lay on. My mind snapped back to the time I'd held Edmund in my arms in much the same way. 'Help is coming.'

He coughed, and a red bubble dribbled from his mouth.

'My sword,' he croaked.

I twisted around and saw it a foot away. Snatching it up, I pressed it into his hand. I knew what was coming. Leif had told me about Valhalla and how the warriors would enter with their swords. Harmod was dying, and there was nothing I could do about it.

'Go,' I said. 'Valhalla is calling you.'

He gave me the briefest of smiles as his head lolled to the side and the light in his eyes faded. I carefully lowered his head to the grass and closed his eyes. Looking up, I saw Torin and Leif watching me, and I shook my head.

I saw the anger and pain rush through them both as they circled as one and sought comfort in killing the enemy, their wild screams vibrating through me.

With the battle lost, Ozur had called for a retreat, his bloodied face the last thing I saw as he jumped on a horse and galloped into the tree line. We were victorious, but it had come at a heavy cost—the death of the jarl's firstborn son.

⁓

The boatbuilders had been hard at work crafting a funeral pyre for Harmod since our return to Hedeby. It stood fifty metres south of the ramparts, close to a row of funeral chambers holding the ashes of previous jarls and their families. It was a strangely comforting place just beyond the walls of the fortress.

I paused, taking in the last of the day's sunshine, watching the craftsmen bind the wood in a specific way as Ingrid's servants fetched artefacts from the hall.

'What are you doing out here, Edith?' Leif stepped into place next to me, making me jump.

'I…I don't know what to do or say to make this better,' I said.

'Why would you want to make it better? Death is a part of life, and Harmod had a good death—a warrior's death.'

I mulled over his words, but they didn't take away the ache in my heart.

'You lost your brother,' I said softly.

'I will see him again in Valhalla.'

It was at times like this I remembered the differences between us. The people of Hedeby believed in their gods and the glory of death, whereas I held on to Christian beliefs and wept at loss. I hoped that Baldred had been true to his word and was still looking after my family's tomb.

'Why are they placing the wood like that?' I asked, pointing at the pyre.

'The fire needs to be extremely hot, hot enough to burn flesh and bone to ash, so they construct the pyre to ensure the fire burns fiercely enough.'

My stomach churned, and I regretted asking.

Leif continued. 'Harmod's ashes will fall to the ground along-side our ancestors', but the smoke from the fire will carry him to the afterlife.'

It was a nice image to think of Harmod floating off to Valhalla and watching his friends celebrating his passage.

'What about the pots?'

Leif looked across at the servant who was placing a bronze kettle and a shield at the foot of the pyre.

'Harmod will take these treasures into the afterlife with him,' he said.

'And the first thing he'll need is a kettle?'

Leif laughed, and my heart warmed at the sound.

'Maybe I could leave his ale jug for him, as I filled it up often enough.'

'I think my brother would like that very much.'

We watched the builders for a moment longer as they tied down the pyre and secured the trunks at the base. It was a sturdy construction and a fine resting place for a warrior and son of Jarl Aaric.

'I have something to tell you,' Leif said, but by the hard set of his jaw, I didn't think it was good news. 'My father has told me that when the seven days of mourning are over and the celebrations begin, I am to claim Harmod's wife and home. He said it's my duty.'

A strange sensation settled in the pit of my stomach, and my head spun as I listened to what he said. I knew I had no claim on Leif; he was a Viking, and I was a slave with a secret, but my heart threatened to break in two anyway.

'Torin is older than you; wouldn't it fall to him?'

'My brother is promised to another, and Father can't break that alliance.'

'What about Eric?'

Leif chuckled and slipped his hand into mine.

'I'm not sure a ten-year-old husband is what Gerda expects.'

I cherished the feel of his hand in mine and the warmth of his touch as the sun set around us and the black cloak of night descended on the land. My father had sent me out to find a suitable husband, and I believed with all my heart that I'd found one. The small fact that he was a Viking set on invading my home and was now sworn to another was unimportant, to my mind.

'I could talk to Jarl Aaric,' I said, thinking about my conversation with Ingrid and the seer. If I was truthful and told the jarl that I was a princess, then he couldn't deny what an important alliance that would make.

'My father likes you, Edith. He has nothing but praise for you, but you're a slave girl, and there's no way he will accept you as good enough for one of his sons.'

I jerked my hand away as I bristled at what he said.

'That isn't how I feel,' Leif said, quick to correct the harshness of his words. 'I would marry you tomorrow if I could.'

I smiled across at him, but it didn't reach my eyes. For the first time since I walked into Hedeby, I felt alone.

'I better go,' I said.

'Edith, please don't leave like this. My feelings for you haven't changed.'

To confirm what he said was true, he grabbed my face and crushed his lips to mine. The urgency of his kiss spoke volumes, and I knew he felt the same way I did. I kissed him back with as much need and desire, running my hands into his hair and pulling him closer still.

He circled his muscular arm around my waist and lifted me easily off the ground, carrying me across to an empty barn and pushing open the door with his free hand. Straw covered the floor, and the air smelt of animal faeces and rotting veg, but I didn't care. My heart thundered, and my face felt hot to the touch. Leif lowered me to the ground and lay by my side, kissing my neck as his hand explored the curves of my body. My skin tingled at his touch, and I ached for him to loosen my dress and find my soft skin beneath.

I grappled with his tunic until it cleared his head, and then I discarded it on the floor. His torso was muscular and smooth with only two or three small scars from his battles. I pulled him close to me and kissed his neck and chest. He moaned, and it sent a rush of warmth through my body. My hands glided down to his waist and fumbled with the laces on his trousers, impatient to finish what we'd started.

'I'm falling in love with you,' he whispered into my hair, kissing my jawline. He slid the skirts of my woollen dress above my knee and slipped his hand beneath the folds of fabric. I gasped as he found what he sought and moaned as he moved with me. Frustration filled my belly when he took his hand away, but as he yanked down his trousers and pushed himself inside me, I felt whole again.

We writhed together to a silent beat, exploring one another, caressing and enjoying each other's bodies. I was vaguely aware that I was racking up the sins; a princess who was not a virgin was as much use to a kingdom as the plague, but I wasn't in my kingdom, and it felt far too good for me to care. Leif built up his pace until he was sweating and panting above me. A strong sensation stirred inside me with the power to curl my toes and make me groan. As the feeling grew and grew in intensity, I cried out in pleasure and he exploded within me.

We lay in each other's arms for a long time afterwards, not saying anything but enjoying the silent companionship. I felt weak and powerful at the same time. Leif stroked my hair and kissed my cheek, his strong arms wrapped around me. He'd shifted my dress back down over my legs to keep me warm, but I glowed from the inside out.

'What are we going to do?' I asked him.

'I wish I had an answer,' he said. 'Maybe the seer would know.'

I cringed at his mention of the seer and untangled myself from his arms to straighten my hair and dress. Ingrid had asked me to find her if I returned from battle, and that time had come. Maybe Leif was right; maybe the seer saw this liaison unfolding in her dreams along with the death and destruction that followed me wherever I went.

He looked like a lost little boy as I left him at the barn door.

'We'll find a way,' I said, kissing him gently. 'I promise you.'

∽

The seer was snoozing in the corner of Ingrid's chamber when I entered. Her soft snores were strangely soothing as I waited for Ingrid to arrive. Looking around the chamber, I was once again drawn to the swathes of fabric and softness of the furnishings. The sign of nobility for the Vikings was like that of the kings of England. Riches and treasures were how you proved your worth. Instinctively, I felt for the pouch at my hip. The outline of my mother's jewellery reassured me of my own status and wealth.

'Thank you for coming, Edith.' Ingrid glided into the chamber, followed by two of her servants carrying a wooden chest.

'I survived the battle, my lady.'

'Indeed. Solveig must be a fine mentor.'

The smile that tugged at my mouth was genuine. Solveig was a fabulous mentor, and friend, although I was fairly sure she'd deny the latter unless her life depended on it.

'I made you a pledge to speak more about your seer's prophecy,' I said, glancing across at the sleeping woman.

Ingrid instructed the servants to drop the chest in the centre of the room and then ushered them out with strict instructions that we were not to be disturbed. For a moment, I wondered if she was entertaining the notion of killing me, carving me into tiny pieces, and putting my remains in the box.

'She knew you were coming,' Ingrid said. 'She told me there was a slave who wasn't a slave heading for Hedeby and that everything would change.'

I stiffened. She was definitely building up to chopping me into chunks.

'Nothing has changed, my lady. I'm still the same slave that Jarl Aaric found in the market that day. Being a princess means nothing without a kingdom, and I'm far away from my home and my people. All I want to do is continue keeping myself to myself.'

'Is that what you think you're doing?'

My brow wrinkled in confusion as I waited for her to elaborate.

'You hadn't even set foot inside the town's borders before you impressed the jarl with your watchfulness. You saved Eric from certain death by being wary of your surroundings and appreciating how important he is to Hedeby, and you've stolen my son's heart with your beauty and wise ways. *Not* very slave-like, Edith.'

A giggle tore up my throat and erupted as a laugh. Ingrid was startled at my reaction and sat with a slump of her shoulders on the edge of the bed.

'I'm sorry, my lady. I mean no disrespect to you. When I was a young girl, my father would recite a single phrase to me over and over. It's the last thing he ever said to me… Well, it was a special saying, but one I never truly understood until this very second.'

'What did he say?'

'He told me to be watchful, wary, and wise. I think that he believed those skills were what made a worthy leader.'

Ingrid appeared to mull over what I'd said for a long moment before speaking.

'I am of a mind to believe that you, Edith, are a worthy leader, but I need to know what you plan to do.'

'My lady?'

'I need to know if you are going to destroy my family.'

13

The shock on my face seemed to push Ingrid to carry on with her story.

'The seer told Jarl Aaric to visit the slave market that day and look for a girl standing apart from the others. She told him he would find a prize to rival all others. When he returned to Hedeby with you, I assumed that, being an English slave, you would give him the information he needed to raid to the west, but…'

I waited for her to continue, clutching at my apron until my knuckles turned white.

'The seer came to see me after my husband left for the slave market. She told me of another dream she'd had—the one where the slave was not a slave and would either unite or destroy us all. You must see my predicament, Edith. You are a slave who is not a slave, you have the resources to bring a great army to these shores in retaliation for your incarceration, and you have the power to tear my family apart.'

She sucked in a deep breath, and I realised she was struggling to keep her emotions in check. Ingrid, the great lady of Hedeby, wife of a jarl, was on the brink of falling apart, and I was the cause of her pain.

I knelt at her feet and took her hands in my own. I didn't care how inappropriate it was for a slave to comfort her mistress in this manner; I only wanted her to know the truth—the whole truth.

'My lady, when Harmod died in my arms on the battlefield, I felt his loss like a sister would. My heart broke for the pain I knew it would cause you, Jarl Aaric, and the boys. I've experienced this pain myself. I saw my sisters murdered in front of me, and my parents killed, and their bodies defiled. I wept over my mentor's body. He'd been at my side since before I could walk. I lost my entire family in one night, and my only surviving relative took my crown.'

Ingrid's face drained of all colour as I told my story. I didn't want her pity though—I wanted her to understand that I wasn't in Hedeby to find retribution. I was here to find peace.

'When pirates kidnapped me, I vowed to escape and find the man responsible for the deaths of my family, but many moons passed. I began to forget who I was and where I'd come from. Jarl Aaric took me away from the market, and I feared I'd never see England again. I started to lose hope, but then you included me in your community. You helped me to become a shield-maiden, and you invited me into your home. You saved me, my lady.'

Ingrid squeezed my fingers as a single tear trailed down her cheek.

'Don't cry for me, my lady, for I must be honest with you. I did want to learn from your warriors, build my strength, and eventually escape, but instead I fell in love with Hedeby and your way of life, and I fell in love with your family. You have taught me how to be a worthy leader, and if I do ever get to go home and become queen of Northumbria, it will be because of you, and that's something I will never forget.'

We both sat in silence, gripping each other's hands, an understanding forming between us. I was about to tell Ingrid about my devotion to Leif when the seer cleared her throat. Neither of us had seen her wake, stand, and saunter to our side.

'I see blood, lots and lots of blood,' she said. 'Over the great sea, a man covets what is not rightfully his. Two will become one, but there will be a great loss.'

Ingrid jumped to her feet and ushered the seer to sit in her stead.

'What are we to do?' she asked the seer.

'The slave must return to her roots,' she said. 'Her story is just beginning.'

'What do you mean?' I was confused by her riddles.

'This is just the start for you, warrior slave girl. A great journey is upon you, but it will bring deceit, death, and haunting memories.'

'The only way I can go home is with Jarl Aaric's army when he raids in the spring.' I paused to reflect on what I was about to say. Honesty had won me the respect of the lady of Hedeby, so I needed to continue down this path, but I wasn't sure how she would take my news.

'I would be honoured to accompany Jarl Aaric into any battle, but I won't betray the people of England.'

'I understand your allegiance to your people, Edith,' Ingrid answered, 'but weren't these the men responsible for the murder of your family? Didn't they hand your crown over to your uncle?'

We talked at length with the seer, trying to interpret her visions to see how best to return me to my home. It was looking more and more likely that the only way I'd ever see England again would be at the head of an invading army.

'I don't know the identity of the elderman who hired the bandits,' I said. 'And I don't think my uncle was that interested in finding him either. He was more concerned with wearing my father's crown. The men of the council may be corrupt and insincere, but the villagers aren't. It's the common people, the men and women of Northumbria, who will suffer at the hands of an invading army. I've heard the stories: death, rape, and destruction follow every Viking that sets foot on the land.'

Ingrid paced the floor once again with her hands clasped at her waist. The seer watched her like a hawk as if she could see or hear what the lady of Hedeby was thinking.

'What if our army didn't invade with the intention of destruction?' she said, coming to a standstill. 'What if they invaded with the aim of overthrowing a king and placing a queen on the throne of Northumbria?'

The air left my body as I processed what Ingrid was saying. She was asking me to command a Viking army who would fight for me and my claim on the throne. I wanted to pinch my skin to check I was still awake.

'Jarl Aaric would never agree to that,' I said, trying not to get carried away with the plans and thoughts that invaded my mind.

'He would if he knew the truth,' she said.

Ingrid swirled her long dress behind her as she glided across to the wooden chest that the servants had brought into her chamber. She opened the catches and raised the lid.

I strained my neck to see the treasures contained within. Luscious fabric of the most brilliant blue spilled out of the chest, and bronze tankards, jewels, and coins nestled within the folds.

'Edith, you are a shield-maiden of Hedeby, but you are also a princess of your own lands. I free you from slavery and gift you a dress worthy of your status.'

She pulled the blue dress from the wooden chest and held it out to me. It was the most beautiful garment I'd ever seen, something my mother would have worn. Silver cord edged the hem of the skirt and sleeves and ran in a long V-shape down the front of the bodice. I took the dress from Ingrid and inhaled the scent of spices.

'It belonged to an Arab trader,' Ingrid said, noticing my confusion. 'I took it in payment for a horse.'

I didn't own a horse or anything else that would serve as payment for such a dress.

'I can't accept this, my lady. I have nothing to give you in return.'

'You can give me a whole new world, Edith. We will have a celebration for Harmod soon, and I want you to wear the dress that night when you attend the great hall. In the meantime, I will speak to Jarl Aaric about the details of your trip to England.'

I thought about my mother guiding my father's hand when it came to matters of the witan, and I recognised the same gesture at play here. In England, women were not accepted as equals. The men sneered at them and disregarded them, thinking them uneducated heathens, and yet the real heathens from the North revered their women and listened to what they had to say. I hoped to bring some of these Viking ways to Northumbria if I returned as its queen.

'Thank you, my lady.' I bundled the dress into my cloak and hurried back to the barn to contemplate everything that had happened. The funeral of the jarl's eldest son was set to take place at dusk the next night. A week of mourning would follow, and then the celebrations would begin. Ingrid had one week to convince Jarl Aaric that I was worthy of his help, and his army.

It had been relatively easy staying out of Jarl Aaric's way for seven days. Solveig took me beyond the ramparts to continue with my training by day, and Leif found me in my room at night. Nothing more had been said about his duty to take Gerda as his wife, and I hoped that once the jarl heard of my inheritance, he would let his daughter-in-law choose another husband to comfort her other than Leif.

'The celebrations begin at nightfall,' Leif said as we lay together in my cot, our lunchtime liaisons becoming my favourite part of the day. 'Will you be coming up to the great hall?'

I thought about my vow to Ingrid, and my pulse raced at the idea of stepping inside the jarl's hall dressed once again as a princess.

'Yes, I'll be there. Your mother has requested my presence.'

He raised an eyebrow, and I giggled at his expression.

'We have become great friends, Leif. Don't worry.'

A shout beyond the walls of my room attracted our attention, and we jumped up to investigate. Fastening my leather tunic around me, I secured my sword belt to my waist. If the cries we heard were from enemy invaders, then my skills as a shield-maiden might be put to the test.

The commotion centred around the main courtyard, where the market traders were set up outside the great hall. Four men in nothing but rags knelt on the floor in front of the jarl and his guards. A trader was arguing with Aaric about the quality of the goods he was offering even though the men appeared seconds from death.

I inched to the front of the crowd that had assembled to watch the events unfold; no doubt they hoped to see blood spilled at some point. Slave traders were a common sight in the market square, but with this being the day of Harmod's celebration, emotions were running high.

The trader was a weaselly man with greasy black hair scraped back into a ponytail. He wore a woollen tunic and a huge fur cloak, clearly hoping to make himself look bigger than he was. A whip hung from his belt, and stains covered the length of it. I'd seen the pirates on the ship punish the slaves using this weapon, and it turned my stomach to recall the memory of how they carved skin from the bone with a single strike. Watching the man haggle and barter with the jarl took me back to my days on the ship and being paraded in front of the slave markets. My heart went out to the poor men kneeling in the dirt.

'They are hardworking slaves,' the trader was saying.

I scrutinised the line of men and shook my head. Jarl Aaric would never buy men in this state. They were nothing but skin and bone, obviously denied a good meal along their journey. Working the land would be impossible for these unfortunate wretches. The merciful option would be a quick death.

I was about to leave when one of the men lifted his head to look out at the crowds. My heart slammed into my chest as I recognised the curve of his nose, the cut of his jawline, and the roll of his shoulders. His hair was matted and his face smeared with grime, but I would have known him anywhere.

'Baldred!' I ran forward and knelt in front of my old friend. He flinched back instinctively, but as his sunken eyes searched my face, I saw the flicker of recognition.

'My lady?' His voice was so weak when he spoke, and relief flooded through me that his words couldn't possibly have reached the ears of the Vikings standing close by.

'Hush now,' I said. 'Don't talk. Save your strength.'

Jarl Aaric strode over to my side, and I stood to speak with him.

'This man was a soldier in Bamburgh,' I told him, unsure if Ingrid had told him everything he needed to know to piece it all together. 'He was a strong man, loyal and honest.'

'A trustworthy soldier?' Jarl Aaric asked me with a lingering look. His eyes revealed everything to me as I looked between the jarl and Baldred.

'I would happily place my life in his hands, my lord.'

Jarl Aaric nodded his satisfaction and returned to negotiate with the trader. I scanned the other men but didn't recognise any of them as my father's men.

'What happened to you, Baldred?'

My old friend slumped further over as he struggled to hold his own weight up. The bones of his shoulders protruded through the thin slip of a tunic he wore. I called to a young girl to fetch me some water and set about helping the men drink their fill. The trader eyed me with distaste, but as I grabbed for the hilt of my sword, he soon turned the other way.

I pulled a rag from my pocket and cleaned Baldred's face.

'How do you know this man, Edith?' Leif approached us warily.

'He was a soldier in the king's court,' I said. It felt like I was betraying our love by keeping my secret from him. Tonight, I would enter the great hall dressed as a princess, and he would know, but until then I had to keep up the ruse. 'We worked alongside one another.'

Jealousy burned in Leif's eyes, but I couldn't begin to pacify him now. Baldred needed me at this moment, and I had to honour my friend.

Baldred's eyebrows squished together, and I'm sure he was wondering why I was pretending to have worked with him and why his princess was dressed like a Viking warrior, but now wasn't the time. I needed to get him safely away from the slave trader and the curious crowds. I was desperate to hear how he came to be on these shores and in such dire need.

'Get him cleaned up and fed,' Jarl Aaric shouted. 'I will want to speak with you both later.'

I nodded my consent and vaguely wondered what price the jarl had paid for Baldred's life as the big Viking supervised his warriors while they manhandled the trader and the remaining poor wretches toward the gate.

I helped Baldred to his feet, and we walked through the streets to my barn. The crowds parted like water around a rock as we made our way through Hedeby. Their faces shone with bewilderment at their jarl's decision to save this weakling for anything other than a sacrifice to the gods.

Once in my room, I lowered my friend onto my cot and poured him some water. He guzzled from the mug and happily took the bread I gave him.

'What happened to you?' I asked him, still trying to take in the sunken cheeks and frail limbs.

'I discovered something dreadful, my lady, and I tried so hard to get people to listen to me, but instead I was sentenced to death for treason. I managed to escape before they could cut off my head, but I didn't get far before the pirates found me.'

I pressed my hand to my mouth. Baldred was the most loyal soldier on my father's guard, and the thought of him committing any treasonous act was unthinkable.

'What did you do?'

'When we heard about the raid on Elderman Wood's estate, a few of us asked King Aelle if we could ride out to your aid.'

My heart swelled at the thought of him worrying about me.

'The king told us we were foolish to think you were still alive,' he continued. 'But we were relentless in our request. In the end, he conceded and allowed five of us to ride to the Wood estate. There was nothing left of the place but bodies and burnt buildings. The pirates set a torch to the barns, and by the time we arrived, it was nothing but ash. The house was intact, but you were nowhere to be seen. We found your dress and feared the worst after seeing the body of your maid and Elderman Wood.'

'What did my uncle say?'

'He told us that we should have listened to him and saved ourselves a trip.'

Thoughtful as ever.

Baldred grabbed my hand and squeezed my fingers, leaning closer as if he had a great secret to tell.

'My lady, there's more. With a heavy heart, I carried on with my duties and even set a rose for you in your family tomb, but not long after the pirates' attack, I overheard your uncle and Elderman Parish talking in the corridor. I shouldn't have been listening, but when I heard mention of your name, I couldn't stop myself.'

'What were they saying?'

'They spoke of your marriage and how easy it had been to rid themselves of the last princess. Elderman Wood's lands, or what was left of them, now belonged to King Aelle, as he was your next of kin, and they were congratulating themselves on how everything had worked out.'

A red-hot rage washed over me, and I almost asked Baldred to stop. My uncle had chosen to marry me off so he could be rid of me. I was sure now that he never intended to give me the crown. He wanted it for himself, and he'd taken it with no appreciation for my father's wishes that I rule Northumbria upon his death. For Aelle to choose Parish as his right-hand man seemed appropriate. They were both corrupt. Elderman Parish was a name I knew well. He had served my father for as long as I could remember and was always the last to voice his opinion. To my young eyes, he had seemed like a vulture sat high in the trees, watching everyone else pecking at the bones and waiting for his turn to strike. He'd never spoken to me directly, choosing to push me aside if he saw me in the corridor. To him, women were insignificant.

Baldred continued. 'Your uncle was asking him if the bandits had been dealt with, and I thought for a moment that he'd found and punished the heathens responsible, but then Elderman Parish said something that chilled me to the bone.'

I took a breath to steady my nerves and nodded at my friend to carry on.

'Parish told the king that the havoc caused by the Vikings across the realm meant that bandits were happy to take whatever coin they could get. He bragged about the small price he'd paid on Aelle's behalf to hire the group that killed your family.'

My head swam, and I sat on the cot next to Baldred so I didn't fall to the floor. The bandit I'd met in the woods that day told me it was an elderman who had hired them, but I never thought it possible that my uncle, the king's own flesh and blood, would be the one to order the murder of his brother, sister-in-law, and nieces. He had hired thugs to tear us apart and annihilate us. They had torched my home, mutilated my parents' bodies, and caused the death of half the guard.

A sense of clarity settled over me as I gazed at the frail and bruised face of my friend. There was nothing left for me in England except my crown, and I was going to tear it from Aelle's cold, dead hands.

14

I smoothed down the fabric of the dress with my hands and spun in a full circle so Baldred could give me his honest opinion. It felt strange to be wearing something so fancy again after such a long time. I'd grown used to the woollen dresses, and the trousers and leather tunic of my shield-maiden's wardrobe.

'What do you think?'

'You look beautiful, my lady. Like a proper princess again.'

I giggled and brushed out my hair, letting it fall in long ringlets rather than my braids. The last time Baldred had seen me, I was wearing a wedding gown, and he was walking me up the aisle. I'd been wed to an old man so that Aelle could get me out of Bamburgh, and it only dawned on me after Baldred's revelation that my uncle and Elderman Parish probably set the bandits upon Elderman Wood's estate in a bid to finish what they started. Now I was an orphan, a widow, a shield-maiden, and a queen-in-waiting.

There was one finishing touch I needed to make before I could leave. I dug into the small pouch I'd discarded with my servant's dress and tipped my mother's amulet and bracelet from the bag. Running my thumb over the precious stone, I remembered with fondness the moment my mother had given me the gift.

I put the bracelet on and slipped the amulet over my neck so the stone sat close to my heart. Now I was ready.

'I'll be back as soon as I can to check on you,' I said, making sure he had water and food to hand. I hadn't left Baldred's side since dragging him away from the slave trader, and I was nervous to be leaving him now.

'From what you've told me about Ingrid and the jarl, it's important that you attend their celebrations tonight. Do you know what you're going to say?'

I shook my head. Ingrid's task was to convince Jarl Aaric to invade England to help me claim my crown rather than to take treasures, and before we'd spoken, I'd been troubled about how I could take on such a mission without compromising my soul, the people of Northumbria, and my friends' lives. All that had changed now. My only remaining friend was here with me by some twist of fate, and although I cared deeply for the fate of my people, I held no regard for the witan who managed the kingdom with my uncle. In truth, I didn't care about the damage a Viking army might cause if we invaded. Buildings could be rebuilt, and crops replanted. I only wanted revenge. My mind was consumed with rage at Aelle and Elderman Parish and the many ways I was going to make them both pay for what they had done.

There was a light tap on the outside of the barn, and my pulse raced. Ingrid had told me to make my way up to the hall after darkness had fallen and everyone was inside. She didn't want the people of Hedeby to see me until the jarl made his speech, and she didn't want me getting my head cut off by the guards, who would take me for an intruder—a well-dressed intruder. I couldn't let whoever was outside see me like this, not yet. I worried that it was Leif, but I knew he would be with his family to start the celebrations for Harmod.

'Edith, are you there?' Solveig's voice hissed through the door, and I relaxed a fraction. 'I've come to escort you to the hall.'

I opened the door a crack to see Solveig dressed in her best leathers and full war paint, a spear dancing in her hand. My throat went dry as I took in the fierceness of her appearance.

'Are you here to escort me or kill me?'

She laughed and brushed past me into the barn.

'I'll happily do both, girl. You know that.'

I smiled and my heartbeat slowed down.

'This is your soldier friend?' She stood over the cot and studied Baldred for a moment. He tried to lift himself, but Solveig placed a hand on his shoulder to stop him.

'No, stay where you are. It's important that you regain your strength; your princess is going to need you.'

I balked at her words.

'You know?'

She turned to face me, her eyes taking in every inch of my dress and hair. I couldn't tell from her expression if she approved or wanted to run her sword through my breastbone.

'Ingrid told me everything and asked that I look out for you. She is unsure how the Vikings will take the news, and I'm here to...'

'Protect me,' I finished for her.

I still didn't know if Jarl Aaric agreed with Ingrid's idea, so when I stepped into that hall, I could be sealing my doom. My stomach churned, and I wiped my sweaty palms on the blanket over the end of the cot, not wanting to spoil the beautiful dress I wore.

'Precisely. If all goes to plan, then you'll have a Viking army at your back, but if the warriors can't see the benefit for their families, then you'll have something else in your back, and that's where I come in.'

'Thank you, my friend,' I said. 'I'm in your debt.'

She laughed and strode across the floor toward the door.

'You can repay me with lots of treasure when we get to England, and perhaps I could have your soldier when he's feeling better.'

Baldred's face emptied of colour, and I suppressed a giggle. I didn't doubt that Solveig and Baldred would be perfect together once he was back to his full strength, but I also appreciated that Baldred had never come across an opinionated female warrior. I would delight in watching my two friends get to know each other better and witness Baldred trying to grasp the Viking ways.

Solveig stepped out into the street to check it was empty, ushering me forward. Baldred gave me an encouraging smile as I vanished into the night.

The noise of laughter and song carried across Hedeby and enveloped me in its tender embrace as we wound our way through the deserted streets. These people were my people now, and I wanted to do the right thing by them.

I approached the giant doors of the hall. My skin began to itch, and my stomach tightened. A million what-ifs streamed through my mind.

'Ready?' Solveig asked as she gripped the iron handles.

'Ready.'

The doors swung open. Jarl Aaric and Ingrid were sitting on their thrones at the head of the hall. The fire blazed in the centre of the room, and all the tables were full of Vikings sloshing their horns of ale in the air.

I took a step forward, preparing myself for whatever was to come, and at that moment, an overwhelming feeling of being in the right place came over me. I pushed my shoulders back and stood tall, and as I glided forward, a hush settled over the great hall.

Solveig led the way, heading straight for Jarl Aaric, and I followed at a slower pace, taking care to hold my frame tight and my head high. Whispers erupted around me, but I tried to tune them out. The only voice I needed to hear tonight was Jarl Aaric's. In my peripheral vision, I saw Leif rise from his position between Torin and Gerda, but I refused to look over.

Jarl Aaric was on his feet by the time I arrived at the platform. Ingrid remained in her seat but nodded at me as I stopped in front of them. Behind them, the seer was resting on her stick and watching the Vikings' reactions.

Silence fell once again as everyone waited for a worthy explanation as to why their shield-maiden now looked like a Saxon princess.

'Many moons ago,' Jarl Aaric boomed, his voice sounding even louder against the blanket of silence, 'I brought a slave back to Hedeby who has since become like family to us. She has fought by our side and defended our home. She trained as a shield-maiden and is worthy of our respect.'

He reached for my hand with his, which I accepted, and then I stepped up onto the stage beside him. I saw the faces of the warriors I'd fought beside. I spotted Torin, Leif, and Eric, and I witnessed the turmoil in their expressions.

'Our warrior slave girl was kidnapped from her home, shipped across the world, and found her way to Hedeby, and I believe the gods sent her to us.'

There was a rumbling of discussion around the room as the Vikings thought about their jarl's words.

'Odin chose to send Edith to us as a slave, but he knew the truth. He knew that she was, in fact, a princess of England.'

The rumbles grew in volume until the chatter was deafening. The men and women I'd fought with talked openly about me, considering the possibility that I was a servant of Odin, their god of gods. I didn't dare look at Leif in case my betrayal shone in his eyes. I could have told him the truth about who I was, perhaps I should have done so, but Ingrid and the seer guided me, and I had to stand by the decisions we'd made together.

'Do you plan to ransom her, Father?' It was Torin who had spoken, and I swallowed down the unease that crept into my stomach at the murmurs of agreement that rippled through the crowds.

Jarl Aaric laughed, and it melted some of the fear that invaded my body.

'Edith is not a prisoner,' he said. 'She is an ally, and our plans haven't changed. We will head to England in the spring but with a different goal.'

He took a step back, leaving me isolated in the middle of the stage. Solveig had moved to the foot of the platform, ready to defend me should I need it, but as I surveyed the Viking warriors, the army that relished a battle and did not fear death, I knew exactly what to say.

'My name is Edith, daughter of King Osberht and Queen Eadgifu of Northumbria. Before I arrived in Hedeby, my father, mother, and two sisters were murdered. The men who usurped my father's throne also tried to kill me, but I disguised myself as a servant to escape and was sold as a faceless slave.' The room remained silent as I told my story. 'My Uncle Aelle took my crown for himself, telling me I was too young to command a kingdom, but that was the old Edith, a different Edith. The one who stands here today may be the last princess of Northumbria, but she's also a proud shield-maiden who has fought in battle and has the scars to prove it, and she wants to honour her new family.'

There was an expectant air in the room; everyone was listening to what I had to say and seemed eager for more. My father would have been so proud.

'Jarl Aaric wants us to raid England in the spring, but I ask him, and all of you, to consider an alternative action. I ask that you follow *me* to England but not only to gather spoils. I ask that you help me take back my crown, kill my uncle, and avenge my family.'

The room erupted into great cheers as the Vikings toasted the possibility of a bloody battle. I held my hands in the air to call for silence.

'I ask you to fight for something that has no value to you, but I swear that I will repay you with more riches than you've ever seen, and land to farm. I swear fealty to Jarl Aaric and honour him with this pledge.'

Jarl Aaric was by my side and cheering along with his warriors. Pride bubbled up inside me at what I'd achieved. I was going home and bringing a Viking army with me to avenge my family.

'We will sail for England, and we will fight for Edith,' Jarl Aaric shouted. 'More than that, she is giving us the opportunity to set up a permanent residence in her kingdom.'

That was what Ingrid had wanted all along. She'd told me I would give her a whole new world, and now I understood what she meant. Conquering Aelle and reclaiming Northumbria meant that I would be in a position of power and able to gift parcels of land to the Vikings. From the stories that had travelled the realm prior to my world falling apart, I'd heard about the invaders' desire to farm and settle.

I held my hands up again, and the hall fell silent once more.

'I would also like to offer another prize to the people of Hedeby, if they are willing. I would offer myself as a bride to Leif, son of Jarl Aaric, in the hope that he would rule beside me.'

When I looked for Leif's reaction, I found his seat empty. Torin was facing the open door. I'd missed my chance. In all the excitement, Leif had slipped away.

The rest of the hall snatched up their ale and burst into song, happy to align their lord with a princess. I glanced behind me to where Ingrid sat, and the need for her to comfort me was overwhelming. Had I secured an army at the cost of love? A wave of exhaustion washed over me, and I fought to keep the tears at bay. I'd opened my heart and Leif hadn't heard me. Upon seeing my discomfort, Ingrid rose from her seat and ushered me into their private chamber. Jarl Aaric followed, the seer and Solveig shuffling in behind him.

'I'm so sorry, my lady. I know I should have spoken to you about Leif before my outburst, but I feared that he would be passed over to Gerda.'

Jarl Aaric waved his hand in the air as if dismissing my comment.

'Gerda will find another to fill her heart,' he said. 'Leif is a good choice for you, and I am happy that he will become a king in England.'

'He might not agree with you, my lord. I wasn't honest with him, and I think he believes I've betrayed him.'

Ingrid took my face in her hands and smiled down at me like my mother used to do.

'Perhaps it's not us you need to convince, Edith. Go, find my son, and tell him your plans, and how you feel.'

I pulled away from her and sprinted for the door, gathering up the skirts of my dress as I ran. The Vikings cheered as I rushed through the great hall, but I was on another mission now, one to convince the love of my life that it was a good idea to follow me into battle.

∽

I checked Leif's private room, the stables, and even the ramparts, but he was nowhere to be found. He either knew I was looking for him and was avoiding me in an elaborate game of cat and mouse, or he'd left Hedeby. I rushed through the south gate and walked out toward the earthen wall. It was the first place he'd taken me when I'd arrived here, and I hoped that he would be there.

I spotted his outline first, hunched over with his head hanging low and his hands pulling at tufts of grass. For a Viking warrior and son of a jarl, he made it too easy to get close to him before he noticed me. There was a flicker of something in his eyes when he lifted his head, and I saw it as a mixture of pain and pride.

'Can I join you?' I asked him, gesturing at the ground.

He shrugged, and I took that as a yes. Dropping down onto the cold earth, I tucked my knees up under my chin and folded my arms around my legs, hugging them close. The fabric of my dress rustled as I moved.

'You look beautiful,' he said in a whisper.

I smiled in the darkness and hoped that all was not lost between us. If he could still think I was beautiful dressed in a fine garment rather than my shield-maiden leathers, then I would cling to that.

'Who knew?' he asked. 'Who knew you were a princess?'

'The seer pieced fragments together, but it was your mother who asked me outright. She was worried that I would bring an English army to Hedeby and harm you.'

'Why didn't you tell me?'

I'd expected this question, and yet I still wasn't sure how to answer. In hindsight, I knew I should have confided in Leif about who I was, but there was no guarantee that he would have still loved me, and the fear of rejection was too great.

'You knew the slave, the girl who served ale and cleaned out the pigsty. You knew the shield-maiden who stood by you against Ozur's men and who cradled your brother as he died. How could I tell you that I was none of those things?'

He fidgeted and then faced me, still looking warily at my dress.

'You are all of those things and much more, Edith. I prayed to the gods that you would be mine one day, but I didn't know how that would be possible because you were a slave. I told Gerda that I was in love with someone else but would marry her to honour Harmod. My parents think I'm a noble son for helping Gerda, and yet inside I'm mourning for you.'

I slipped my hand into his and squeezed his fingers.

'If you'd waited around a bit longer tonight, you would have witnessed the rest of my speech. I talked about farmland and riches, but I also offered another gift to your people. What do you think it was?'

He shrugged the way I'd seen Eric do, and my heart melted at how young and vulnerable he seemed for the first time.

'I offered myself as a bride so that when I take my crown, I'll have a king to stand beside me. I asked your people to accept me as your wife, Leif—and they agreed.'

He leaned over and kissed me, pressing his lips to mine and spreading warmth and desire through my body.

'Are you happy to have a princess as a wife?' I asked him as he gathered me up into his arms.

He chuckled. 'I'm happy to have my warrior slave girl.'

15

Hedeby was alive with activity as the snows began to melt and the first buds were seen breaking through the frosty ground. The promise of spring sat on the horizon, and with it came an air of hope.

Baldred was recovering well. Jarl Aaric had included him in the plans for our upcoming invasion, drawing on his expertise of the coastline, the newly built fortifications at Bamburgh, and the finer details of the men in power. I'd worried that my friend would resist, as these were his kinsmen, but like me, he had lost all faith in what was behind us and only held on to the hope of a prosperous future.

Bundled up in my furs to stave off the crisp air that still clung to the early mornings, I sauntered down to the harbour to see the longboats. I'd never seen anything so beautiful as the boats built by the Vikings. They sat sleek in the water, the keels almost as long as the great hall itself. Their square sails, attached to sturdy masts in the centre of the boat, were being tied up by the men working to ready the ships to depart. Ten boats moored in the waters of Hedeby's port, twenty oars apiece. At the prow of each longboat, the boatbuilders had sculpted a ferocious dragon head, intricately carved out of the wood. The sight of these boats floating out of the mist would instil fear in any man.

From the jetty, I watched furs, weapons, and livestock being loaded into the belly of each longboat. It wouldn't be long before the jarl gave the order and two hundred warriors took to the seas to fight for my crown.

Aaric and Baldred talked of landing on the coastline under cover of darkness and attacking Bamburgh while the eldermen slept in their beds, but part of me wanted Aelle to see me coming. I wanted him to watch the boats appear on the horizon and fill every inch of the sea, and I wanted him to fear what was about to happen.

Having his throat cut while he slept was too easy a way to die. When the light left my uncle's eyes, it would be my face he saw standing over him, and I wouldn't grant him a swift death. I vowed to make him suffer, along with Elderman Parish, for what they had done to my family.

'Preparations are going well, girl,' called Solveig as she leapt from the nearest longboat and approached. 'You have a fine army at your command.'

I smiled at my friend, who refused to treat me any differently even though she now knew my true identity. Some of the Vikings didn't know how to approach me since I'd stood in front of them in the great hall. It was going to take time and patience to reassure them that I was still the warrior slave girl they fought beside against Ozur's men. I'd taken the fine dress off as soon as I could and now wore my shield-maiden outfit as I walked around Hedeby. Looking like a Saxon princess wouldn't win me any favours here.

I studied Solveig as she walked toward me. She wore her hair loose, her face free of her trademark black paint. Since Baldred had emerged from my barn washed and dressed in Viking attire, Solveig had been smitten. Although she would never admit her feelings, I saw how she watched him, and I noticed the subtle changes in her—the lack of war paint being one.

'You look lovely today, Solveig,' I teased. She hated me mention-
ing her appearance in any way other than to tell her how fearsome she
looked ahead of battle.

She snarled at me. 'Where are your fine jewels today, my lady?
Left them with your servants?'

I laughed and embraced her. Never had I felt such a connection
to a person. Edmund had been an incredible mentor to me, but I was
nothing more than a child when in his care. The bonds of friendship were unknown to me, as the royal court remained cut off from
the real people beyond the fortress walls. Baldred had only bonded
with me due to the horrific circumstances we found ourselves in at
that time. I often wondered if our paths would have crossed had
our husband-grabbing mission succeeded. He would have been just
another soldier, just another face in a long line of guards assigned to
protect and serve the Crown.

It was hard to think about how different my life was now
compared to then. I'd survived so much and suffered at the hands
of cruel men, but in the end, this had made me stronger—mentally
and physically. My mother would have rolled her eyes in horror if she
could have seen me standing beside a fierce shield-maiden, both of
us dressed in trousers and tunics with swords at our hips, but I also
hoped that once she recovered from the shock of my appearance, she
would have been mightily proud of the strong woman I'd become.

'Is everything set for tomorrow?'

I took a deep breath and gazed out over the water. The next day
was Frigga's Day, the sacred day for the goddess of marriage, and I
would marry Leif in a Viking wedding ceremony that was to be the
talk of the lands. Allies of Jarl Aaric had already started to arrive by
land and water, eager to see the union between Viking and Saxon.

'Ingrid has everything under control,' I told her. 'I'm to meet her
in the bathhouse shortly, and I hoped that you would join me.'

'You want me to be one of your bridal party?' The shock on
Solveig's face made me giggle.

'Of course I do. You are my most loyal friend, and besides, I'm not sure I can do this without you by my side.'

'I thought you wanted to marry Leif,' she said.

'I do. I'm just nervous about the ceremony. I might look like a shield-maiden, but in all honesty, I'm terrified. I've only ever seen Christian weddings, so I've got no idea what to expect.'

Solveig linked her arm in mine and turned us away from the harbour, heading back into Hedeby.

'There's nothing to worry about, girl. I'm sure your Christian priests used blood sacrifices all the time back in England—oh, and then there's the part where you have to strip naked in the great hall and chase a goat. Only then will the jarl let you marry his son.'

She laughed at my horrified expression. It was for this reason I knew I needed her by me throughout the ceremony. If anyone could make light of the proceedings, it would be Solveig.

'If I see a single goat, I'm running,' I said with a chuckle.

We made our way toward the centre of Hedeby at a relaxed pace. The speed with which everything was happening made my head spin most days, and I wanted to savour a few moments of tranquillity. I loved the way the small houses crowded together in this part of town, and how each street led down to the harbour. It made walking through the settlement simple, which was something I'd also loved about Bamburgh. You couldn't get lost once you'd deciphered the layout.

The bathhouse was a small hut located behind the great hall with a single door and a vast amount of straw on the floor. There were two large circular wooden basins big enough to fit a single person. Both were full of water, but steam rose from the basin on my right. Ingrid was waiting for us and burst into a flurry of activity as soon as we entered the room.

'The bathing is an important part of the ceremony, Edith,' she told me, stripping off my furs as she went. 'You must shed your clothes and status of a maiden and then wash away your old life. This will purify you so you are ready to enter your new life.'

I liked the sound of that—rinsing away all the heartache, horror, and deceit from my former life and emerging as a new Edith, a strong, fierce Edith.

With Ingrid and Solveig's help, I shed my shield-maiden clothes until I stood naked in the small room. I stepped into the steaming basin and sank below the water, submerging my head and letting the liquid wash over me. The warm water was glorious against my skin, and as my face broke through the surface, I felt lighter than I had in a long time. One of the maids ladled two large stones out of the fire that blazed in the corner of the room and dropped them into my bathwater. The heat radiated through the basin and melted away all of the tension in my body.

'I'll have new clothes brought in for you,' Ingrid said as she handed me a bar of soap. 'You'll have a fresh shield-maiden outfit to represent your new life, and I've also sent for a dress you can wear tomorrow. Everything is in place.'

'Thank you, my lady. I'm not sure I could have arranged everything so well if it had been left to me, and I certainly don't want to offend anyone by slipping into Christian ways.'

Solveig giggled, and Ingrid threw her a sharp look.

'It will be perfect in every way,' she said, turning back to look at me. 'You will sleep in the great hall this evening, and we will help you prepare in the morning.'

I sank back into the water and sighed, thinking about my mother, father, and sisters and how much they would have loved to be a part of my wedding. We'd set out on a husband-grabbing mission many moons ago, and here I was on the eve of my nuptials to the perfect husband. I'd just had to sail across an ocean to find him.

'Time to move to the next basin, Edith. You've washed away your journey as a maiden, and now you must plunge in the cold water to end the cleansing process.'

I stepped out of the warm water and shuffled across the straw, dropping into the second basin, which had been filled to the brim with icy water. The temperature took my breath away, and as the cold enveloped me, I hoped this was a quick ceremony.

Before I lost the feeling in all my extremities, Ingrid ushered me out of the water and covered me in a blanket. Her maid combed my hair as I tried to stop my teeth from chattering.

Changing into the new woollen trousers and tunic that represented my transition from maiden to wife was surreal. When I was a young girl in Bamburgh, I'd placed far too much attention on the dresses, shoes, and accessories I wore. I'd bicker over a dress with my sisters and squabble over a bracelet, but in reality, the clothes we wore didn't matter. It was the heart and soul of who wore them that counted. I'd survived plenty of heartache along this journey, but it had taught me the most valuable lessons, and for that I was grateful.

'I need to take your old clothes, Edith, and anything that represents your old life.' Ingrid picked up my old shield-maiden outfit and the servant's dress I'd brought with me at her request, and with it my mother's amulet and bracelet.

'No! Please, you can't take them.' I snatched for the jewellery and Ingrid squealed in fright at the vehemence in my voice. 'They're all I have left of my mother.'

Ingrid's face softened at my words, but she kept hold of the jewellery.

'You can't have anything from your old life, Edith; however, I will keep them safe for you, and perhaps you could hand them to your own daughter one day.'

My heart ached as she left the room, taking my precious memories with her, but as Ingrid was the lady of Hedeby, I was powerless to challenge her. The wedding was a Viking ceremony, and I couldn't risk alienating anyone in advance of us sailing for England.

Solveig slipped her arm through mine and supported me as we walked to the great hall. She didn't need to say anything, and I didn't need to answer. Solveig understood what the amulet meant to me and how painful it was to have it taken away.

Hanging garlands of flowers and greenery festooned the great hall, and lavish floral displays, bread, and meats decorated the tables. I'd never seen so much ale in my life.

Leif had been sent out with his brothers to sleep elsewhere, and I took his cot for the night. Lying awake in the middle of the night and listening to the soft snores of the maids in the next room and Solveig tossing about on her bed, I couldn't stop myself thinking about what was to come once we landed on the English coast. Bamburgh would be well defended, and I knew that many men and women would die because of me. It was a sobering thought that didn't sit easily with me.

A whispered conversation pulled me from my thoughts, and I swung my legs over the edge of the bed to investigate. Pulling back the curtain which separated the sleeping quarters from the great hall, I saw three burly men skulking in the shadows, their swords drawn.

Before I could grab for my sword, the tip of an axe brushed against my throat.

'Hush now, girl. We don't want to wake the entire town.'

The intruder took a step closer, and I gasped. It was a face I recognised, one I'd seen across a battlefield some time before. Ozur and his men had somehow managed to infiltrate Hedeby and enter the great hall. How many men did he have? Were we cut off? The panicked thoughts flooded my brain.

'What do you want?' I asked through gritted teeth.

'I understand that Leif, son of Aaric, is to wed tomorrow, but I don't seem to have received my invitation.'

The axe dug a little deeper, and I sucked in a breath.

'Probably because you weren't invited.'

He sniggered as he walked behind me, his arm enveloping my shoulder with his axe at my neck. I wasn't sure he knew I was the intended bride, so if I could pull off my slave act one more time, I might survive the night.

'You're brave for a servant,' he said, wrapping his free arm around my waist. 'I like a woman with fight in her bones.'

He hauled me off my feet and proceeded to carry me through the great hall. His companions approached the black curtain, inching closer to Jarl Aaric's private room. No matter the outcome, I couldn't let them kill the jarl.

'Attack! We're under attack!' I screamed as loud as I could. At the same time, I hooked my fingers around the wooden handle of the axe and pushed it away while Ozur was disoriented.

He was quick to recover and snatched at me again, binding his muscular arm tighter around my waist and snarling into my ear. We weren't far from the main doors when they burst open and the guards rushed in with their spears, axes, and swords. I spotted Baldred near the front with a burning torch in his hand, and as his eyes circled the room, I prayed he wouldn't see me for fear of his reaction. Too late.

'Princess!' he cried, tossing the torch into the fire grate and swinging in my direction.

'Princess?' Ozur spoke into my ear, and a cold chill settled in my bones. 'Well, what a prize I've captured this evening.'

Jarl Aaric, Solveig, and all the household were awake, armed, and advancing on Ozur. His accomplices had doubled back to flank their lord as he crept closer to the doors. With an axe at my neck, nobody dared engage him.

We stepped out into the courtyard where a circle of warriors was gathering. There was no escape for Ozur and his men, and from the lack of fighting, I assumed that this was the sum of his raiding party.

'What do you want?' I asked again.

'I came to kill Jarl Aaric, but I seem to have found something far more valuable. A bargaining tool.'

'They will not bargain for me,' I said. 'I'm not a princess anymore. I'm just a slave, and they don't care if I live or die.'

Ozur chuckled in my ear once more. 'Oh, I doubt that. Judging by the look on Leif's face, I'd say you're far more than *just* a slave.'

In the darkness, I made out Leif's form and the murderous gleam in his expression as the flames from the torches danced in their holders.

Ozur held my life in his hands and could use it to destroy everything we'd built. My crown drifted further from my grasp with every bite of the axe.

'You destroyed my home, killed my sons, and drove me from my land,' Ozur screamed across the courtyard as Jarl Aaric emerged from the hall. 'Now I will do the same to you.'

Leif stepped forward into the circle, and Ozur jostled me in his arms, tightening his grip and lifting the axe, forcing me to lean my head back slightly.

'I am a son of Jarl Aaric. If you want your revenge, then take it out on me.' His eyes were cold as he stared at my captor.

'Now, why would you want to fight on the eve of your wedding, Leif?' Ozur licked the side of my face and ran his free hand across my dress to cup my breast. I could hear Leif's sharp intake of breath.

I wriggled and fought against Ozur's hands until he resumed holding my waist, the stench of his breath invading my nostrils as I waited to see what he would do next. He could destroy Leif with one swipe of his axe, taking my head off and killing his bride with one blow. Was that enough revenge for the man who had systematically tried to invade Hedeby for many moons?

'Enough.' Jarl Aaric stepped into the circle, which was now fully lit by rows of blazing torches. Solveig was circling around the back of the men toward me, and I hoped she would reach my side before my head rolled across the earth.

'You come into my home in the middle of the night and threaten the life of an ally, you disrupt our sacred celebrations, and you dare to talk to me about revenge.'

I could see Ozur's two men being held to the left of where we stood. Jarl Aaric strode over to them, drew his axe from his belt, and buried it into the skull of one of the men. The sickening crunch of bone breaking echoed across the open space. Ozur's grip on me tightened. Aaric wiggled the blade until it popped out and let the man's body slump to the floor. His companion squared his shoulders in readiness for death, something that always surprised me about the Vikings. There was no fear in their eyes when they took their last breath. Aaric's axe did its job, and the second man fell to the floor beside his friend.

'Now, Ozur, you are alone,' shouted Jarl Aaric. 'With nowhere to go and nobody to command. It's over. Drop your axe and you may live.'

I could almost hear the thoughts stumbling through Ozur's mind as he calculated his chances. He was trapped with no means of escape. He knew it, and I knew it, but he was a Viking, and fighting was what they did best.

'Yes, Jarl Aaric. It does appear to be my time to enter Valhalla, but maybe I'll take one last soul with me when I go.'

He pulled back on the axe slightly, and I felt his arm tense as he readied to strike. There was nothing I could do as my eyes met Leif's. Horror was etched in every crease on his face as he launched himself toward me, but I knew he'd be too late.

16

Leif's piercing cry filled the air as Ozur jerked back his blade to take off my head. A million images soared past me as I prepared for the strike: my father standing in front of me, his hands on his hips and a huge smile on his face; my mother sitting on her throne waving at the people, who adored her; and Edmund watching me spar with a guard, a look of pride on his face.

If I was about to die, then so be it. Perhaps I would make it to Valhalla for being a fierce shield-maiden. Shield-maiden. As the thought popped into my head, I heard the swish of a blade, felt the cool breeze as it brushed my cheek, and the spray of blood coating my skin.

My eyes stayed on Leif as he came closer and closer to me. I wasn't falling, there was no pain, and I could hear the roar of the crowds. I was alive.

I looked down at my feet and Ozur's severed head staring back up at me, his eyes frozen in time as Leif gathered me in his arms.

Solveig stepped into my view as she wiped the blood from her blade. Relief flooded through me as I buried my face into Leif's chest. Tears flowed down my cheeks, but I didn't want anyone to see me weep. I wasn't meant to die today, which gave me hope that our mission to take Bamburgh was going to be a success. Their gods were on our side.

'Are you all right?' Leif asked me as he kissed my hair and wrapped his strong arms around me.

'Yes,' I said in a whisper. 'Thanks to Solveig.'

'She will be rewarded,' he said. 'If it wasn't for the shield-maiden, we wouldn't be holding our wedding in a few hours. Maybe when you're my wife I can keep you out of trouble.'

I giggled and kissed him. It felt good to be in his arms, and I wished it was morning already so that we could be married.

'Leif! Shoo, go back to bed,' Ingrid said as she separated us. 'You'll have plenty of time for that tomorrow.'

Ingrid ushered me to my bed too, and I pressed my fingers to my lips, wanting to remember the feel of my husband-to-be's kiss.

⌒

Frigga's Day was bright and pleasant. The cold winds had changed, and there was a hint of spring in the air. Hedeby was buzzing with activity and cheerfulness as the wedding guests wandered around town telling their stories, reciting their poems, and drinking ale. Solveig told me that Leif had risen early to perform a sacred part of his ritual.

'He has to dig up a corpse and steal his sword?'

Solveig chuckled. 'It's not stealing,' she said. 'He enters the grave, which represents death as a boy, and emerges into his new life as a man with his ancestor's sword.'

It sounded similar to my bathing ritual, and I was suddenly thankful that I didn't have to dig up an ancestor as my part of the celebration.

We waited for Ingrid in her private room, which I'd been allowed to use for my preparations. She had disappeared after breakfast, and I was becoming anxious that she'd changed her mind about me marrying her son and stolen him away.

Sensing my nervousness, Solveig helped me with my outfit, a plain white woollen dress with minimal embellishments across the bodice. It was nothing like the elaborate gowns worn in Christian weddings, and I once again marvelled at the pagan way of valuing the process over material possessions. I did feel naked without my mother's jewellery but understood the necessity for this celebration to be perfect in every way.

As I slipped my feet into my shoes, Ingrid entered the room with a beautiful bridal crown. Clover leaves and green silk cord entwined to form a circle with bright flowers placed along the edge.

'I hope you like it,' Ingrid said as she stood in front of me. 'I've also had something else added to the crown.'

Looking closely at the intricate design, I spotted my mother's amulet woven through the silk cord. The jewel sat at the front, balancing on my forehead when she placed it on my head.

'Thank you so much,' I said, fighting back the tears. It was the most wonderful thing anyone could have done for me, and having a family heirloom with me helped me to feel my parents' presence.

'Are you ready?' she asked.

I nodded and took the flowers from Solveig. 'I'm ready.'

We walked in a procession through the streets and down to the harbour where a longboat awaited us. Dressed in flowers, it appeared very different from the other ships, which were ready for battle. Solveig helped me aboard, and once everyone was in, we sailed out along the river toward a small beach further along from the town. At the water's edge, the gothi waited for our arrival, and as our longboat headed for the beach, Leif's boat drifted into view and sailed alongside us. I smiled across at him as the ships ran onto the sand and we disembarked.

Together we strolled along the beach to where the gothi waited by an altar, a goat tethered by her side. I gave Solveig a pointed stare as soon as I spotted the goat, and she stifled a giggle as we joined the rest of the wedding party.

I followed the ceremony with relative ease as the gothi summoned the gods and goddesses by slitting the goat's throat and pouring its blood into a small bowl. Using a bundle of fir twigs, she dipped them in the blood and sprinkled both of us. I knew my family would have been horrified by the pagan rituals when they held such devout Christian beliefs, but I had to hope that they would have understood my reasons.

Leif took the sword he'd dug up from his ancestor's grave and handed it to me.

'For his sons,' Ingrid had explained to me.

I was flustered when the gothi turned to me, expecting my offering. Was I supposed to bring something too? I looked at Ingrid as the panic rose within me, but she stepped forward and placed my mother's bracelet in my hand.

'Edith has no sword to offer Leif, as her father is not with us,' she told the gothi. 'She does have this token from her family, which will act as the transfer of protection from her parents to Leif.'

The gothi nodded her acceptance and exchanged the offerings. Leif secured my mother's bracelet on his arm alongside his arm ring that showed his fealty to Jarl Aaric, and I handed my sword to Solveig for safekeeping.

We then exchanged rings, something that I did recognise from Christian weddings in England. We placed them on the tips of our swords and switched them as the gothi passed her blessings over them.

As I slipped the ring on my finger, the crowds erupted into great cheers and Leif stepped forward to kiss me. I was married at last.

The celebrations raged on with the brullaup, which meant that Leif's family raced against my family, but as I didn't have any, Baldred and Solveig stepped up and challenged Torin and Eric to the race. They hurtled along the beach, pushing and shoving one another as the crowds cheered. Once at the marker, they made their way back to us, and everyone screamed their support for Solveig, who burst ahead of the boys.

She crossed the finish line victorious, and the guests scooped her up and carried her at shoulder height all the way along the beach back to town.

'What did she win?' I asked Leif.

'The losing family gets to serve the ale at our wedding feast,' said Leif, slapping a hand on Eric's shoulder as he hurried past us. 'And she gets to be served by the jarl's sons.'

Once back in Hedeby, the Vikings lined the courtyard as we made our way to the great hall. Ingrid had told me that I wasn't allowed to enter until my husband helped me, so as I arrived at the door, Leif blocked my way and laid his sword in the doorway. Taking my hand, he helped me cross the threshold to another great cheer.

Everyone crowded into the hall with great excitement, and Jarl Aaric ushered me to the stage where the first cask of honey ale waited. I poured the first jug and asked Leif to join me as I recited part of the Valkyries' drinking song.

'Ale I bring thee, tree of battle,

Mingled of strength and mighty fame.

Charms it holds and healing signs,

Spells full good, and gladness-runes.'

I handed the ale to Leif, and he drank it in one go, slamming the cup on the table with a roar. The roof nearly lifted with the sound of the Vikings' cheer. The wedding was done, and now it was time for the celebrations to begin.

My head was still pounding from the aftereffects of the ale a week after the celebrations had come to an end, and I was sure the thumping sound would be with me forevermore. I'd embraced married life easily and found it most pleasurable having someone to support, comfort, and love you every day of your life.

Jarl Aaric had gifted us with a home of our own in town over-looking the harbour, and I was overjoyed to be able to curl up with my new husband without the prying eyes of the jarl's servants.

Our time spent at home was even more precious, as we set sail for England at the next full moon, which was two nights away.

Preparations were nearly complete, and two hundred Viking warriors would join us. Ingrid would stay behind with a small guard to protect Hedeby and keep up with trade negotiations in the jarl's absence while we plundered my homeland and took back my crown.

I hadn't given Aelle much thought in recent weeks, as the wedding had occupied so much of my time and energy, but now, as I carved the fish for supper, I thought about my uncle and how I would feel seeing him again.

Forgiveness would never be something I could consider given the crime he had committed, and so death was the only option. I'd told Leif that I was the one who had to kill the pretender king so that he knew who had defeated him. Leif understood my desire for revenge but counselled caution.

'Your uncle is a clever man,' he'd told me as we lay in each other's arms the previous night. 'He will have built up a loyal army and have men around him that are just as devious.'

I knew he was right, but it didn't deter me from the desire to destroy him. After listening in on Jarl Aaric's gathering and discussing the raids with Baldred, I knew we would be heading further along the coast to Alnmouth, landing there to gather ourselves and send scouts ahead to check on Bamburgh and its defences. Baldred had been gone a long time, and nobody knew what provisions Aelle had put in place since the soldier's escape.

From memory, the only way out of Alnmouth on foot was by a long road to the north, so if Jarl Aaric wanted his scouts to go by land, we could be camped some time. Would Aelle hear of our army and march out to meet us? Or would he lock the doors to his fortress and hide himself away?

∽

Hedeby faded into the distance, and it was harder than I'd expected. Eric and Ingrid remained on the jetty until they were specks, yet I couldn't look away. Before we launched the longboats, Ingrid made a sacrifice to the gods for our victory and safe return, and right now I was praying to those same gods that we all survived.

It wasn't until that moment that I gave returning to Hedeby any consideration. If I won my crown, then I'd be required to stay in Bamburgh as queen with Leif by my side. There was every possibility that some of the men who wanted land would stay with us. I wasn't sure how many would return to Hedeby with Jarl Aaric.

Of course, if our mission failed and Aelle won, then I would either die or retreat to Hedeby with a heavy heart. Could I continue my life as a Viking, fishing from the river, fighting in the jarl's battles, and raising a family? It was a question I couldn't answer. Not yet.

Solveig and Baldred had chosen to sail with Leif and me, and I was grateful to have my friends with me on this journey. On my previous voyage across the ocean, I'd been incarcerated within a wooden cell below decks, only able to feel the spray on my face when I was dragged from my cell to serve the captain.

The design of the longboats meant that you could smell the ocean and feel the splash of the waves on your skin with every row of the oar. The Vikings powering the boat were relentless in their work, pulling the heavy wooden oars through the water like a knife sliding through a fish's underbelly. The breeze was light, which meant rowing was a necessity; once we reached the open waters, the current and wind would carry us to our destination.

I looked out across the water at the nine boats beside us, and my heart swelled with pride and love. Growing up in Bamburgh, I'd felt safe and cherished, but I'd had that ripped away from me. Only now was I starting to feel like I'd found my way home again. It had taken a while, but I finally realised that home wasn't a place, it was the people around you, and as I watched Leif standing at the prow, I knew he would be in my heart forever.

'What's going on in that mind of yours, girl?' Solveig sat down next to me. 'You look like you're carrying all of Odin's worries.'

I smiled at my friend and sank lower into the hull, drawing my fur cloak around me to stave off the wind.

'What if I can't do it?' I asked her. 'What if, when I come face-to-face with Aelle, I can't kill him?'

She shrugged. 'I'll do it for you,' she said in her usual matter-of-fact manner. 'That's what shield-maidens do. We look out for one another.'

I chuckled at her sincerity and knew that should it come to it, Solveig would plunge her sword in my uncle's chest to honour me.

'And what if I'm not a good queen?'

She took a dagger from her belt and cut into her palm, drawing blood. Reaching over, she took my hand and repeated the action, so I too had a small cut in the palm of my hand. She then pressed our hands together and lowered her forehead to rest on mine.

'We're bonded as shield-maidens forever,' she said. 'I will honour and serve you, protect and obey you, within reason, and I will always be honest with you.'

My chest tightened at her words. 'Thank you, Solveig,' I whispered.

'Don't get me wrong. If you mess this up, I'll be the first person to tell you.'

We laughed as the wind picked up and the square sail billowed. The Vikings lifted their oars from the water and let Thor carry us. With the god on our side, we should reach our destination in one piece—and then the hard work would begin.

~

Darkness enveloped the boat as it lurched through the waves. Swells as large as the fortress walls back at Hedeby replaced the calm seas. The cries of men tightening the halyard ropes and managing the sails as the wind and rain buffeted them floated through the air like a wailing spectre.

The rain hammered down on us, soaking us through, and the ocean invaded the hull of the boat. I clung to the side, swiping at my face to try to clear my vision, but the weather was relentless.

'Thor is testing us,' Solveig shouted above the roar of the sea. 'He wants to make sure we are worthy of winning this great battle.'

Leif was hanging on to the mast as he tightened the sails, calling orders to the men on our boat to tie everything down. Anxiety marred his face as he stared out into the blackness. There were many other ships out there battling with the conditions just like we were. Would we all be in one piece come morning? Were Jarl Aaric and Torin still out there?

I tried to let my eyes focus on any shapes on the waves, but there was nothing but a black expanse of water rising and falling all around us. My stomach churned with every drop as I fought to hold on to the dried fish we'd eaten earlier in the day.

'What if we're blown off course?' I called back at Solveig, who was winding a rope around her waist to avoid getting swept overboard. Baldred followed her actions and began tying himself to the stern. 'We could end up miles from Bamburgh.'

'It's an adventure, Edith,' she yelled, lifting her face to the sky and letting the rain drench her. A flash of lightning lit up the sky, and Solveig momentarily resembled a murderous warrior calling to her gods. A wide grin spread across my face at the sight of her. Yes, it was an adventure. We would survive Thor's test, and it didn't matter where we ended up because together we could take on the world.

I laughed out loud and howled into the night sky. Leif smiled at me as a wave crashed across the boat, soaking the men and washing a few shields overboard.

'Our warrior slave girl is talking to Thor,' he called out to the men. 'She's telling him that we will survive this night and be victorious.'

The men cheered, and across the black water, our fellow warriors cheered back. Staring death in the face, we battled all night with the ocean until our muscles ached, our skin wrinkled, and our energy was almost spent.

Then, like a gift from the gods, the sky began to lighten as the sun rose from the sea and the churning mass of waves stilled.

Although spaced out across the ocean, our boats were intact and our men safe. We'd passed Thor's test and awaited our prize, and as I considered what that prize might be, I heard Leif cry out from the bow.

'Land!'

17

The small settlement of Alnmouth sat at the mouth of the River Aln, a perfect base from which we could scout Bamburgh. Our boats glided up onto the sandbanks as the sun was beginning to rise, and two hundred warriors silently jumped from the ships and infiltrated the village.

I stayed on the beach with Baldred and Solveig as Leif joined his father and brother in the raids. There was nothing of value in this settlement, nothing that a Viking warrior would want, and on my request, the Vikings had been told to capture but not kill.

Ever mindful that Alnmouth would be under my command when I took my crown, I wanted to protect the people, but I knew that Jarl Aaric's army needed the thrill of battle to satisfy their needs.

'I assured them of all the glory and blood they could imagine but only when we arrive at Bamburgh,' I told Baldred as we set about securing the longboats.

'Do you honestly think they'll be able to resist killing everyone in that village?'

'I have to hope they can,' I said. 'If we're to unite the Saxons and Vikings, then we have to find some balance. Maybe there's land that needs farming here.'

'The eldermen will stand against you, Princess. You must prepare yourself for that,' he said.

'I know,' I replied with a shrug. 'I've got to get my crown before I can even think about the eldermen. All except Elderman Parish, of course. I've got a special gift for him.'

Once all the boats were secure, we made our way over the grassy bank of the river toward the village. Plumes of smoke rose into the air where two of the buildings blazed, and I prayed that Jarl Aaric hadn't gone against his vow and burned the villagers alive.

Upon closer inspection, I saw a huddle of men, women, and children herded inside the tiny church and managed to calm the churning nerves that swirled through the pit of my stomach.

Jarl Aaric strode across the muddy village, his axe drawn but clean, dragging a priest behind him. The man's eyes bulged, and he muttered incoherently, clutching the wooden cross that hung around his neck until his knuckles were white.

'I found one of your Christian men, Edith,' Jarl Aaric said with a wide grin, dropping the man at my feet. 'He'll tell us what we need to know or I'll cut his heart out.'

I'd helped Jarl Aaric to understand the English language during my time in Hedeby, and he spoke it perfectly now, making sure the priest could understand him and the seriousness of the situation. The colour drained from the man's face as he listened to our conversation.

'Please, don't kill me,' he pleaded, pressing his hands together in prayer.

Jarl Aaric snarled at him, making him jerk backwards and fall in the dirt. The warriors around us laughed, but my heart went out to the man.

'Nobody is going to kill you,' I told him, kneeling to hold his hands. His instinct was to pull away at the sight of me, and I had to remind myself that I had travelled to England as a Viking. My braided hair, leather tunic, and sword gave me away as a shield-maiden, not a princess.

'Does Aelle still rule Northumbria?' I asked, ignoring his attempts to wriggle free of my grasp. At the sound of my English accent, he stopped fighting me and snapped to attention.

'Yes, he does,' he said, confusion wrinkling his brow. 'King Aelle resides at Bamburgh, which is a good six- or seven-hour trek from here.'

'Does Elderman Parish still live?'

'I believe so.'

'And what of King Osberht's tomb?'

The priest made the sign of the cross and bowed his head.

'King Osberht was a good and honest man. His body remains at Bamburgh as far as I know,' he said. 'May I ask how you know of our king?'

I smiled at the priest, who studied my face with growing curiosity. He glanced up at Jarl Aaric, a silent question hidden in his eyes. Jarl Aaric nodded at me, and I took a deep breath. Once I opened my mouth and spoke the words, it would begin. Word would spread, and Aelle would know I was back. Once I told the priest the truth, there was no return.

'My name is Edith, daughter of King Osberht and Queen Eadgifu, sister to Cynethryth and Ealhswith, and the last princess of Northumbria.'

The man scrambled to his knees at my feet and began praying out loud. The Vikings laughed at him but watched in fascination as this holy man crossed himself over and over.

'My lady,' he said, finally recovering himself. 'The death of your family was heartbreaking for the people of Alnmouth, but then we heard that you were also killed by the pirates who attacked Elderman Wood's estate.'

'Not killed,' I said, getting to my feet. 'Kidnapped and sold into slavery.'

'Oh, my lady, you must have been terrified.'

'I…adapted,' I said. 'It was Jarl Aaric here who saved me and helped me return home.'

The priest took a fleeting look at Jarl Aaric and nodded. 'We thank you, sir, for returning our princess to us.'

Jarl Aaric slapped a huge hand on the man's shoulder and wrenched him off the ground and into a bear hug, much to the horror of the tiny priest.

'It's only right that we should bring your warrior queen home,' Aaric said, his voice booming across the village.

'Queen?' The priest looked from Jarl Aaric to me and back again.

'King Aelle hasn't been entirely honest with the people of Northumbria,' I said in response to the priest's unspoken question. 'It was he who had my parents murdered, it was Aelle who sent bandits to meet our convoy and kill my sisters, and it was also him who had Elderman Wood killed, but he made one fatal mistake.'

'What was that, my lady?'

'He underestimated me.'

~

The tiny church was nothing more than a wooden hut with a cross above the door. The villagers were crowded together in small groups, eyeing with fear the Viking guards who stood at the doors.

I entered the building behind the priest, who had just about recovered himself from hearing the news of how I came to be in his village.

'People of Alnmouth, I have great news to share,' he said, placing his hands on the heads of those he walked past. The children watched me with wide, frightened eyes, and I hoped that between us we could convince the people of Alnmouth that we were not the enemy.

The priest approached the altar and addressed the crowds.

'We've all heard the news that has travelled from York of the great heathen army that occupies the city, and we all feared that the men from the North would find their way to our settlement before too long. I can assure you that the men you see here today are not part of that army.' He paused and gazed around the room, and I realised he was passing on the news in the same way he would a sermon. 'These warriors here with us in Alnmouth are escorting a precious cargo.' He ushered me forward, and I slowly made my way through the villagers until I stood by his side. 'This is Princess Edith,' he said with an excited pitch to his voice. 'The last princess of Northumbria. Taken by pirates, shipped across the great sea, and sold into slavery, only to be rescued by a Viking jarl and returned to us. Praise the Lord.'

'Praise the Lord,' the crowd repeated as they all turned to look at me.

'It's true,' I said. 'Aelle usurped my father, King Osberht, and wiped out my family. I've returned home to claim the legacy handed down by the late king. I'm here to take my crown.'

Everyone began talking at once as they analysed our words and debated the truth in them. The Vikings on watch drew their swords, silencing the chatter instantly.

'How do we know you speak the truth?' asked a tall man with a shock of red hair.

'I need you to trust that I am who I say I am. I can show you my mother's amulet, I can tell you stories of my childhood at Bamburgh, and I can describe in great detail the deaths of my mother, father, and sisters if that will help.'

Murmurs swirled through the group.

'What do you want with us?' asked another man with wisps of grey hair and a leathery face.

'We need to assess Bamburgh's strengths and weaknesses before we attack, and to do that, we need to make camp close enough to reach the fortress with ease. We've chosen Alnmouth as the base and ask that you accommodate us.'

'How can we trust that the heathens you travel with won't slit our throats when we sleep?' asked the red-haired man.

'You have my word that these warriors will not harm you in any way. We have a single mission, and that's to overthrow Aelle and seek revenge for what he did to my family. If you can allow us to stay here until the time is right, then we will offer you our protection against other Northmen that may venture into your village.'

The people nodded their consent, and I celebrated that as a small victory. If I had to win Northumbria over one settlement at a time, then so be it. Alnmouth was mine, and now it was time to plan for Aelle's destruction.

Baldred, Torin, and Solveig took a handful of men and set out for Bamburgh. They borrowed horses from the villagers and even took a local guide with them to help navigate the long road that looped to the north around the ford.

'Baldred will have insight into the fortress from a Saxon soldier's perspective,' Jarl Aaric told me as we sat in the priest's humble home. 'Torin will be able to look at it from a Viking standpoint.'

'Once they return with the information we need, then we can evaluate the best time to attack,' added Leif.

The priest placed bread on the table and three cups of mead, which we gratefully devoured. It had been a long time since our last meal thanks to the raging storms we'd encountered, and I hadn't realised how hungry I was until that moment.

Leif slipped his hand into mine and kissed my forehead between mouthfuls. I saw the priest cross himself, and I hid my smile.

'Father Owen, do you believe in the sanctity of marriage?'

'Of course, my lady,' he said with a splutter.

'Then why do you cross yourself when my husband shows me affection?'

The colour drained from the priest's face as he looked at Leif and then back at me.

'My lady, I mean no disrespect, but these men are pagans, and you are a good Christian woman. Surely you're not expecting me to believe that you are joined in holy matrimony?'

'That's exactly what I'm telling you. We were married in Hedeby before we travelled here, and Leif will stay with me in Bamburgh once I've defeated Aelle.'

Jarl Aaric rose from his chair and walked over to where Father Owen sat on a small stool in the doorway.

'The gods blessed their wedding,' he said. 'Are you saying that your god would disapprove?'

The priest fidgeted on the stool and tugged at the wooden cross around his neck, an action I was starting to notice as a sign of anxiety. If the man felt nervous or threatened, he clung to it.

'Not at all, Jarl Aaric, but perhaps we could perform a blessing here in the church to show the people of Alnmouth that your union is agreeable in the eyes of our God.'

I liked the idea of having our marriage recognised by a Christian priest. Although my faith had been ripped away from me along my journey, I understood the value it had here in England. I wasn't sure that Leif would go so far as to be baptised, but blessing our marriage might make it easier for the people of Northumbria to accept Leif as their king.

I looked across at Leif, hoping to sense his reaction as he lifted my hand to his mouth and kissed my fingers. It was the simplest of acts, but it spoke volumes. He understood my need to placate the people of Northumbria.

'We agree,' I said, squeezing Leif's hand. 'You can bless our union when the others get back from their scouting.'

Darkness had blanketed the sky by the time Baldred and Solveig returned to camp. Tents were set up along the grass banks down by the river, leaving Alnmouth relatively empty of warriors. Two hundred men took up a lot of space, and the villagers had been accommodating with water, timber, and horses. The nervous glances from the people of Alnmouth didn't help to settle my nerves. How was it possible that I could feel like such a stranger in my own country? I might look like a Viking shield-maiden, but in my soul, I was still a Saxon princess. Or was I? I hoped the blessing might help the people to see that I only had their best interests at heart.

'What news?' I asked Solveig as she strode into Jarl Aaric's tent with Torin and Baldred behind her.

'Your uncle has built solid defences around the town,' she said, much to my dismay. I'd hoped the building work had been slow during my time away. 'The gate is well-protected and offers no cover for us to attack from. We saw about one hundred and fifty men at his disposal. I would recommend invading by sea. They appear to monitor the road more than the water.'

'There's something else,' Baldred added. 'Aelle has erected beacons along the shore as a warning system. If we are spotted, the guards will light the torches and every town between Bamburgh and Whitby will know we're coming.'

'We could send a small group overland to take out the beacon,' Torin suggested as he spread out various cups, pebbles, and sticks on the table to act as a map of the rocky headland. 'That way, it would allow our ships to land without alerting the fortress.'

'Agreed,' said Jarl Aaric. 'Torin, you and Baldred will go by land and take out the beacons along the coast. Solveig will join Leif and Edith on the boats.'

'Yes, my lord,' they all said in unison.

I slipped away from the tent and followed Baldred as he went to water the horses.

'Did you see Aelle?' I asked. I wanted to be sure he was at Bamburgh when we attacked, as I couldn't risk him escaping.

Baldred shook his head. 'We only saw the guards and the men on the high towers. There were four soldiers at each beacon, but that was it. I couldn't get a look inside the fortress.'

'No matter. If he believes there's a threat of Viking invasion, he'll either flee or barricade himself inside the fortress.'

'What if he rides out to meet us?'

I laughed. My uncle was a clever and manipulative man, but I couldn't see him at the head of an army. My father had trained along-side his soldiers, willing to fight with them if necessary, shoulder to shoulder. Aelle had found this amusing and took great pleasure in calling his brother a glory-seeking fool.

'No, he'll squat inside the walls and rely on his army to keep him safe. Aelle was always an intelligent man who preferred to use his brain over brawn. It's up to us to break down the barriers.'

'What if he's grown bold over the years you've been gone, Princess?'

I hadn't considered that. The man I remembered was calculating and relished the finer things in life, but he was no fighter. Was it possible that becoming king had made a man of him? I couldn't think about the possibility that Aelle had become a match for my father, the greatest king and warrior Northumbria had ever seen. I'd make sure my uncle was remembered for another reason altogether.

'We'll have to see what happens, my friend, and hope that King Aelle is sensible enough to fear a Viking army. You never know; he might ride out of the gate and surrender.'

We both laughed at the absurdity of my words, although I couldn't help but think it would save so much bloodshed if he did.

'Edith, my father needs you,' Torin called across the sand to where I stood brushing down the horses. I nodded and left Baldred to his work. It must have been hard for him to go back and see his old home and old friends through enemy eyes. I wasn't yet sure if I, myself, would be able to keep my emotions in check when Bamburgh floated into view.

I swept the fabric of Jarl Aaric's tent aside and entered the small space. Leif and Torin stood behind their father, who was sitting on an upturned ale barrel with a deep groove wrinkling his brow. Opposite him sat a large man I didn't know. He was clearly a Viking warrior, as he wore leathers and weapons and had his beard braided with rune stones. He stood up as I entered and turned to greet me.

'Edith, this is Halfdan, one of the men in the great army that currently holds York.'

I bowed my head and gestured for the giant man to sit. I'd heard the stories of the great army. Ivar the Boneless led them in a bloody and merciless battle to take the largest city in Northumbria, a city that would eventually fall under my responsibility. I was certain that Jarl Aaric had realised this small fact but, like me, hadn't raised the question of what to do about this army once I took the crown.

'We've heard of your great victories, Halfdan,' I said, taking a seat next to him. He towered over me like a giant bear, and I suddenly felt very childlike. 'You have achieved what so many men before you have failed to do.'

He grinned at me, and I couldn't avoid staring at the gaps in his mouth where his teeth had been knocked out. This man had seen many battles judging by the scars on his face and arms, and the deep muted stains on his tunic.

'What brings you to Alnmouth?'

'I'm to find out why a large Viking force has landed on these shores,' he said. 'Ivar has moved his army south and takes Nottingham as we speak, but he is concerned that while he is busy fighting the Saxons, he will be usurped by his kinsmen. He doesn't want to divide his army and send men to kill you.'

I flicked my gaze to Leif, Torin, and Aaric.

'We are here on a separate mission,' Jarl Aaric said, handing Halfdan a mug of ale. 'Our shield-maiden here has a claim to the crown of Northumbria, and we are merely helping her achieve that goal.'

Halfdan swung his big, bearded head, a look of mild interest on his face. 'You're a princess?'

'I am,' I said with a nod. 'King Aelle usurped the throne from my father, and I'm here to take it back.'

'Impressive for such a little thing,' he said.

Leif sniggered. 'She's tougher than she looks, believe me.'

Halfdan laughed out loud and raised his mug toward me. '*Skal*,' he said, saluting me before drinking the ale. 'Perhaps we can offer some assistance,' Halfdan said reaching for the jug of ale to replenish his mug. 'I have a small group of men that can be here in three days if you need us.'

'That's very kind of you,' I said. 'We have two hundred warriors with us, so I'm hopeful that we will be victorious.'

Halfdan smiled at me with that toothless grin. 'We are allies, Princess. If you need me, then I'm at your disposal. My brother Ivar would be delighted to hear of the union between Viking and Saxon, as it would be of great benefit to us all.'

Smiling at the burly man, I felt reassured that the greatest tactical mind to set foot on English soil was on our side. Halfdan drained his mug and stood. We all followed him out of the tent and to the horse he had waiting.

'It was a pleasure to meet you, Halfdan,' I said as the big man climbed upon his horse and turned the steed toward the road south. 'Out of interest, how many men do you have with you?'

He grinned at me again and began to trot away. I didn't think he was going to answer me until he finally called back before bursting into a gallop.

'Three hundred,' he cried with a hearty laugh.

Jarl Aaric, Leif, Torin, and I watched the warrior depart at speed down the sand toward the road with open mouths and bewilderment on our faces. Another three hundred men with weapons and an appetite for battle, and they were mine if I needed them.

18

Father Owen was right about the Christian blessing being something the people of Alnmouth could get behind. The villagers prepared the small church with flowers and laid out food and mead for anyone who joined the celebrations.

Solveig, Torin, and the majority of our army chose to stay on the beach far away from the Saxon god and the Christian ways, but Baldred and Jarl Aaric remained in the village with Leif and me. Baldred gave me away—again—but Aaric was more intrigued with the strange customs of the English.

The lack of swords and blood sacrifices baffled him, but he kept silent and watched from the back of the church. Poor Leif was subjected to the full force of Father Owen's prayers, and I was certain that if our hands weren't bound together in ribbon, he would have bolted for the hills.

'What we've done today is a good thing,' I said to Leif as we disappeared into the night, leaving the villagers to their revelry in our honour. 'If the people of Northumbria are happy that our marriage is blessed in the eyes of their god, then it makes it easier for them to accept you as their king.'

'I know,' he said, kissing my fingers. 'I'm just not sure my father's men would agree with you.'

I giggled as I remembered the look on Torin's face when Leif told him about the blessing. There was going to have to be a balance between us all if we were to succeed in letting the Vikings farm the land and set up homes. I'd heard the snide comments from a few of the Saxon churls as I walked through Alnmouth earlier and was grateful that Jarl Aaric hadn't overheard them. Otherwise the unstable peace might have ended then and there.

'We're to sail along the coast in the next few days, so it's right to let the villagers see us as an ally rather than a domineering force. We need the people on our side. Or rather, I need the people on my side.'

Leif stopped walking and cupped his hands around my face in the way that made my heart flutter and my stomach roll over.

'Once you wear that crown, the people of Northumbria will flock to your side,' he said, leaning down to kiss me gently. 'And if they don't, Solveig will kill them all.'

I laughed at him even though I knew there was probably some truth in his joke. Solveig was fiercely loyal to the Vikings, and now to me, and she wouldn't allow anyone to get in the way of our mission.

'Thank you,' I said, wrapping my arms around his neck and pulling him closer. 'I'm so glad you're here with me.'

A snapping twig off to our left wrenched our attention back to the present moment, and we both spun around to see three village boys running off through the long grass. I giggled at the thought of us being the centre of attention and the young people of the village watching our every move like we were some sort of entertainment. Leif was preparing to chase after the youngsters when I spotted two horsemen talking to Father Owen out by the road into Alnmouth. I tugged on Leif's arm, and we stepped into the shadows to watch.

Something didn't feel right about this meeting in the darkness, and when I saw the priest fiddling with his cross and tugging the hood of his cape further up over his head, I had the impression he was anxious about being out in the open.

'Who are those men?' Leif whispered as we crept slightly closer through the tree line to get a better look.

Although the sky was dark and the shadows engulfed everything around us, I could still make out the crest on one of the men's chests. It was an image I knew well.

'They're soldiers from Bamburgh,' I said with a heavy heart. If my uncle's soldiers were in Alnmouth, then there was every possibility that they knew we were here, unless they'd avoided the coast and come along the north road.

The beach was full of longboats, tents, and Vikings. Hundreds and hundreds of Vikings. It wasn't a sight they'd miss easily.

'I'll warn my father,' Leif said, moving off toward our camp. I stayed put. I wanted to see if these men were just passing through and exchanging pleasantries, or if there was more to their visit.

Edging closer, I managed to hide behind the trees along the side of the road. Father Owen had his back to me, but I could clearly see the two men on horseback. One was a young soldier, barely older than I was, who watched the road as if expecting an invasion, his hand never leaving the hilt of his sword. The other man was a more seasoned soldier with dark brown hair and a square jaw. He reminded me of someone, but I couldn't place who. He was firing questions at Father Owen, who played relentlessly with his wooden cross.

'We saw him leave York,' he said. 'But our scouts tell us he never returned. King Aelle wants to know where he is.'

'I understand from my parishioners that he passed through the village earlier but didn't stay,' Father Owen replied.

'If we find out you harboured that vile Norseman Halfdan and went against the orders of your king, then you'll hang—priest or not.'

I clenched my fists at the tone in the older man's voice. He was talking about the Viking who rode up from York to offer us his army. Why was Aelle so worried about a single warrior?

'I promise you, the man you call Halfdan has no interest in Alnmouth or Bamburgh. They hold York. Is that not enough for the heathens?'

'Our sources tell us they have marched south but left Halfdan behind. King Aelle wants to be sure they don't venture any further north than York. He plans to drive them from the city but can't afford to have any rogue armies in the field who can surround us as we advance. It's tactical, Priest. Your king doesn't want any surprise attacks that may threaten his crown, but you don't need to worry yourself with such matters. Your only task is to tell us of any Viking activity in the area, and if you don't, then you'll pay with your life.'

Father Owen tugged on his cross and glanced over his shoulder toward Alnmouth where the celebrations for our blessing still raged on, and I held my breath to see if he would betray me.

'There is something King Aelle needs to know,' he told them, leaning in closer to their horses. 'Princess Edith is alive. She's here, and she is not alone. There is a large Viking force with her.'

The words pouring from his mouth wounded me more than I thought they would, and I tore the ring of flowers from my head which Father Owen had placed there only a few short hours prior.

The older soldier jumped down from his horse and grabbed Father Owen by the shoulders, shaking him as he spoke.

'Why did you not alert us to this immediately?'

'I had to be sure she was who she said she was. If I'd approached the king only to discover she was an imposter, then he would not have been pleased. I thought it wise to wait, find out for sure she is the last princess, and then inform the king.'

'Are you certain it's Edith?'

I bristled at the sound of my name on the soldier's tongue. Who was he to talk of me in such a familiar way?

'It is her, Lord Parish,' Father Owen said.

I slapped my hands over my mouth as Elderman Parish's son interrogated Father Owen. Now that I could place him, the resemblance was uncanny. He had the same cold, unwavering eyes and angry temperament as his father. I was overcome with rage as I stared at the man striding about the road, barking orders at the priest.

'She is to be watched at all times until King Aelle decides what to do with her,' he said. 'We'll return to Bamburgh with the news, Priest. It's up to you to prepare the villagers to fight with us when we return. The king will want to march out at the first opportunity to meet this Viking army of hers and defeat them before they have a chance to strike.'

Inch by inch, I drew my sword from my belt. I was close enough to hear their conversation, but once I broke from the cover of the trees, Parish would have plenty of time to arm himself. There was going to be no element of surprise. If I wanted to kill this man, like his father had murdered my family, I would have to be smart about it.

'Of course. I will begin preparations at once,' Father Owen said with a little bow. 'Praise our victory. Praise the Lord.'

Both soldiers crossed themselves as Father Owen scurried off into Alnmouth to rejoin the villagers and begin his surveillance duties. If I was going to strike, it had to be now.

Picking up a pebble from the ground, I hurled it at the feet of the younger soldier's horse, causing the animal to skitter and lurch farther along the road. By the time he had it under control, I was halfway across the grass and pressing down on Parish as he grabbed for his own horse and steadied it, ready to mount.

His eyes found mine as I skidded to a halt before him with my sword pointing at his chest. The recognition was instant.

'Princess Edith,' he said, dragging his gaze over my shield-maiden outfit and along the length of my sword. 'How lovely to see you again.'

'Tell your man to climb down from his horse,' I said, keeping my voice calm and steady. Parish did as I asked, and the young soldier landed on the floor with a soft thud. 'Tie your horse to this one and send them into the village.'

He did as he was told, and in my peripheral vision, I saw the horses trotting off between the outlying village barns until they were out of sight.

'Do you intend to kill us, Princess?'

'I don't want to kill your friend,' I said, inclining my head in the direction of the boy. 'You, on the other hand, are going to die a horrible, bloody death.'

Parish laughed as he held his arms wide in surrender, and it made my blood boil to see the amusement dancing in his eyes.

'You don't think I can kill you?' I asked him.

'Princess, you're a gentle soul, and even though your heathen friends have you dressed up like a man, they can't take your womanly nature away from you.'

I tilted my head to the side and watched him drop his hands and curl his top lip. The man believed he was superior to me in every way, and it oozed from every cell in his body. His stance, his mannerisms, his speech—they told me everything I needed to know. I was a silly Saxon princess playing with a pointy object, and any minute now he would put me over his knee and punish me.

Before Parish had a chance to draw breath, I'd unhooked my axe from my belt and hurled it at him. It buried itself in his chest, throwing him backwards into the dirt. The young soldier yelped and ran off into the darkness. The warrior in me knew I should track him down and kill him too, but the young girl who sought revenge sauntered up to Parish, who lay in the mud, gasping for breath.

I stood over him like a bird of prey hovering over her kill. Blood trickled from the corner of his mouth, and that superior expression I'd found so repulsive was replaced with one of fear and horror. I revelled in his pain and knelt to press the axe even further into his breastbone.

His bloodcurdling cry echoed through the night air.

'Your father hired the men who murdered my sisters, my mother, and my father the king. They tried to kill me, but they failed, and that was their first mistake.'

His eyes widened as I brought my sword to his throat.

'I'm going to make sure your father understands how it feels to lose family, and I'm going to make it perfectly clear that he's next.'

With one slash of my sword, I slit his throat and let the air and blood bubble and gurgle until Parish was silent. I watched him for a while longer, wishing I felt the satisfaction I craved, but this was a hollow victory. Using my axe, I cut off his head and carried him by his hair back into Alnmouth.

The villagers were dancing and singing around the fire when I arrived. The quieter men and women who clung to the outskirts saw me coming and backed away, their eyes fixed on the prize in my hand.

I grabbed a rake from the ground and snapped off the prongs, creating a long stake. Spearing Parish's head on the top, I lifted it while pushing the other end into the ground. I'd chosen to display the severed head right outside the church door, to be sure that Father Owen saw it the moment he stepped outside.

The singing and dancing grew quieter as more and more of the villagers noticed me until eventually they began screaming and running back to their homes. The roaring fire illuminated the blood that coated my clothes and splattered my face, and I knew that to the people of Alnmouth, I must look like the devil reincarnated into the body of their princess.

Father Owen stumbled out of the church to see what the screams were all about and upon seeing the head on a spike, he sank to his knees, clutching his wooden cross.

'You're next, Father,' I hissed at him.

'No, please, my lady, have mercy.'

'Why? You betrayed me. You would sell me to my uncle even after I told you what he did to me.'

'I'm sorry, my lady. You must understand. King Aelle is nothing like your father. He rules with violence and fear, and we must obey, or there will be consequences.'

'You've obeyed him for the last time,' I screamed.

As I drew my sword back to strike, I heard Solveig's voice behind me. It pulled me back into the moment, and I gawked in horror at the terrified priest in the dirt at my feet.

'Go,' I whispered, pushing my sword back into my belt with shaky hands.

Father Owen scrambled to his feet and ran inside the church, followed by a large group of villagers who craved sanctuary from their deranged princess.

'Edith?' Solveig stepped in front of me with a raised eyebrow before glancing across at the severed head. 'Is that your handiwork?'

I nodded, and she laughed out loud, startling me.

'I'm impressed, shield-maiden,' she said, throwing an arm around my shoulder and steering me away from the village. 'You really are a warrior queen, aren't you?'

'He had nothing to do with the death of my family aside from having a corrupt father, and I killed him for it.'

My hands trembled as I allowed Solveig to manoeuvre me out of Alnmouth and over the dunes. I slumped to the ground and curled up in a ball.

'It's all right,' Solveig said, sitting down next to me but allowing me space. 'He is the first Saxon you've killed since coming home, girl. Fighting in battle with the jarl against a faceless enemy is hard enough, but you work through it. When it's your kinsmen, that's a different thing.'

I listened to her and understood the wisdom in her words, but I couldn't find the power to speak. Shock waves ricocheted through my body, and I struggled to keep my hands from shaking so violently. The blood that covered my fingers and clothes left a lasting reminder of what I'd just done. I jumped up and began stripping off my tunic and trousers right there on the beach.

'Edith, it's all right. I promise you it's going to be all right.'

'I'm a monster,' I cried, fighting against my friend, who had stopped my hasty undressing and was holding me in a tight embrace. 'I'm no better than Aelle.'

I sobbed then, great big hacking cries of pain and torture. The tears weren't for the son of Elderman Parish, whose head now rested on a spike in a Saxon village. They were for my mother and father, for Cynethryth and Ealhswith, for Edmund. I feared that the pain would grow so big that it would engulf me and I'd never find my way back again, but as I wept, Solveig clung to me. She was the anchor that kept me tethered to the real world; she was the grounding force that I needed if I was ever going to recover from what I'd done, and what I was becoming. For that was the most terrifying thought of all—I was no longer a Saxon princess in my heart and soul, I was a Viking, and I'd taken pleasure in murdering that man.

As my sniffles subsided and the energy left my body, I slumped back into the sand as if I'd just marched all night, physically and mentally drained.

'You truly are a warrior queen, Edith,' Solveig said, squeezing my fingers. 'From what you've told me, I know your father would be proud of you.'

I looked across at my friend as the light of the moon hit her face, and I saw the sincerity and love in her eyes.

'I'm a murderer. How could he be proud of that?'

'You're avenging your family, you're honouring them and their memory by seeking revenge on what was done to them.'

'You can dress it up however you like, Solveig, but I coldheart-edly killed that man out on the road. There was no great battle, only a broken girl with the power to wield a sword.'

'Just look at the sight in front of you,' she said, sweeping her arm out toward the beach. 'Two hundred men sailed across the sea to fight by your side. So you murdered a soldier, someone who would run and tell your uncle all about us. It doesn't matter. You are in command of a Viking army, and they believe in you enough to wield their swords with you.'

My gaze travelled along the beach to where the torches burned outside the many tents and the warriors sat around the campfires telling stories and drinking ale. The mood down there was buoyant and hopeful; they were happy to be here on the eve of battle. A thought struck me, and I jumped to my feet, startling Solveig, who snatched her axe from its sheath.

'There were two of them,' I said. 'Two soldiers, and one ran away.'

'He'll go back to Bamburgh and warn Aelle.' Solveig put the pieces together without me saying another word. 'We must tell Jarl Aaric.'

By the time we reached the jarl's tent, Leif had told him about the two strangers talking to Father Owen, and Solveig happily added my gruesome tale to the mix.

'You did the right thing, Edith. One less captain to fight in battle.' Jarl Aaric slapped his hand on my shoulder, and his praise seeped into my bones. Solveig was right; I'd done what any good warrior would have done for the good of her army.

'With any luck, it will take the boy many hours to reach Bamburgh without his horse, which gives us back our advantage,' Leif said.

The assembled group nodded their agreement and turned to Jarl Aaric, who was staring at Torin's makeshift map. We waited patiently for him to assign his orders. The lines in his forehead crinkled, and the gleam of strategy shone in his eyes, reminding me of my father and the reason I was standing on this beach in the first place. The ferocity of my emotions after killing Parish scared me. If I resisted that much to disposing of one captain, then how was I ever going to kill Aelle and Elderman Parish? I needed to embrace who I was, channel my fury, and turn it into cunning and wisdom. I needed to stop dividing myself between two worlds and pick one.

'Torin, you and Baldred must set out for the beacons at once. Do not allow them to be lit,' Jarl Aaric said. 'We will ready the boats and sail before the moon begins its descent. Tonight, we take Bamburgh.'

19

The beach was alive with activity as we doused the fires and readied the longboats. Torin and Baldred had already ridden off into the night but not before barricading the doors on the small church, locking Father Owen and his congregation inside. We couldn't risk another churl giving away our plans to any passing soldier or merchant who could forewarn the king.

Leif helped Solveig and I board the ship, and I took a moment to kiss the husband I'd barely seen since arriving in England. I knew the dangers we faced, and I worried that I was wasting every moment I had with Leif.

'I know what you're doing,' he said as we launched our boat into the black ocean and began rowing north along the coastline. 'You kiss me like you're saying goodbye.'

I shook my head, but in my heart I knew he was right. He was a strong and capable warrior, and although I was trained, and had survived my only battle back in Hedeby, I was still much smaller and weaker than the men we would be facing.

'You will survive this battle, Edith. You are fast, fierce, and have knowledge of the ways of these men. You can use that against them.'

I'd never thought about it like that before. In England, the women were weak in the eyes of the men and would never be found on a battlefield. Seeing me, or Solveig and the other shield-maidens who had voyaged with us, in the middle of an army should give them enough cause to falter, which is when we would strike.

'Use anything in your power to win this fight, Edith. You are the strongest woman I've ever met, and I thank Odin and Freya every day for bringing you to me.'

I circled my arms around his waist and watched the sleek shapes of our longboats cut silently through the water. It would take Torin and Baldred a couple of hours to reach the beacons by land and about the same length of time for us to reach the beaches below Bamburgh. With the gods on our side, we should begin our raids under the cloak of night.

I dozed on and off as the soft sound of the oars sweeping through the water lulled me. Leif's body heat contributed to my comfort, and for the first time in ages, I felt safe and protected. I prayed that the soldier I'd allowed to run free was slow on his feet and hadn't managed to find transport back to the fortress. Our success relied on Torin and Baldred killing the guards on watch at the beacons.

The moon was high in the sky when Bamburgh came into view, perched in its defensive position on top of the outcrop. The beacons remained dull against the darkness, but we were still waiting for a signal to confirm our advance.

As my eyes adjusted to the dark coastline, a single torch flickered in the sky.

'There,' I said, pointing at the small light.

We watched as it floated in the air before descending the outcrop toward the beach and away from the beacon. It had to be one of our friends who was carrying the torch to our assigned meeting point.

The warriors guided the longboats up onto the sand, and we dropped from the boats, snatching up our shields and weapons.

Torin ran into view, clutching the flaming torch, and approached Jarl Aaric.

'Five guards at this post and four at the beacon further along the coast. We've taken care of them. The way is clear,' he said.

We knew the main gate would be heavily guarded, but we hoped the men on duty would be dozing and unaware of the great army sweeping through the sand dunes toward their ramparts.

Jarl Aaric divided the army into two groups. I followed Leif and Solveig around the northeast side with the ocean on our right and the fortress walls high on our left. Jarl Aaric took Torin and the rest of the army toward the main gate. The village sat to the southwest of the fortress, and with any luck, the people would be asleep and oblivious of what invaded their king's home.

We were to advance first, slipping over the ramparts and penetrating the fortress through the back door. Once inside, it was up to us to open the front gates and let in the main force of our army.

The boatbuilders had fashioned us three ladders, which we set against the walls in readiness for the attack—starting our raid from this position brought forth all the horrific memories of that fateful night. Parish's bandits had used grappling hooks to climb over the back walls and burn the fortress buildings before hunting down my mother and father, and now here I stood, in the same spot, about to follow a similar strategy. My stomach rolled at the thought, but I shook it off as Leif began to climb.

Fifty of us scaled the ladders and dropped soundlessly onto the platforms running around the circumference of the fortress. Tall towers were spaced out at various stages to be used as a lookout for the soldiers on duty. In the pale moonlight, I made out a handful of guards chatting softly to our right with another group over to the left. I counted only five per tower and nodded at Leif as he motioned for me to move ahead.

With Solveig at my back, we ducked low and crept along the platforms until we were in position. A torch secured to the wall within the tower illuminated the men inside. Most of them were not much older than me. Leif and his group had circled in the opposite direction toward the next tower. Without making a sound, I darted forward, grabbing the hair of the boy nearest to me and slicing his throat before he could raise the alarm.

Surprised faces peered out into the darkness as, one after another, we cut the guards down. With the tower secure, we moved forward to the next and repeated the action. It was only when we moved to the final tower near to the main gate that an eagle-eyed soldier spotted our advance and raised the alarm.

As the bells rang and men shouted from all corners of the fortress, I ran for the stairs leading into the courtyard. These were steps I knew well and had run up and down a thousand times before, but this time was different. Solveig and my warriors followed as we met up with Leif in the centre and turned toward the gates.

The sound of swords clashing behind me drew my attention as Aelle's guards engaged with our group. If we didn't get the gate open, then we would be up against the might of the king's army and cut off.

'Get to the gate!' I roared above the din.

Solveig sprinted for the group of soldiers guarding the entrance. She twirled and hacked down two men, screaming like an untamed beast at the other bewildered guards. Leif was by my side as we engaged with four armed men who charged at us from the gatehouse.

Not once did I think about these men being my kinsmen; I only saw them as the enemy—Aelle's men. We fought with passion and aggression, and the Saxon men fell around us until a pile of bodies blocked the courtyard. Solveig had cleared the gate and was raising the wooden post that secured it when an arrow struck her in the back.

'No!' I screamed on seeing my friend falter and fall.

Pushing my way through both Saxon and Viking men, I reached Solveig and dragged her to the side of the opening. Two warriors took her place and hoisted the wooden post, flinging open the gate.

The sight that greeted me turned my blood to ice.

Jarl Aaric and his army were engaged in a bloody battle of their own against the strength of Aelle's men beyond the fortress walls. The boy must have made it back to Bamburgh in time to warn my uncle. Torin charged into view covered in blood, burying his axe in a Saxon soldier. Baldred was by his side fighting hard with a man who could have been his friend in another life.

The noise was immense from the cries of men and the clash of swords. Jarl Aaric's booming voice called for a retreat, and one by one the warriors withdrew toward the beach below.

I spun toward the courtyard where Leif was disposing of the few men left inside the walls.

'Leif, help me carry Solveig,' I shouted above the noise.

He buried his sword in a soldier's chest before sprinting to my side and helping me gather the shield-maiden from the floor. She moaned as we moved her, but I couldn't think about the pain we were causing or the blood that coated my hands where I pressed them against the wound. My only aim was to get her clear of Aelle's army and back to Alnmouth where we could fix her up.

'Fall back!' Jarl Aaric bellowed again.

We fled, running over the dunes and down to the waiting long-boats. Viking bodies littered the ground outside the fortress, arrows buried in their chests. Aelle had known we were coming and had waited in the darkness for the opportunity to strike. My heart ached at the sight of the fallen men who had believed in me and followed me into battle. They had died in a foreign land and for what?

'Leave me,' Solveig whispered as we half carried, half dragged her toward the boats.

'Never,' I snapped. There was no way I was losing Solveig on this or any other night. 'We've got too much work to do, and I need you.'

She huffed and wheezed as we secured her into the hull of the boat and cast off. I glanced back up the embankment. Aelle's army was standing on the outcrop holding their swords aloft and cheering their victory. My eyes searched for the one face I wanted to see, and just when I thought he'd sent his men to fight without him, I saw him.

He was sitting on top of a white horse with my father's crown on his head. His uniform was clean, proving he sat back to watch rather than engage in the fighting. He'd always been the tactical one, whereas my father was more hands-on. The rage built up within me until all I could hear was the roar in my head.

I screamed as the Saxon army laughed and jeered, and I vowed to return and slaughter them all.

The arrow wasn't very deep, so the damage was minimal. Solveig's shoulders were tight, and she winced when she moved, but luckily, we'd managed to stem the blood loss and bind the wound enough to allow it to heal.

'It's not your fault,' Solveig said as I sat on the end of her cot in the tent outside Alnmouth. 'Nobody could have predicted that the boy would be picked up by Aelle's scouts on the road.'

It was true. Baldred had found the boy boasting of how he had alerted the king to our whereabouts when he and Torin snuck up on the beacons. They'd managed to kill them all before they could light their torches, but it hadn't deterred Aelle or his men from swarming up from the town to defeat us.

'I know. I just feel responsible. None of you would be here if it weren't for me.'

'Yes, we would,' Solveig said. 'Jarl Aaric was always heading to England on his raids, but with you as his ally, he has a greater cause to fight for—land.'

She was right, as always. Ingrid had said the same thing—*you can give me a whole new world*—and I still wanted to deliver on that oath. To settle and farm here was a dream for many of the Vikings who travelled with us, and I was able to make that happen.

'What is the jarl going to do?' Solveig asked, shuffling in her cot so she could sit upright.

'I don't know,' I said, dropping my head low and allowing my braids to fall forward and sweep the floor.

'Stop it,' Solveig snapped. 'You are a queen, Edith. A *queen*. Start acting like one.'

I jumped at the severity in her voice but lifted my head and shoulders in response. She was staring at me with the ferocious gleam in her eye that I'd learnt never to ignore.

'What are you going to do to make this right?' she continued. 'How are you going to beat Aelle and take the crown that you deserve?'

Her abrupt manner and honesty were having a strange effect on me, and my pulse quickened as I strategised over the various options open to us.

'Halfdan,' I said, remembering the Viking warrior who had offered his help. 'The great heathen army is sweeping south now, but they already hold York. Tactically, they hold the strongest position in the north. If we can combine our Viking forces, we can annihilate Aelle and offer the great Viking army all of Northumbria.'

'If you do this, you will not be able to claim the crown as a Saxon. The might of Halfdan and Ivar's armies will not kneel before you.'

I knew she spoke the truth. If I allied with Halfdan, there was every possibility I was forfeiting my crown, but if I didn't join with him, Aelle would grow stronger, and I couldn't allow that to happen.

A deep sense of calm washed over me, and I knew what I needed to do.

'I'm prepared to give up my birthright and the crown of Northumbria if it means destroying my uncle and allowing the Vikings to stay in England. Jarl Aaric will understand. He wanted Leif to be a king, but perhaps we were not destined to rule in England.'

'Then you better tell your husband,' Solveig said with a smile. 'He'll support you, Edith, and he'll be happy if you are happy. It's what he lives for.'

I grinned at my friend.

'What of you and Baldred?' I asked, changing the subject and teasing my friend. Instead of getting defensive as I expected, she began laughing.

'Your Saxon soldier is a good man,' she said with a wink. 'I'll make a warrior of him yet.'

We laughed together, as I did not doubt that before the spring was out, Baldred would be a fully-fledged Viking. I was overjoyed that my two friends had found one another. After everything they had been through, they both deserved all the happiness in the world.

'Stop stalling, and get off with you,' Solveig said, pointing at the tent opening. 'Halfdan won't come if you don't ask him.'

I nodded and rose from the cot. It was time to let go of any semblance of Saxon princess that remained within me and turn into a ruthless, cunning, and fierce Viking. It was time to change the course of history.

⸺

We dispatched a messenger to track Halfdan down. Two days later, he arrived. The great warrior seemed bigger than I remembered as I greeted him on the road leading into Alnmouth.

'Thank you for coming,' I said as he slid from his horse and joined me on the roadside.

'Why are we meeting here, Princess?' he asked, looking around at the lack of a welcoming party. 'Are you ashamed of me?' His laugh boomed across the countryside, and a faint smile tugged at the corners of my mouth. Setting aside the reputation Halfdan had for his ferocity and murderous tendencies, I liked him and found him to be good company.

'I wanted a private word before you meet with Jarl Aaric,' I told him.

We walked toward a fallen log behind the outermost barn of the village and sat in the early morning sunshine. The rain had been torrential the previous night, and the mixture of soil and the warmth from the sun left an earthy scent lingering in the air.

'The jarl is going to ask for your help in defeating King Aelle,' I said, watching the big man's face for any signs that he was tempted by the offer to come. 'We suffered a defeat recently and lost many good men. I hoped that you would be true to your word and offer us your army.'

'I've already told you I would be willing to help,' Halfdan said, folding his giant, muscular arms over his chest. 'So why do you seek me out behind Jarl Aaric's back?'

I didn't want him to think I was deceitful toward Aaric, but I also didn't want him to think this was some small battle that had little value to their cause.

'When we last spoke, you offered us three hundred men, which is what Jarl Aaric will ask for,' I reminded him, at which he nodded. 'But I would like you to offer us the strength of your entire army.'

Halfdan was silent for a long moment, but then he started to laugh. It was almost a giggle at first but then quickly erupted into a hearty laugh that rose up from his belly.

'You want the great army to march on your command?'

I tried to control the frantic beating of my heart and squared my shoulders as I answered him.

'That's exactly what I'm asking. I want Aelle to be stripped of his land, title, and head, but I need a mighty army to do that.'

'My three hundred men aren't enough for you then, Princess?' He was teasing me.

'Of course they are,' I said with a smile. 'But I want Aelle to tremble in his shoes, I want him to fear death, and I want him to see the strength of the Viking army marching for his door.'

'What do you offer in return?' His gaze drifted down the full length of my body, and I was quick to steer the conversation down a more respectable route.

'I've spoken with my husband, as it was always our aim to reclaim Bamburgh and rule as king and queen of Northumbria once my uncle was defeated, but we understand the need for some of the Vikings to settle here and farm the lands.' I paused to make sure I had his attention. 'If you and your brother will join with us and usurp Aelle, then I will stand down from my claim on the crown and allow you to rule Northumbria.'

Halfdan's eyebrows rose almost to his hairline as he processed what I was saying. Any Viking would be mad to turn down the offer of a kingdom, but I also understood that he was merely a lieutenant under his brother's control.

'It's a tempting offer, Princess,' he said. 'Ivar desires to invade Mercia and eventually take Wessex, but I appreciate the value of holding a seat of power in the north. You've given me plenty to think about.'

In the distance, I spotted Jarl Aaric's guards heading toward the road, no doubt wondering why their guest was delayed.

'Think on my words, Halfdan,' I said, motioning for us to stand and make our way to the welcoming party.

I was acutely aware that I was handing over my legacy and relinquishing my father's wish to see me on the throne of Northumbria. If he were watching over me from beyond the grave, then he would have seen what I'd gone through at the hands of my kin, and I hoped he would have agreed with my decisions. Having lived as a Viking for so long now, I'd realised one vital thing: they were never going to stop coming to these shores nor give up on that dream to set down roots and build communities across the world, and I wanted to be a part of that transition.

Leif had told me only the other day about the settlements in Ireland that were thriving, and the longboats heading to the south and the east. The Vikings were a force to be reckoned with, a destructive and fierce wave swarming across the lands, but at the core of that, they were simple people looking for better farming lands and opportunities for their families to thrive.

I'd brought Jarl Aaric's army to the shores of England with the guarantee of riches and a new world. My pledge to his people was to make Leif a king of Northumbria, but now I was going back on that promise. In my quest to seek revenge for the murder of my family, I was willing to hand over everything that was mine to a Viking, and I wasn't even sorry.

20

'I fell in love with a warrior slave girl, remember?' Leif said to me that night as we huddled together in our tent nestled between the sand dunes.

'I know, but when you found out I was a princess with a claim on the crown of Northumbria, you must have been thrilled at the prospect of being a king.'

Leif kissed the top of my head as I lay in his arms. We'd spent the day with Jarl Aaric and Halfdan, working on the plans to attack Aelle and take Bamburgh, and not once had Halfdan mentioned my offer or the possibility of bringing more men back with him. I wasn't sure if he was still mulling over my words, had dismissed what I'd said, or was waiting for the right time to broach it with Jarl Aaric.

'Being a king, or a jarl, is not something I crave, Edith,' Leif said. 'If I become jarl, then it's because my father and brother have fallen in battle, and if you believe that giving Halfdan the crown is the right thing to do, then I'll back you, but don't start doubting yourself or your ability to strategise.'

He was right. Releasing my claim on the crown freed me to think about a different future, one that allowed me to be and do anything I wanted. I remembered my sisters telling me how grateful they were to be younger, so they didn't have to worry about the responsibility or strain of ruling a kingdom. Part of me was disappointed that I would never sit on my father's throne, wear his crown, or assemble my own witan, but I knew that what I offered Halfdan would benefit more people in the long run.

'My father will understand your reasons better than anyone, Edith. He was the one who found you all those moons ago and brought you back to Hedeby. He can claim credit for everything you do.'

I chuckled at his words. It was exactly what Jarl Aaric would do. He was in the perfect position to tell everyone that it was his idea to bring the last princess of Northumbria home and take over the kingdom, and if that's what he had to do, then so be it.

'You don't think he'll be mad at me and cast me out, do you?' That was my biggest fear, the possibility of Jarl Aaric not understanding and tossing me aside. What if he made Leif cast me away too? I could lose everything and everyone—again.

'There's no way he would turn his back on you now, Edith. You are family, and don't ever forget that.'

I loved hearing those words. Family was important to me, and having lost one already, I certainly didn't relish the thought of having another one ripped away from me.

'I love you,' I said, stretching my arm across his chest and snuggling closer. His body heat enveloped me in a warm cocoon, and I savoured the feel of his skin against my own. Married life wasn't what my mother had told me it would be. It was better than I'd ever hoped for. A Saxon marriage meant the woman was seen but not heard, ran the home, bore children, and stayed in the background, but a Viking marriage was entirely different, and I was free to express myself, fight, travel, and follow my dreams.

Not for the first time, I thanked all the gods, pagan and Saxon, for sending me down this path. I'd embraced the pagan beliefs with ease and knew that this was one aspect of my life that my parents would never have approved of. I was also convinced that Father Owen prayed to his god that I might be struck down by lightning. Perhaps one day there would be unity between all of us.

'Everything will work out as the gods desire it,' Leif said eventually, and I knew he spoke the truth. I just needed to believe.

∽

The villagers of Alnmouth remained distant and cold toward us as we used their settlement as a base camp for the battle ahead. Father Owen was unable to look me in the eye since I'd threatened to take his head from his shoulders, and I was under no illusion about who was feeding information to Aelle's scouts at every opportunity.

'He was seen out in the fields again,' Torin said as we assembled in Jarl Aaric's tent later that night. 'My man tells me there were two hooded individuals with him who rode away when they spotted him watching their exchange.'

'He thinks he's doing the right thing for his people,' I said in his defence. As much as I disagreed with the way he betrayed me, I understood why he did what he did. 'Aelle knows we're here, so there's no information that Father Owen can send on that will benefit the king.'

'I know that,' Torin said. 'I'd just really like to kill the priest anyway.'

That got a cheer and laughter from the warriors in Aaric's tent as they drank ale and debated the options open to us. We'd been sitting in this tent for hours and were no closer to deciding when to march. Halfdan had departed to York with an agreement to return within the week, which in my mind gave us the time we needed.

'Father Owen is no threat to us. In fact, we could use his treachery to our advantage,' I said, finally finding my voice and strength. 'If we know that Halfdan will arrive with more men by the next full moon, then we could begin our march a day early. Father Owen will report our advance and tell Aelle that we have no more than one hundred and fifty men. By the time he realises that more men are following behind, it'll be too late.'

'I like that, Edith,' Jarl Aaric said, prodding at the makeshift map on the table. 'Aelle will expect a smaller army and not be fully prepared for the might of warriors that turns up at his door.'

'I suggest we draw him out of Bamburgh,' Leif added, stepping up to the table. 'There's a field south of the fortress with good tree cover that Halfdan can use to hide his forces. Aelle will see our one hundred and fifty Vikings on the field and assume he has us matched.'

'Then we call forward the rest of the army once Aelle shows us his strength,' Jarl Aaric responded.

'It will be his weakness,' I said. 'If he thinks we are a smaller group, he will push forward all his men to make himself look like a powerful force. We need to let him show his hand, allow his soldiers to feel a moment of power and glory as they outnumber us, and then blow the horns and call Halfdan's men to the field.'

There were murmurs of assent from all the warriors around the table, and Leif winked at me as we revelled in our joint strategy. We'd come up with the plan as we lay in each other's arms the previous night and had only hoped that Jarl Aaric would see the strength in our scheme.

'Excellent,' he said, slapping his hand on Leif's shoulder. 'Now we wait for word from Halfdan.' He turned to leave, and I knew it was time to tell him what I'd done.

'My lord,' I said, stepping up to the front of the group. 'I need to tell you something important.'

Jarl Aaric stopped just inside the tent flap.

I closed my eyes and blurted everything out in a verbal deluge, not stopping until I'd emptied my soul and revealed my sins.

'I know you wanted Leif to rule in England, and I can't apologise enough for taking that away from him, but believe me when I say I've done this for him, and you,' I finished.

I was physically and mentally drained, and under the steady gaze of the jarl, I awaited his response.

His booming laughter wasn't what I'd expected.

'You're still our warrior slave girl, aren't you, Princess?' He chuck-led. 'Before we sailed from Hedeby, the seer came to me with another prophecy. She told me that the slave that wasn't a slave would deliver us to the new world at great cost. I feared she was talking about my men being lost at sea or killed in battle, but now I realise that the cost was not mine to bear. The cost was always going to be yours.'

He walked forward and pulled me into a hug, crushing me to his chest like a father would.

Tears sprang up in my eyes, and I blinked them away before this great warrior saw me weeping. The seer had never steered the jarl or Ingrid wrong, and it seemed that she still held my destiny in her hands from across the ocean.

'I will always remember the day I found you in that slavers' market as a gift from the gods, Edith. You are like my daughter, my family, and the gift you give my people will be talked about for gener-ations to come.'

Now I did weep. The tears flowed freely down my face as Jarl Aaric kissed the top of my head before striding out of the tent with Torin and his men close behind. Leif was the only one to remain, and it was his strong arms that circled me as I allowed myself to cry. I cried with relief that my honesty was well met, and I cried for the legacy that I'd lost.

～

The sun was shining on the day we were to leave Alnmouth and begin our journey north to the fields just outside Bamburgh. I knew our destination well, having learnt to ride a horse on that land as a child with my father and Edmund by my side. The area was ideal for battle due to its tree-covered perimeter to the east, and the higher level to the west, which would give you a bird's-eye view of the entire expanse. Aelle would approach from that side with his army and be able to see our small group of warriors before sending his men down into the valley.

Our plan relied in part on Aelle's desire to see the Viking strength for himself and his need for another victory. He'd watch us march into that field and assemble our shield wall, he'd see the remains of our army, one hundred and fifty men and women at most, and that's when he would assume triumph.

There was always going to be an advantage to fighting your family, and that was understanding how they thought. Throughout my childhood, I'd watched my father, my uncle, and the men of the witan debate matters for the good of the kingdom. I'd seen them decide the fate of men and turn away from the people who truly needed them; through a child's eyes, it was all inconsequential, but I'd taken it all in and processed their words and actions on a subconscious level.

I could see the corruption within the ranks of the eldermen and the poverty within the communities. The church was rich in treasures and faked morality and yet brushed aside the sick and frail members of their congregation.

They used land and women as bargaining tools to gain power and privilege, but all that was about to change. The important men of Northumbria had taken no notice of a little girl running through the corridors of Bamburgh. Even as I came of age and could be married off, they still only saw me as a game piece. With that invisibility came a great gift; they never bothered to stop their discussions, continuing to speak freely about their ill-gotten gains whenever I was around. Nobody cared about the king's daughter.

What they didn't take into account was how that young girl would evolve and grow into a formidable force wielded against them.

I'd left the English shores as a broken princess and a slave and returned as their worst nightmare. I relished the thought of putting an end to them all.

'Ready?' Solveig interrupted my thoughts as she threw a blanket over the horse I was grooming.

'I'm ready for anything,' I said with a feral smile.

Solveig laughed and patted the horse to move him along. A procession of warriors was travelling with Jarl Aaric and his sons on horseback with the rest of us marching on foot. Leif had offered me his horse, but I wanted to be with the men, and with Solveig and Baldred. He understood my reasons better than I did sometimes, and for that I was grateful. Leif needed to be with Jarl Aaric for the ride into battle, for the sake of the Vikings who fought beside him, and so that Aelle didn't see me until the last minute.

We believed that although the king was aware of my presence, he still clung to the outdated values of the Saxons that I'd be left behind in a Viking tent to cook and clean.

'Today we march, tomorrow we fight, and only the gods know how these days will end,' Solveig said.

I glanced across at her as she fiddled with her belt and adjusted her tunic. Her raven hair was partly braided, but loose curls tumbled over her shoulders, and her face was clean. We wouldn't apply our war paint until the eve of battle. She appeared wistful, if that was possible. I'd only ever known my friend to be fierce, moody, and loyal, but there was something different about her this day.

'Baldred has asked me to wed,' she said, finally lifting her eyes to meet mine.

'That's wonderful news, Solveig,' I said, reaching forward to pull her into an embrace. Her shoulders tensed, and I was quick to step back. 'What is it?'

'What if we die tomorrow?' she said. 'What if Baldred is killed by his own men and goes to his heaven, and I fall on the battlefield and go to Valhalla? How can I wed a man when I know we can never be together forever in this life and the next?'

'What if you don't?' I said simply. 'You can't live your life by the what-ifs, Solveig. What if we'd never met, what if my family was never murdered? All these scenarios happened, and they changed our destiny. If I could bring my family back, then I would, but then I would lose you, as we would never have met. Don't rule your life by what if. Embrace the right here, right now, and live it to the absolute fullest.'

My friend studied me for a long moment, and I wondered if she'd missed my meaning, but a single tear fell from the corner of her eye and trailed down her cheek.

'I couldn't imagine my life without you in it, Edith, and I thank Odin and Thor every day for bringing you to us. Thank you for your counsel, my friend.'

She swiped at the tear on her cheek.

'Will you marry Baldred then?'

'I will,' she said with a wide smile. 'I will wed your funny soldier and enjoy whatever life the gods allow us to have.'

I clapped my hands together in joy. Seeing my best friends united was the best thing that could happen, and yet if we did all die tomorrow, then the joy we felt would be wasted.

'Come with me,' I said, grabbing her arm and pulling her back toward the village centre. 'It's not ideal, but I've got an idea that will start you off on your new journey with Baldred.'

Father Owen's face drained of all colour as we stood in his small church.

'You want me to do what?' he asked again.

'I want you to bless Baldred and Solveig as if you were doing a Christian wedding.'

Solveig shuffled from one foot to the other, keeping one eye on the priest and one hand on her axe. A wedding blessing by a Saxon priest might not be what she had expected, but it might just give them both the drive and passion to survive the battle as a pair.

'Please, Father Owen, it would mean so much to me,' Baldred said, pressing a small pouch of coins into the priest's hands. Father Owen's face changed as he felt the heaviness of the purse, and I was momentarily reminded of the corruption within the witan.

'Can you do this one thing for us before we leave you?' I asked him.

Squirreling the coin purse away into his long tunic, he nodded at the groom and bride-to-be.

'Of course I can bless your union,' he said. 'It's the least I can do for a once loyal subject of the Crown.'

He smiled at Baldred and then squinted across at me, and I didn't miss the loathing in his expression. At this point, I no longer cared what the holy man thought of me; he had made it clear with his betrayal where his loyalties lay, and I would never forget it nor forgive it.

Wrapping Baldred and Solveig's hands together, Father Owen performed a blessing and united my friends in matrimony under the laws of the Christian faith. Although Solveig remained cold and unsmiling throughout the process, I knew she understood that it held meaning for Baldred. If we survived the battle, then they could return to Hedeby and enjoy a full Viking ceremony as I had done with Leif.

'You are now husband and wife in the eyes of God,' Father Owen concluded, stepping away from the couple.

'Congratulations,' I said with a smile.

Baldred swept Solveig into a tight embrace and kissed her tenderly, and something melted within me. Love could conquer all. Two young people from different countries and cultures had united because they loved each other with all their hearts.

Jarl Aaric's horn blasted from beyond the church. That was the signal for us to leave Alnmouth and begin the march to battle.

'Time to go,' Baldred said, kissing Solveig's hand and walking to the church door.

As I followed the newlyweds, I heard the smooth pull of metal against leather and turned in time to see Father Owen drawing a dagger from its sheath and lunging forward.

As one, Solveig and I heaved our swords free and thrust them headlong. Blood pooled at the corner of Father Owen's mouth as he was impaled on two sword points.

Solveig removed her weapon first and snatched hold of the priest by his tunic.

'You deserve to die for what you've done to your princess,' she said, spitting in his face and spinning around to storm out of the church. Baldred followed but only after I gave him a meaningful look that told him I was safe.

'Why?' I asked him as I withdrew my sword from his belly. 'Why did you betray me?'

I cradled him as he dropped to the floor, his blood the brightest red against the pale tunic he wore.

With bloody hands he reached for my arms and leaned closer so he could whisper in my ear. 'Aelle is evil,' he said with a gasp. 'Tax is high, soldiers come and take what little we have, his men are always watching, and I was afraid.'

It was only then I realised what this man must have been going through since I walked into his village and told him who I was. It was worse than I thought. Aelle ruled Northumbria through fear, and men like Father Owen did the only thing they thought they could to stay alive. I couldn't blame him for trying to protect himself or the people of Alnmouth.

'I forgive you,' I said, stroking his face with my free hand.

'Thank you, Princess,' he said with a faint voice. 'I'm sorry for the part I played, truly I am. I know you will make your father proud.'

His head dropped back as the final breath left his body, and his words rattled around the small church. I closed his eyes and laid him on the floor beneath his altar. When the villagers eventually found him, they would blame us, but I had no time to stop and explain myself. The horn sounded again, and I rushed from the church with a mixture of sadness and hope in my heart.

21

We passed many settlements as we marched to battle. The Viking army was a terrifying sight to behold, and the wide eyes of the villagers proved it as they turned and fled as we thundered by. If our plan succeeded, then these people would become subjects under Viking rule, and part of my heart ached at that thought.

I knew I'd done the right thing in offering up my crown, but I also knew that I would still work behind the scenes for the good of the people. I'd heard that Ivar was merciless and a fierce war machine, but Halfdan was different. If I could convince him to rule the lands with a fair hand, then these people—my people—would survive to live another day.

'What are you thinking about, Princess?' Baldred asked as we walked along shoulder to shoulder.

'I worry for Northumbria,' I said with a faint smile. 'I worry that this land will run red with the blood of innocent people if we fail tomorrow, and I worry most of all that Aelle will triumph.'

'That's a lot of worry for such slender shoulders to carry, Princess.'

I giggled at his words, and he blushed.

'Forgive me, Princess. I talk out of turn again.'

'No you don't, Baldred. You're one of my most trusted friends, and your honesty is what I've always loved about you. Solveig is a lucky girl.'

He blushed again, but the twinkle in his eyes told me how devoted he was to my mentor and friend.

'She's like nobody I've ever met before, Princess. She's strong, passionate, and…'

'Headstrong?' I added with a chuckle.

'Indeed. It's what I love the most about her.'

'You make a formidable team,' I said, glancing toward the front of the Viking army in search of Leif's blond hair. 'Stick together and you'll never falter.'

Baldred followed my line of sight and shifted his shield to his other hand before leaning closer to me.

'We are all stronger together, Princess. Leif is your anchor just like Solveig is mine. We will fight for our honour, we will fight for your family, and King Aelle will not win this battle, I promise you that.'

'I hope you're right, Baldred.'

His words touched a part of my heart that I hadn't explored for a while. My family was the reason I was on these shores and marching with a Viking army. I couldn't allow my uncle to get away with what he had done to my father, mother, and sisters. They couldn't rest in peace until I had avenged them, and understanding that made me appreciate Baldred's words even more. Together we would stand and together we would be victorious.

By the time we made it to our campsite for the night, I was tired deep down in my bones but mentally awake and eager to strategise. Leif and Torin had ridden on ahead to scout out the battlefield, and Baldred was checking up on movements at Bamburgh.

'The gods will protect us,' Solveig said as we lay on our backs staring up at the stars.

'How can you be so sure?' It often amazed me how the Vikings put so much stock in their pagan beliefs and saw so many omens in everyday items.

Solveig sat up and crossed her legs, pulling her dagger into her lap as she did so she could caress the blade.

'It was the gods who sent you to us, Edith, and they have not left your side. Can't you see that for yourself?'

Her fingers glided over the blade in her hand, and I lifted my arm to stare at the scar in my palm. We'd made a pact with blood that we'd stand together through anything, and as I trailed my own finger over that scar, I smiled.

'I don't know if it was your gods, my god, or dumb luck that brought us together, Solveig, but I'm glad we are. Tomorrow is going to be the beginning of the end for Northumbria. Either Aelle will win, and he'll pour his wrath on the land, or we'll win, and the Vikings will rule.'

'Halfdan sent word that he would join us in the battle, but he still hasn't confirmed that he does so for your crown. Maybe he doesn't want to be king.'

I laughed and pulled myself up to sit beside my friend. The camp lay stretched out before us with small fires flickering as far as the eye could see. Rumbles of conversation and laughter drifted through the dark sky as I surveyed the Viking army.

'No man, Viking or Saxon, would turn down a crown. Halfdan has made his decision—he's just stalling, which tells me he's unde-cided whether to let Ivar take it or claim it for himself.'

'You think he would defy his brother to become a king?'

'I think men are strange creatures when it comes to power. They would turn on their own family to get what they want, and they don't care about the consequences.'

'You're talking about your uncle, aren't you?'

The smile I offered my friend didn't reach my eyes. I was growing weary of thinking about Aelle and wanted this over with.

'He murdered my entire family and tried to kill me too. He usurped my crown and has plundered his own people. I'd say he is a classic example of how men who crave power become evil and corrupt.'

'Well, let's hope Halfdan does a better job if we win tomorrow. If not, we'll have to kill all the men and let queens rule the world.'

I laughed at the wicked gleam in my friend's eye. She always knew the right thing to say to pull me out of my musings.

'Thank you,' I said, reaching for her hand and squeezing it tight. 'I don't know what I'd have done without you.'

'You'd probably still be a slave girl slopping ale all over the jarl's floor and bedding down with the pigs.' She laughed and stretched her arms to the sky. 'Let's get some sleep. Tomorrow is going to be a long day for both of us.'

She rose and walked to the tent she shared with Baldred. Her raven hair blended with the darkness and only her pale face could be seen in the light of the moon. I knew her well now and understood her quirks and mannerisms, whereas when we first met, all I saw was a terrifying shield-maiden. She'd moulded me into her image, and pride bubbled up inside me as she waved at me before seeking out her bed.

I was a shield-maiden. I was a princess. I was Edith, a strong-willed and fierce warrior who would take charge of my own destiny and show the world what I was capable of.

I was ready.

∽

The sun rose slowly from the east as Jarl Aaric's army readied themselves for the battle to come. Solveig woke me before dawn to ensure I was suitably dressed and prepared. My leather tunic was well-worn by now and sculpted to my curves. It was like a second skin. The Saxons fought with metal plates attached to their chests, which made movement cumbersome, and although they might protect against a direct blade to the heart, they didn't protect against an axe to the back.

'Remember what I told you,' Solveig said as she tightened the straps around my wrist. 'The best way to a man's heart is through his fourth and fifth rib.'

I chuckled at her words but secured the information away in my mind in case I needed it on the battlefield.

The tent flap shook as Leif swept it back and grinned at us while we checked our weapons. He looked more handsome than ever. His blond hair was tied back into a long braid, and he wore a tiny silver rune charm in his beard. Two blue stripes decorated his face, travelling down his forehead, over both eyes, and ending at his jawline.

'Thought I might find you two together,' he said as he strode forward.

He tasted of dried berries as I draped my arms around his neck and kissed him.

Solveig made her excuses and left the tent with a wink in my direction. I took advantage of some alone time with my husband.

'Are you ready?' he asked as he trailed kisses down my neck.

'I'm ready for anything,' I said with a light moan. The desire to stay in the tent with Leif and abandon the battle tugged at my heart. 'But I'm not ready to lose you,' I added.

Pulling back, I gazed into Leif's eyes and held his face between my hands.

'Be careful out there,' I said tenderly. 'I've lost everyone I ever loved, and I have no intention of losing you.'

He grinned and kissed me full on the lips. 'You're not losing me today or any other day, warrior slave girl. Today we change history.'

I shrieked as he scooped me up and spun me around. We fell in a tangled heap on the floor of the tent gasping for breath and laughing, all thoughts of the impending battle forgotten momentarily.

'I love you, Princess,' he whispered in my ear.

My carefully secured tunic fell apart as we tore at each other's clothes, eager to be close one last time before marching into battle. Our lovemaking was fast and frenzied as we kissed and caressed with passion and devotion. I didn't want it to end, but the sound of the horn blasting to signal our advance brought us both to a speedy climax.

Leif helped me reattach my arm shields as I tried to tame the hair that had come loose from his braid. Our rosy cheeks and warm glow gave us away the moment we stepped out of the tent, and Solveig was quick to cover her giggle behind her shield.

'Be careful,' Leif said as he kissed me one last time. 'I'll see you on the field.'

He walked away to the head of the army, and a deep chill crept up my spine. What if that was the last time I saw him alive? What if either of us fell in battle? I was about to call after him when Solveig seized my arm.

'Stop it. You will see him again, girl. Chasing after him is a Saxon princess thing to do, and today you're a Viking shield-maiden.'

She was right. The fear of being left alone again was strong, but I knew from experience that I was a survivor and I would endure this day.

Baldred burst through the gathered Vikings with a clay bowl in his hand and a wide grin on his face.

I reached into the bowl, taking a decent amount of the blue war paint and smearing it across my face in a band covering my eyes. Baldred fidgeted from foot to foot as I worked.

Solveig dug out her trademark black paint and did the same. Both of us studied Baldred as he squirmed and jiggled and looked on the verge of internally combusting.

'Oh, for Odin's sake, Baldred, what is it that has you grinning like a baby?' Solveig said with a feigned harshness to her voice.

'Halfdan has arrived,' he said in a rush.

I whirled around to see the huge warrior sitting astride his horse, heading through the crowds toward Jarl Aaric, Leif, and Torin.

'He came.' I was relieved that we had his army at our back because three hundred extra fighters would make a difference, but part of me wanted to know if he'd taken my deal. Was Ivar with him? Did he bring more men? Was my crown now his?

'Yes, he came,' Baldred said with a gasp. I watched my friend lift his eyes to the heavens and sigh.

'What is it?' I asked.

'Yes, Baldred, what on earth has you dancing around like your trousers are on fire?' Solveig added.

'Come and see,' he cried, grabbing my hand and pulling me along behind him. Solveig secured her paint pot in her tunic and followed with a shake of her head. Clearly she was used to Baldred's excitable nature more than I was these days.

We pushed our way through the wave of Vikings that waited for the battle horn to sound and stumbled out of the back of camp where the road snaked up the hill before swinging off to the left toward the sea.

The open road, rolling countryside, and muddy puddles were all I could see, and I was about to reprimand Baldred for his actions when a deep rumble filled the air.

'Take a look,' Baldred said, letting go of my hand and pushing me gently up the road. I studied him for a moment thinking he'd finally gone crazy; my brow creased with concern that my friend had flipped, but then the rumble grew louder and louder until it vibrated through the ground and into my body.

I walked up the road which crested the hill, and there on the horizon I saw the source of the rumble. Thousands of Vikings marched toward us, their heavy boots pounding the earth and the pommels of their axes beating against their shields.

I'd never seen anything so incredible. Even watching my father's army march out of Bamburgh with all their pomp and ceremony didn't compare to this spectacle. Viking men and women covered the road, the fields, and every inch of land from left to right, and they marched for us.

'Odin is surely with us today,' Solveig said in a whisper.

'Halfdan brought the entire army,' Baldred said, his excitement returning. 'Ivar stayed behind in York, but he saw the benefit of capturing the north, so he let the army march. They march for you, Princess.'

From somewhere behind us the sound of the battle horn broke through my thoughts. It was beginning.

'Time to go,' Solveig said, placing a hand on my shoulder. 'This army will reach the valley after we've engaged in battle, but at least we've seen them with our own eyes.'

It was all part of the plan. We would show Aelle our small army and tempt him to push all his forces forward, thinking he had us beaten. He would never know about the thousands of warriors who would surround him until it was too late.

As we turned to leave, a group broke away and headed to the south. Halfdan's colours covered their shields, and I remembered him telling Jarl Aaric that his army would be the one to ensure nobody could retreat.

My heart raced and tremors of adrenaline coursed through my body as we followed Jarl Aaric's army into the valley.

Any vestige of the demure Saxon princess was long gone as I strode into battle with my sword at the ready.

❧

We gathered in the valley, tramping through the puddles left from the recent rainfall, and came to a halt beyond the tree line. We needed Aelle to see all the army and not believe that we had left half of our warriors concealed in the trees.

Solveig, Baldred, and I positioned ourselves at the back of the line so we could keep the army in front of us and the open space stretching to the trees behind us.

The valley was open on three sides, but a high outcrop stood across the plain, sweeping down to the left and leading onto the field ahead of us. From Aelle's point of view, it would feel like he was sending his avenging angels swarming down from heaven to defend his realm. From our perspective, we could see the strength of his forces as they would be forced into single file to descend the outcrop.

Jarl Aaric, Leif, and Torin left their horses in the woods and joined the army on foot. From my position at the back, I could see

Leif's blond hair and Jarl Aaric's wide frame as he pointed his sword to the sky.

Following the direction of his blade, I glimpsed a figure on horseback watching us from the safety of the hill. Aelle wore fine clothes and a red cloak with my father's crown perched on his head. My blood boiled on seeing him again. The lack of protective clothing meant he had no intention of joining the fight and was quite happy to watch events unfold from his perch. Yet again, I'd been right about my uncle. Knowing that Halfdan's army was moving to intercept and would make sure he never made it back to Bamburgh gave me great comfort.

Other men on horseback joined the king, and I recognised Elderman Parish as he circled his horse toward the young soldiers who watched us from above. I prayed that he was foolish and arrogant enough to join in the fight, as meeting him in the middle of a bloody field would make my day complete.

'Archers.'

The command to send a deluge of arrows down on us was given, but we were ready, and no sooner had the first arrow left its quiver than Jarl Aaric responded.

'Shield wall!'

As one, we moved to interlock our shields over our heads. The *thunk-thunk* of wood against wood reverberated around the valley as we braced for the first wave.

The odd stray arrow found a victim, but the majority thundered down harmlessly into the wooden shields protecting the army.

'Archers.'

Again they let their arrows fly, and again we averted any danger. I moved my shield just enough to get a better look at Aelle and his corrupt eldermen as they watched their efforts go to waste, and a wide smile spread across my face at the frustration etched across my uncle's brow.

'He's angry,' I said. 'He'll start sending his soldiers down into the valley soon.'

More arrows fell from the sky, and yet again, they landed upon the shields. Jarl Aaric roared with laughter at the head of the army, and the warriors followed his lead. The sound was deafening as one hundred and fifty Vikings jeered at the onlooking soldiers.

As I predicted, Aelle raised his hand and a branch of his army broke away and ran down the hillside into the valley. I counted no more than one hundred at most. Was he going to test us with short, sharp bursts, or did he have another plan up his sleeve? From my position, I saw that it was Parish shouting orders, and I prayed to all the gods that the murderous elderman would find his way onto this battlefield.

Leif and Torin engaged with the advancing soldiers as we swarmed forward as one. More arrows flew in our direction, and we used our shields to defend those who were in the thick of the fighting.

Above the din, I heard Parish call forward the rest of the king's guard, and they poured down the hillside to join the fray.

Drawing my sword from its sheath, I ran toward the oncoming soldiers with a loud cry and a feral smile on my face.

22

My blade sliced through the belly of a boy no older than fifteen. His wide eyes told of the horror he felt at being in the middle of a battle. Somewhere out there his mother prayed for his safe return, and yet I was the one to end his life: Edith, his princess and kinsman.

I hadn't bargained for the mixed emotions that raged through me as I cut down soldier after soldier. Saxon blood soaked my clothes and spattered my face and hair. There was no way these men would ever recognise me as their rightful queen.

Solveig fought to my right and Baldred to my left, and as I glanced across at my friend, I saw the pain in his expression too. We were English subjects hacking down our countrymen. How had it come to this? I lifted my eyes to the hilltop and saw Aelle still sitting on his horse, watching the battle rage. He was the reason for all of this. Aelle and Elderman Parish had set the wheels in motion when they murdered the royal family and usurped the crown. They would both pay for what they had done.

'Edith!'

I whirled around to see Solveig wrestled to the ground by two soldiers and burst into a run. I buried my sword into the back of one man and, pushing against his falling body, I propelled myself into a spin until I was dragging my dagger across the throat of the other.

'Between the fourth and fifth rib, wasn't it?' I said with a smirk, extending my hand to help Solveig to her feet.

'Absolutely. It's the only way to a soldier's heart.'

We laughed together and stood back-to-back as more soldiers swept across the field. It seemed to be a relentless wave, and yet the stream of men descending the hillside had stopped. Aelle remained on the hill with a large group of soldiers, clearly keeping some loyal guards back in case of trouble.

I twisted in a full circle, looking for Leif, but instead my eyes met with another only a few yards away on the outskirts of the battle. Elderman Parish stood on the sidelines with blood smeared across his cheek and mud splattered over his uniform. It took mere seconds for me to register that he was smiling at me in the way a predator smiles at its supper.

'Princess, what a surprise to find you here,' he shouted above the cries of battle that raged on. For a moment, it felt like we'd both stepped inside a bubble and nobody else existed.

I moved away from the fighting so I could stand face-to-face with the elderman.

'You're surprised to find me here, my lord, or surprised that I'm still alive?'

He gave a curt nod and laughed.

'Indeed,' he said, wiping at the grime on his face. 'You have proved most difficult to kill so far.'

'I'm sorry to have caused you so much upset, my lord. Of course, the fact that I am alive can only mean pain and death for you and Aelle,' I said calmly.

'You think yourself a warrior, Princess? Edmund wasn't that good a teacher.'

'He was a worthy mentor, but more of a stepping stone toward the teachers I've since met on my journey.'

'When will you learn that women should be seen and not heard?' he spat. 'You fight with heathens, girl. You'll die like one too.'

He took a step forward, then stopped short as Solveig stepped up beside me.

'Nobody calls the princess *girl* except me,' she said with a wicked gleam in her eye.

'Filthy heathens,' Elderman Parish repeated. 'You'll die screaming.'

'You mean like your son did?' I asked.

Parish had the decency to look pained at the mention of his son, and I couldn't resist the opportunity to twist the knife further.

'He squealed like a pig when I drew my blade across his throat,' I said. 'But thrusting his head on a spike certainly kept the crows away.'

Elderman Parish roared in anger as he ran at me, his sword above his head, ready to strike me down. I blocked his first strike and ducked his second, managing to drag my sword along his thigh. He crashed to one knee with a cry.

'If I have to cut you down one piece at a time, I will,' I hissed in his ear.

He lashed out with his sword and caught me on my left shoulder. The blade stung, but I brushed it off. Nothing was going to stop me from my revenge.

Staggering to his feet, he regained his composure and advanced again. The ground churned up beneath our feet, and the mud clung to our shoes as we circled one another. In my peripheral vision, I could see Solveig engaging with soldiers as they made their way to the elderman's aid. Baldred was nowhere to be seen, and Leif's blond hair was no longer in my line of sight. I couldn't think about them now. I couldn't think about anything but killing the man in front of me for all the pain he had caused.

His blade arced through the air, and I blocked it again; the bite of metal on metal ricocheted through my arms. Through gritted teeth, I pushed against his sword as he tried to bring it down on me, but he was much bigger and stronger. He twisted the hilt of his sword, and it flipped my own weapon out of my hands. The look of satisfaction on his face filled me with such loathing.

He prepared to strike me down, but I didn't falter. I tugged my axe from my belt and slit the elderman's throat before he could bring his weapon down upon me. He stared in horror as I pushed against his chest. Stumbling backwards, he fell into the mud, clutching at the gaping wound at his throat.

I knelt next to him, keeping my eyes on his.

'That's for my mother and father,' I said, pressing the axe against his chest. 'And this is for Cynethryth and Ealhswith.' Using all my weight, I cracked the axe into his breastbone, splitting his chest wide open. The sound of his last gurgling breath leaving his body should have satisfied me, but instead I felt empty. It wouldn't be over until Aelle was dead.

I stood over Parish's body and raised my head to the hilltop. I had to get to the king and finish this.

The king's eyes met mine across the battlefield as if he sensed my hatred. There was no shock or surprise in his expression, merely recognition. His eyes flicked to the body at my feet and then back to me. He wasn't a stupid man, he knew why I was here, and I hoped he understood that I wouldn't stop until he was dead.

He sat a little straighter in his saddle and addressed the young army at his side.

'To the death!' he cried.

༄

My limbs ached from fighting, and the thick mud pulled at my feet, trying to drag me into its sticky embrace. Hundreds of bodies littered the grassland as their lifeblood soaked into the earth. Warriors in mid–battle cry lay face down in muddy puddles, still clinging to their axe and shield, and the sound of conflict floated across the grey English sky like one of the king's banners.

Aelle remained on the hilltop protected by his witan, a circle of evil men greedy for power and wealth. The remains of the king's army thundered down upon us as he smirked in triumph.

Over the sounds of battle, Jarl Aaric's horn blasted, and a lightness flooded through me. Halfdan's army had arrived. From the tree line came a mighty roar as hundreds of Vikings burst into the valley. Glancing toward my uncle, I saw that triumphant look slide from his face, replaced with confusion and then fear. I longed to be standing by his side so he could hear my voice. I wanted to scream at him that he had brought this plague of warriors to his land.

His horse skittered, and I wondered if it would throw him over the edge, but he regained control and turned the animal back toward Bamburgh, disappearing from my view as Halfdan's men began to cut down the weary soldiers left on the field.

'Go,' Solveig hollered from behind me. 'Follow him.'

I didn't need her to tell me twice, and I shot off to grab hold of a riderless horse that was racing around the field. Dragging myself into the saddle, I spurred the animal into a gallop, and we tore across the open ground toward the bottom of the hill. The ground was churned up from the king's soldiers, but the gradient wasn't as steep as it appeared from a distance. I urged the beast to climb the embankment and, for a moment, took in the scene from the valley below.

Bodies covered the ground, but the fighting raged on. I spotted Jarl Aaric standing over a fallen Viking as he hacked at the soldiers who attacked them. I couldn't see from this angle who lay at his feet, and I could only pray that it wasn't Leif. There was no way I could tell my husband apart from the others with everyone covered in blood and dirt, his beautiful blond hair no longer a beacon I could see across the battlefield. I swallowed down the rising panic and pushed the animal forward.

I crested the top of the hill and twisted the horse's reins toward the woodland and the road to Bamburgh that lay beyond it. I knew this land; I'd grown up here, running through the trees with my sisters and hunting pheasant with Edmund.

On the horizon, Aelle and his convoy were riding hard toward the fortress. There was no way I'd catch up to them before they reached it and barricaded themselves inside. Who knew if the king had left soldiers behind to defend my old home?

A wave of despair washed over me as my murderous uncle faded farther into the distance. Would I ever get my revenge?

'Odin, help me!' I screamed into the sky with such ferocity that the horse bolted, and I struggled to control the beast before it threw me from its back. Any remaining scrap of the Saxon princess left me in that instant, and I poured all my faith into Leif's gods.

I heard the roar of the Vikings before I saw them. Part of Halfdan's army, which had broken away from the main group who now fought with Jarl Aaric, poured over the horizon, giving chase to a group of men on horseback. I blinked in disbelief as I saw Aelle galloping in the direction he'd just left—heading straight for me.

Drawing my sword, I kicked the horse on and galloped toward the advancing army and the retreating witan. Panic and terror pinched at their faces as they barrelled across the open land, no doubt seeking out any of the king's guards left who could defend them.

Despite being on foot, Halfdan's army swarmed the men before they could get too far. They dragged the eldermen from their saddles and plunged their axes and swords into them, and I felt no remorse. Aelle swerved and outmanoeuvred them until he was within yards of me. He heaved his horse to an abrupt halt as I careered in front of him.

'Going somewhere, Uncle?'

⁓

With the arrival of the great heathen army, the end of the battle was swift. Jarl Aaric marched out of the field in front of his victorious warriors.

I waited for his arrival at the top of the hill and was relieved to see him in one piece although bloody and bruised.

'Edith.' He beamed at me as he strode up to my side. 'You fought well, my warrior slave girl.'

Laughing, I wiped the mud and blood from my face. 'Thank you. How did we fare?'

His face clouded over. 'Torin fell in battle,' he said, placing his big hand on my shoulder. 'He feasts in Valhalla this night with all our warriors.'

Tears spilled down my cheeks, thoughts and memories of Torin and his bride-to-be back in Hedeby whirling through my mind.

'I'm so sorry,' I whispered, thinking of Ingrid's pain when she discovered the news. 'He would never have been here if it wasn't for me.'

'Edith, it was always my intention to raid these lands with or without you, and Torin, Leif, or I could fall at any time. This isn't your fault.'

Exhaustion invaded every cell in my body as I thought about the loss we had all suffered. My entire family had been executed, and Jarl Aaric had now lost two sons and most of his men. Was peace always so tricky and bloody to obtain?

'Does Leif know about his brother?'

Jarl Aaric shook his head. 'I haven't seen him since the battle began.'

An icy trickle of fear trailed a path down my spine. I didn't want to consider that he hadn't made it out alive. I couldn't lose him too.

Seeing the despair on my face, Aaric circled his arm around my shoulder and turned me toward the road.

'We'll find him together, all right?'

I let him lead me away from the battlefield until we were marching in step with the remains of Aaric's army and the strength of Half-dan's men. Huge, muscular Vikings greeted me on the road with a broad smile and a triumphant slap on the back. Whatever Halfdan had told them about me must have been complimentary.

My heart leapt upon seeing the rebuilt fortifications bordering Bamburgh. High walls circled the fortress, but the gates stood open to welcome me home.

My steps faltered as we drew nearer until I eventually came to a full stop just beyond the outer wall.

'You go on without me. I just need a minute,' I told Jarl Aaric when he stopped alongside me. 'I'll meet you inside.'

He left without a word, clearly understanding what a momentous occasion this was for me. On my last visit, I'd scaled the back wall and fought my way to this very spot, almost losing my friend in the process. Arriving at the gates victorious felt strangely overwhelming. Part of me had dreamt about this day as I was shipped from slavers' market to slavers' market, and that same part of me had wondered if I'd ever see these lands again. Yet here I stood, within a few feet of the only home I'd known until I had been welcomed into the hearts of the citizens of Hedeby.

The sound of the ocean far below called me to the edge of the outcrop, where I dropped to my knees and vomited into the earth, the strains of the day catching up with my weary body. With Bamburgh at my back, I stared out across the North Sea and breathed in a great lungful of air to settle my stomach. It felt like a lifetime ago when I'd stood on this very spot and wondered about the raiders from the North that the men of the witan spoke about. I would watch the open water and try to spot the ships that drove fear into the hearts of the people.

Once upon a time, I'd feared these foreign invaders too, praying that they would perish amongst the waves and leave my home untouched. I'd been so naive back then. Danger had lurked much closer to home, and in the end, it had been the fearsome invaders who stood by my side to reclaim what was rightfully mine.

I stood and spun on my heel to look at the imposing fortress. I had to give Aelle credit where it was due; he had done an excellent job of rebuilding the place, even adding extra turrets and stronger fortifications, but something felt different. Perhaps I'd been away for so long that I'd forgotten what it felt like to have a home I cherished. Except that was a lie. I had a home. I'd built a new one in Hedeby, an ocean away, and I loved it.

A single tear trailed down my cheek as I realised with clarity that I no longer belonged in Northumbria. I was no more a princess than Baldred was a lord. In truth, I'd become a Viking and a shield-maiden, and I wanted to go home, but I had to see how things worked out with Halfdan before I could make any solid decisions.

'Edith!' Leif's voice cut through my musings, and my heart melted at the sound. I whirled around to see him pushing his way through the Vikings who were setting up camp outside the walls of Bamburgh.

'Leif!' I threw myself at him, kissing him full on the lips and wrapping my arms around his neck. I never wanted to let him go again.

'Are you hurt?' He held me at arm's length and scanned every inch of me, looking for cuts and wounds.

'I'm fine, just a few scratches here and there. Are you all right?'

He nodded and drew me close to his chest once more.

'Torin's dead,' he whispered against my hair.

'I know. I'm so sorry.'

'Father said he had a good death, a warrior's death.'

I smiled at his words. It mattered to them that their fighters were remembered as being fierce, loyal, and reliable. A good death meant that Torin would be respected forever. I imagined the pyre that would be raised in his honour and the prized possessions that would travel with him to Valhalla.

'He was a good man,' I said. 'He'll be missed in Hedeby.'

Leif tensed against me, and I unravelled myself from his arms.

'What is it?'

'With Harmod and Torin gone, it means I'm next in line to inherit the jarldom when my father dies.'

I hadn't thought about that. I'd been so caught up in my own legacy that I hadn't given much consideration to Leif's. If Jarl Aaric were to die, then Leif would take his place and rule in his stead.

'Will you return to Hedeby?' I asked, swallowing down the churning sensation that ripped through my insides.

Leif studied me for a long while until I started to flinch under his stare.

'Do you want me to leave?' he asked finally. 'Are you sending me away?'

'What? No, of course not. I would love nothing more than for both of us to return to Hedeby, but I don't know what's going to happen here.'

'You have what you want, Edith. We won the battle, and the crown of Northumbria is rightfully yours. Whether Halfdan takes it or not, you completed your mission.'

'I know,' I whispered, turning back to look out across the sea once more. 'I just need to work out if I still belong here. Everything's changed beyond recognition, and I don't just mean Bamburgh. I've changed, Leif. I'm not the same girl that rode out of the gates all those years ago. The young princess that was captured by pirates and stolen by a Viking died somewhere along this journey.'

'What are you saying?'

'I've been reborn,' I said, taking his hands and kissing them. 'You made me whole again, and I know that my place is with you, in Hedeby.'

'What about your crown?'

'If Halfdan doesn't want it, then I'm sure he can find a puppet king to fill my spot until the next power-crazy fool comes along. The games they play for power and wealth don't interest me, Leif. A long time ago I had a young girl's fanciful dream to invade Wessex and Mercia and become queen of all England, but that no longer interests me. I know that someone will get the job done. Perhaps Prince Alfred will rise to fame and glory, or Ivar and his invading Vikings will finish what they started. It's of no concern to me because I won't be here to see it.'

Leif wrapped his arms around me, and we clung to one another as the sea breeze played with our hair and buffeted our cheeks.

'Whatever you decide, I will stand by you,' Leif said eventually. 'But no matter what happens, you've got unfinished business to deal with.'

23

Halfdan had secured my uncle in chains in the main hall where he was overwhelmed by jubilant Vikings who took great pleasure in prodding and poking him with their axes. My uncle had the good sense to keep his mouth shut and endure the discomfort and humiliation.

'Welcome home, Princess.' Halfdan shouted his greeting from the raised platform where a solitary throne stood. My heart ached at the absence of my parents' chairs.

The noise died down, and the gathered men and women parted ways, giving me a clear passage through the hall, past where my uncle was chained, to where Halfdan stood. I rounded my shoulders and glided through the assembled Vikings. I might look like a shield-maiden, and I might be covered from head to foot in blood and mud, but this was my father's hall, and I would honour him by presenting myself as a member of the royal family.

My steps slowed as I drew alongside Aelle, and I couldn't resist looking him in the eye. Dried blood trailed down the left side of his bruised face toward a split lip. His torn clothes looked like he had been mauled by a dog—or a Viking army.

I opened my mouth to speak, but no words came. All that anger drained out of me in a rush as I noted the tiny similarities between him and my father. They had the same colour eyes and curve to their nose, something I'd never noticed before. To see him strung up caused my stomach to churn, and I struggled to stop myself from vomiting at his feet.

Shaking off the feelings, I turned away from him and concentrated all my efforts on walking to Halfdan.

The huge Viking raised his arms as I joined him on the platform.

'I give you Queen Edith of Northumbria,' he boomed to a volley of cheers.

My face must have revealed the surprise I felt at his announcement because Halfdan leaned over to whisper in my ear.

'I have no use for an English crown, my lady,' he said with a wide smile. 'Unlike my brother, Ivar, I have no long-term plans to stay on your island. There are far too many exotic places to plunder across the great sea.'

'Won't your brother be upset with you?'

He laughed and slapped me affectionately on the back. 'My brother sets his sights on Mercia and Wessex and is more than happy to leave the north in the capable hands of a shield-maiden.'

It was only at that moment I realised just how much of a Viking I had become. For the ferocious and tactical genius of the great heathen army to trust my rule meant that the last princess of Northumbria was no more. She had been replaced by a warrior queen who was open to sharing the land and building diverse relationships with the invaders from the sea.

I'd looked out across the ocean and wondered about the dangerous men who raided our shores. At that time, I believed them to be nothing more than murderous thugs, but in truth, they were just the same as us: farmers, families, loyal friends, all striving for something better in this corrupt world. My father had tried to teach me how to be a great ruler, but he meant for me to rule as a Saxon queen and maintain the old ways.

A man walked through the crowd, clutching something in his hand that I recognised. He was jostled and cheered as he inched closer to where I stood until, eventually, he was standing before me holding the object high for all the room to see.

Halfdan took my father's crown from the Viking and turned to face me. My heart pounded so hard that I thought it might break through my rib cage.

'Let us drink to Queen Edith,' Halfdan bellowed as he placed the crown on my head. 'Our warrior queen.'

Everyone raised the roof with their cries of celebration as barrels of ale were rolled into the great hall. The Vikings had made themselves at home in Bamburgh and plundered Aelle's stores to rejoice in their victory.

They drank and laughed, but somewhere deep inside of me, I knew the crown upon my head weighed more than I was able to carry.

～

'So this is it then,' Solveig said as she held my crown in her hands and studied its lines. 'This bit of tin defines you as a queen.'

I laughed at her incredulous expression. She was right, of course. According to legend, the wearer of the crown was given all the power in the kingdom—unless another came along and chopped your crown-wearing head from your shoulders.

My friend had rescued me from the previous night's revelries right before Halfdan's men had the chance to hoist me aloft and parade me through the fortress. They were more invested in my new role than I was. Their exuberant celebrations raged through the night, but we were able to slip away and find suitable lodgings.

Although the fortress interior had been damaged in the fire, the layout remained the same, and it hadn't taken me long to locate my old room.

'Did Leif manage to secure Torin's body?' I was disappointed with myself for not being with my husband when he and Jarl Aaric retrieved Torin from the battlefield.

'He did,' she said, throwing the crown on the bed and flopping down beside it. 'They've managed to gather all our fallen men. Jarl Aaric wants to celebrate them in a festival this night if you can tear yourself away from your queenly duties.'

I lifted my head from the parchment spread out on the table in front of me and set the quill down next to it, my half-written words silenced by my friend's sullen mood.

'What's wrong with you?'

Solveig fixed me with a stare that, once upon a time, would have turned my stomach inside out in fear. She had never held back on me before, so I wondered what could be so bad that it rendered the fearless shield-maiden mute.

'Aelle still lives,' she said, bursting from her seated position and striding back and forth in front of me. 'Our mission was clear, Edith: take back your crown and kill the men responsible for the murder of your family.'

'I know what the mission was, Solveig. It was *my* mission,' I snapped. 'With or without you and Jarl Aaric, I would have found my way back here eventually.'

'Really? You think that without us you would have landed on these shores with the might of a Viking army at your back?'

My shoulders slumped at her words. Who was I kidding? If it hadn't been for Jarl Aaric, I would still be a slave on a pirate ship; without Ingrid, I'd be serving ale in a Viking hall; without Leif, I never would have experienced love; and without the shield-maiden standing in front of me, I would be nothing but a young girl harbouring unfulfilled dreams.

'What's stopping you from cutting his throat?' Solveig's voice lowered in tone and ferocity, and I appreciated the moment to gather my thoughts.

'Honestly? I don't know. When I saw him strung up in the hall, I just felt pity for him. All that rage vanished, and I saw a much poorer version of my father standing in his place.'

'What of your father, and your mother for that matter? Aelle murdered them in cold blood. He had your sisters massacred and then came after you.'

'I know,' I snapped again, frustration bubbling away in the pit of my stomach. 'I understand what you're saying, and I appreciate how ridiculous I must sound, but for all his evil deeds, he's still my only remaining family.'

Solveig's eyes widened at my words, and she crossed her arms and squared her shoulders. I forced myself to maintain eye contact and braced myself for the barrage of abuse that would no doubt follow. I hadn't meant to sound so harsh or disrespect the mighty shield-maiden who stood before me. Instead, Solveig remained calm as she pointed out the obvious to me.

'No, he's not your only remaining family, girl. Aelle was never your true kin. You found a new family, a loyal, strong, and loving family, on the other side of the ocean. We took you in and cared for you, we loved you as one of our own, and we followed you across the sea. That's what a real family does. They support you; they don't kill you.'

She was right. I'd dragged an entire army halfway across the world to help me get my revenge, and here I was trying to justify my uncle's actions.

'I don't know what's wrong with me, Solveig,' I said in a whisper. 'For so long I've been consumed with rage and determination to kill my enemies. Now I'm here, one small step away from achieving everything I wanted, and suddenly I'm afraid.'

'What are you afraid of?'

'I'm afraid of losing myself completely and becoming a person I don't recognise. I have nightmares. I see the faces of all the Saxon soldiers I killed in battle, I hear the cries of the people in Alnmouth as I put the severed head of an elderman's son on a spike in their village. Father Owen's words haunt me in my sleep, and I worry that I'll be damned for all time. It's making me physically sick.'

'Edith, you are a warrior. All warriors are haunted by those they kill in battle, but when you enter Valhalla, you will see them again and be able to drink and rejoice in victory forever.'

'I don't know that I believe in that, Solveig.'

My friend visibly recoiled as I refuted her beliefs. I'd called for Odin's help and my uncle was delivered to me, and yet since being back in Bamburgh, I saw the influence of the Christian beliefs all around us. My father's chapel still stood alongside the tomb containing my family's bodies. Was it possible that this was the reason I felt conflicted?

'Aelle needs to die,' Solveig said. 'It's as simple as sliding a blade into his belly. It doesn't matter if you believe in my gods or your Christian god, it only matters that he pays for what he did to you.'

'What if I can't do it?'

'That's what I'm here for,' Solveig said, drawing her sword from its sheath. 'I would die for you, Edith. We are bound together, and when you are in pain, I also feel it. If you leave this land with Aelle still alive, it will eat away at you forever.'

A deep chill flooded my body at her words. She spoke the truth. I was letting myself get sentimental because I was home and surrounded by familiar walls and landscapes.

I was about to take up my axe and rush off to do her bidding when something she'd said stopped me.

'Why do you think I'm leaving this land?'

She smiled that feral smile that made grown men turn and run.

'That crown isn't what you truly want, girl. You already have everything you desire, even if you haven't realised it yet.'

I looked across at the parchment where only moments ago I was writing a message to Halfdan, asking him to find a replacement for me. I knew Solveig couldn't read it, and yet she'd guessed my intentions. She probably knew what I'd do before I did.

'You want to return to Hedeby with Leif and Jarl Aaric, don't you?'

I sat at the end of the bed and scooped up my father's crown. It felt cold and burdensome to the touch. Throughout my entire life, I'd regarded it with childlike awe.

'I don't belong here, Solveig. I no longer feel like this is my home, and it's making me sick to my stomach to think of ruling over people who don't believe in me.'

My friend sat next to me, setting her sword aside and sliding her arm around my shoulder in comfort.

'These people would come to believe in you once you showed them who you are. It's just fear of the unknown talking, and shield-maidens don't fear anything or anyone. Have you perhaps thought there might be another reason for your sickness?'

I stared at her for a long moment, trying to untangle the riddle of her words, but the wide smile and twinkle in her eyes melted that part of me that wanted to remain mad at her.

'Oh, for Freya's sake, Edith, for someone so educated, you really are hopeless,' Solveig said with an exasperated wave of her hands. 'You're with child.'

I heard her words as clearly as the sea below the fortress, but they swam inside my skull for what seemed like an eternity before registering with my conscious mind.

'I'm what?'

'Me and Baldred have watched you for weeks, girl. You're sick all the time, you look ghastly, your tunic is a little too snug, and all this talk of forgiveness has confirmed the inevitable for me.'

I was with child. Leif's handsome face floated into view as I thought about the new life growing in my belly. Would it have his fair hair and blue eyes? Would it be a leader and change the world for the better?

'I just thought I was weary from travel and battle,' I said eventually. 'It never dawned on me that I might be with child. What do I do?'

Solveig laughed loudly and kissed the top of my head before striding to the door and yanking it open.

'You finish what you started, and then you get your family back home before you grow to the size of a whale and we need twenty longboats to move you.'

Her laughter echoed down the corridor as she left me alone to process what I'd just discovered. How had I missed it? My last bleed had been about three moons before, but with everything that had happened since arriving in England, I hadn't even realised.

I set the crown on my head and picked up my axe.

Placing a hand on my stomach, I smiled. Everything would be different from now on, but Solveig was right about one thing. I needed to finish what I started.

⌇

The great hall was empty as I crept through the doorway. Half-dan and his men were out in the camps beyond the fortress walls, eating and drinking their way through the town's supplies.

If ever another English king wanted to invade Northumbria, then now would be the ideal time, as the entire Viking army was probably too drunk to fight.

The thought amused me, and I appreciated how my strategic mind had evolved over the years. As a child, I'd hidden behind the tapestries in this very room, listening to the witan talk about invading Mercia. At the time, I'd thought them all foolish and wondered why they schemed so ruthlessly, but now I knew better. Finding the perfect time to strike was how battles were won and crowns were lost.

My uncle had fallen foul of that strategy when we held back a vast Viking army until he had shown his strength, and now he was paying for it.

The chains still held Aelle in the centre of the hall, his arms raised above his head, dried blood encrusting his shackles and wrists. His body hung limp, and his feet trailed along the floor. If I hadn't heard the soft rattling of his breath, I might have thought him dead already.

'Have you come to kill me, my dear Edith?' His voice was soft and hoarse, but the venom that dripped from his words was clear.

'I've come to talk,' I said, rounding my shoulders and taking a step forward out of the shadows.

The hall had been rebuilt in the same way as the original, so it felt safe and familiar to me. The ceiling was high with strong rafters where heavy iron candleholders hung at intervals throughout the room. Large, colourful tapestries depicting life in Bamburgh covered the walls, bringing some warmth to this part of the building; however, the finishing touches of my mother's homemaking and the babble of my sisters' excitable chatter were missing from the picture.

'Why?' I said, swallowing down the desire to scratch out his eyes. 'Why did you do it?'

He lifted his head to look at me, and I managed to keep my gaze steady. His face was swollen on one side and the split on his lip I'd noticed yesterday had been matched by another. The men who were assigned to watch my uncle were apparently not being gentle with their ward.

'My brother was a fool,' he said. 'He squatted inside these walls, never listening to the eldermen's pleas to take control of more land. He could have been the most powerful king in all of England.'

'My father *was* the most powerful king in all of England,' I snapped. 'He was the most beloved by all the people, he had the respect of his army, and he did it all to secure the future of his family. Something you could never understand, Uncle.'

Aelle spat on the ground at my feet and laughed; the sound grated on my ears.

'Girls,' he said. 'There was never going to be a future for Northumbria without a male heir.'

My skin began to itch, and the anger I felt at that moment sparked something inside me. Something I'd almost forgotten.

'My father named me as his heir for a good reason,' I said. 'He knew the plans I had to invade Mercia and Wessex and unite England under one crown. He believed in me and my abilities to become a warrior queen.' I gripped Aelle's jaw in my hand and stepped closer. 'He knew what I was capable of, and he knew I'd do anything for my people.'

'You're not fit to rule, Edith. You're nothing but a filthy heathen.'

I grinned wildly at him. It was the same feral smile that Solveig used to terrorise the enemy on the battlefield.

'Oh, my dear uncle, you're so right, as always.'

His eyes flickered in confusion for a moment as I gripped his jaw a little tighter.

'I have no intention of ruling in Northumbria,' I said, taking off the crown with my free hand. 'There are many men who would welcome this prize, and I plan on handing it over to the highest bidder.'

'You can't do that,' Aelle spluttered. 'You wouldn't destroy your father's legacy.'

'*You* destroyed everything my father built, Aelle. Your greed and corruption tainted this land until it was only fit for pirates. In truth, I came home for a single reason, and that was to watch you die.'

I let go of his face and took a step back. Aelle pulled himself up until he was standing on shaky legs. The effort of being suspended in chains had clearly taken its toll on his body.

'Edith, you're the last princess of Northumbria, and whether I like it or not, the people will follow you if you lead them,' he said. 'Put aside your feelings for me and take control of your kingdom.'

I laughed then. It echoed around the great hall and bounced around the rafters. It wasn't the sound of a young girl's laughter; it didn't resemble the sounds that flooded this hall when I was a child. Back then, the walls held secrets and wishes. Three young princesses tore through the corridors full of giggles and dreams. The king and queen of Northumbria ruled with kindness and compassion, and there was a unity and peace about this land that was felt far and wide.

No, this laugh was a sharp sound that wound itself around a fallen king and the monster he had created.

'You don't understand, Uncle. I no longer want to rule Northumbria. I have plans that are much bigger than even you could imagine. I shall breathe new life into this world, but I will also share everything I have before I leave.'

'You wouldn't dare.'

'It's already done,' I said. 'As we speak, a letter is on its way to the head of the great heathen army requesting my replacement. Within a few days, Northumbria will be under Danelaw and will be shared equally between the Anglo-Saxons and the Vikings.'

'You stupid fool!' Aelle screamed, pulling on his chains. 'You've destroyed everything. How could you hand over your father's lands to those barbarians?'

'It was you, Uncle, who taught me how to negotiate with the enemy to get what you want. If you hadn't hired pirates to murder me and my family, then I would never have understood how far I would go for revenge.'

I placed a sword on the floor at Aelle's feet and stretched up to unlock the first chain around his wrist.

'In fact, you could say that you, my dear uncle, are responsible for all of this.'

His nostrils flared, and his eyes bulged as I unlocked the second chain binding him to the ceiling.

'Let's finish this together.'

24

There was a time when my uncle wouldn't even give me the time of day when he came to my father's court. He would bustle into the great hall with an air of importance, believing that his status as a brother to the king gave him power and authority.

A young princess curious about matters of court was of no import to him. He would brush past without ever seeing me at all, just like the other eldermen. They only concerned themselves with listening to their king and then plotting behind his back to undo whatever good he hoped to achieve.

The corruption in the witan ran deep, and in all sincerity, it was the servants and honest folk in the villages that saw it for what it was. The people of Northumbria could only sit back and watch as their leaders raped and pillaged the kingdom.

Aelle had wiped away any semblance of purity when he murdered King Osberht and Queen Eadgifu, and now he was going to pay for that with his life.

It was never going to be a fair fight. My uncle had been chained up and beaten by his Viking captors. His body was weak and broken, and my recent revelations now shattered his mind, and yet he was putting everything he had into burying his sword in my heart.

'Maybe you should have joined my father and Edmund when they trained with the king's guard, Uncle,' I said as I swung my sword at his head, leaving plenty of room for him to duck and stumble to his knees.

The sound of metal on metal had drawn a few curious well-wishers, who now roared their approval at the sight of their queen in single combat with the fallen king.

'Your sword skills aren't up to scratch,' I added, kicking him hard in the shoulder until he fell heavily on his back.

As I waited for Aelle to drag himself to his feet, Leif, Solveig, and Baldred burst into the hall. A steady flow of warriors herded through the main doors and circled the room, hemming us in to what now resembled a fighting pit.

I nodded at Solveig, which was code for *I've got this; don't worry*, and watched her usher Baldred and Leif further into the hall so they could get a better view.

Would I have given Aelle a sword and pushed him into a fight to the death if he had been in full fitness? Yes, I would, because only now did I truly believe in myself and my abilities. It had taken a long time and many frightening moments, but I'd arrived at that place where I understood who I was, what I wanted out of life, and how I was going to get it.

Nothing and nobody would ever make me feel vulnerable again because I knew who I was. The last princess of Northumbria was a legend, a character in stories told around the campfires at night. She died in the forest with her sisters, and from her ashes arose the strongest warrior the world had ever seen.

Aelle's sword swung at me but merely grazed my arm as I spun out of his reach and elbowed him in the face. He must have known he couldn't win, or if he did that the Viking army that now encased us would rip him to shreds.

'What do you want from me?' he asked as he spat a bloody mouthful on the floor.

'I want to watch the light go out in your eyes,' I told him. 'I want you to understand how dangerous it was to underestimate a daughter of King Osberht.'

Leif's voice carried over the cries of the assembled men and women, and I homed in on where he stood with my friends. He smiled across at me as I whirled my sword around in my hand, getting ready to advance again.

He was my future, and once Aelle was dead, we would be able to start a new life with our baby in Hedeby. I hadn't had time to tell him yet, and I relished the thought of his warm embrace when he heard the news.

I turned my attention back to Aelle, who had stumbled further away from me and was dangerously close to the wall of Vikings. His gaze drifted to where Leif, Solveig, and Baldred stood, and I saw the realisation in his eyes as he calculated my one weakness.

He acted before I could reach him, and I watched in horror as he flung his sword with all the remaining strength he had left. I heard my warning scream, but it sounded muffled, almost internalised. The blade flipped through the air over and over, but instead of thinking about where it would land, I lunged forward, sliding my own sword straight into Aelle's belly.

Blood spurted out of my uncle's mouth as he choked and spluttered. I kept my hands on the sword, driving it deeper and deeper.

We fell to the floor in a bloodied heap, and the Viking circle scattered.

'There will be no redemption for you,' I spat at him. 'Your fate is in the hands of the Vikings, and when they've had their fill, they'll throw your body to the dogs and let them feast on your flesh, and then I'll tear your bones apart and send them to every corner of the world. You'll never be allowed to enter heaven, and you'll be cursed for eternity.'

His face crumpled at my words, and I took pleasure in seeing the fear in his eyes.

'Hold him,' I shouted at two men standing close by.

The shouts and commands coming from the other side of the great hall attracted my attention, and I fought my way through the crowds to where my friends had stood only moments before.

I saw Solveig first, her hands covered in blood and her face a mask of terror and tears. She shook her head as I approached, and my heart almost stopped. She knelt on the floor with two bodies in front of her. Blood covered them both, and neither was moving. Leif lay still on the ground, blood spreading behind him. Baldred was pinned to him by a single blade, his eyes open and staring blankly at the ceiling.

'No.' I threw my hands to my mouth and swallowed down the sickness I felt looking at my friend's lifeless body. Solveig was pressing her hands against his chest where the blade protruded. 'He can't be dead.'

'He threw himself in front of Leif,' said Solveig. 'He gave his life to save the jarl's son.'

A man stretched forward and yanked Aelle's sword from Baldred's chest, causing Leif to stir and cry out. I dropped to my knees and pressed my hand against the wound. The sword had punctured his right shoulder, but he was thankfully still alive.

Solveig dragged Baldred's body into her arms and cradled him, stroking his hair and kissing his forehead. I prayed to all the gods that he would blink or cough to give us a sign that he was still alive, but there was no happy ending. Baldred was dead, and my friend was broken.

'He jumped in front of me,' Leif said as he followed my watchful gaze. 'I couldn't stop him.'

'He sacrificed himself for us,' I whispered, wiping at the tears that coursed down my face. 'He saved our family.'

'What do you mean?'

'It doesn't matter,' I said, knowing that this wasn't the right moment to tell Leif he would be a father and that our friend's sacrifice was to make sure that happened.

Baldred had been a dear friend since we encountered the bandits in the forest, and I thought my heart might burst from the pain I felt, but looking at the anguish in Solveig's eyes, I didn't think my pain came close to what she was going through.

Jarl Aaric rushed into the great hall with Halfdan at his back, and they stopped to take in the scene around them. One look at the unlocked chains and they would know exactly what had happened.

'Come outside, Leif. Let's get you cleaned up.' Halfdan ushered Leif out into the courtyard, but I didn't follow. I couldn't leave Solveig or Baldred.

'He died a warrior's death,' Solveig said, her voice calm and steady. She raised her watery eyes to meet Aaric's, and he nodded his understanding.

'Tonight, Baldred joins his brothers in Valhalla,' he said. 'But now, Aelle will pay for what he has done.'

The Vikings cheered as they scooped up the hero's body from Solveig's arms and carried him carefully outside; they were followed by the men dragging my uncle.

As we trailed after them, I saw Baldred's body being taken toward the other fallen Vikings and Torin. I knew he would be honoured as the warrior he was.

Pushing my way to the front of the gathered crowds, I witnessed the rage in Jarl Aaric's expression as he secured my uncle to two posts in the centre of the courtyard. Aelle was on his knees, arms spread wide to either side like an eagle in flight. His dark hair fell forward to obscure his bloody face.

'For your crimes against my people, and for your crimes against Edith, your own flesh and blood, you will die by blood eagle.'

The noise was deafening as everyone cheered at the jarl's declaration. I glanced across at Solveig, who had raised her eyes to the sky as if looking for Odin to personally thank him for what was about to happen.

'What's a blood eagle?' I asked her.

Her dark eyes glinted as she nodded toward Jarl Aaric. 'It's an execution worthy of your uncle, Edith. Just watch.'

There was an excitement in the air that felt like a storm was brewing. Jarl Aaric cut my uncle's tunic from his back to expose the flesh beneath. Using the beautiful dagger he had once handed me at the start of our journey together, Jarl Aaric carved the shape of an eagle into Aelle's skin. My uncle shrieked in pain, which only rallied the cries of the Vikings all the more.

Blood poured from Aelle's back as Jarl Aaric began to pull the flesh away from the bone, revealing my uncle's rib cage beneath. My stomach rolled and I vomited into the dirt, but no matter how horrific this torture was, I couldn't bring myself to look away.

Using his axe, Aaric broke every rib, detaching them from the spine before pulling Aelle's lungs out and spreading them over the ribs like wings. I vomited again.

I had no idea at what point my uncle had died. The pain must have been unbearable, but the nature of this act was to prolong the agony and suffering. Aelle's lifeless corpse hung between the posts like a morbid work of art.

'It's over,' Jarl Aaric boomed, giving me a sidelong look that spoke volumes.

I waited as Aaric left and the Vikings followed. I waited until I could no longer hear their cheers and the world became silent. I waited with Solveig by my side because I knew that one small movement would break both of us.

⌒

Halfdan and his army returned to York, carrying my message for Ivar, with a promise to replace me as queen at the earliest opportunity. He spoke about an Englishman called Ecgberht who might be willing to stand in my shoes under Ivar's command.

I couldn't care less who they got to rule Northumbria; all that mattered to me was that I was far away across the sea. Leaving these shores had become my sole mission since the death of Baldred. Solveig wandered through the camp like a ghost, and only I could see how much pain she was in. Her mask was firmly in place, giving Jarl Aaric and Leif the false reassurance that their fiercest shield-maiden was fine. We needed to go home, and we needed to do it soon.

'The funeral is set for sunset,' Leif said as he joined me on the beach and swept me into his arms. His shoulder was bound, and his motor functions had fortunately not been affected by his injury. He'd had a lucky escape, or rather he'd had a guardian angel watching over him.

I looked out at the three longboats tethered just off the shore. Two of them carried the bodies of Jarl Aaric's fallen army, bound in cloth and each of them united with their weapons. The third boat was more elaborate. It contained a wooden pyre in the centre decorated with wildflowers and carried Torin and Baldred.

'Are you just going to let the boats go?' I asked, unsure of the ritual involved in funerals by sea.

'Yes, we'll light the boats and let them drift out across the ocean. Our men are ready for Valhalla, and there's no better way to arrive than by longboat.'

I smiled, but it didn't reach my eyes. Seeing Baldred bound up ready for his funeral brought back memories of my parents and sisters. It had been Baldred who stood with me throughout that ordeal, and it had been him who tended to their tomb and laid flowers on their graves to honour them. Nobody would be able to leave flowers for Baldred if he was cast out to sea.

'It's what Solveig wants,' Leif said as if understanding my inner turmoil.

'I know. Don't mind me, I'm just getting sentimental.'

He wrapped his arms around my waist and rested his head on my shoulder, both of us facing the ocean, lost in our thoughts.

'Once the funeral is done, we need to begin preparations to return to Hedeby,' I said finally. 'I don't want to delay the journey too long.'

'There's no rush,' he said, kissing my neck.

I moved away and turned to face him, slipping my hands into his.

'There is cause to rush,' I told him. 'I'm with child, and we need to get back before the baby is born.'

Leif's eyes shone with pride as he scooped me up and swung me in a full circle.

'Are you sure?' he asked, pressing his hands against my stomach.

I giggled at his reaction. 'I'm sure,' I said. 'We're going to have a family of our own, and I want to bring up our child in Hedeby.'

'All the battles I've fought, all the memories I've made, and right now, this moment is the happiest I've ever been in my life,' he said. 'I love you, Edith.'

He knelt, sliding his arms around my waist and kissing my stomach tenderly.

'If you are a son, I will name you Baldred,' he whispered.

I lifted my face to the sky and let the tears of joy and grief fall.

☙

Stars peppered the night sky as Jarl Aaric raised his drinking horn to the fallen warriors. We all crowded onto the beach below the fortress to celebrate the journey to Valhalla that our family and friends were taking.

Solveig stepped forward to stand beside Leif and another man who each held a flaming torch. One at a time, they fired blazing arrows at the longboats until they began to burn. Vikings waded into the sea to push the boats out farther from the shore until the current caught them and they drifted away. It was eerily beautiful to watch, and I could almost sense their spirits rising from the boats and ascending to Valhalla.

Once the longboats were fully ablaze, everyone began to disband, and Leif rushed off to find his father and tell him about the baby.

With the funeral preparations and breaking down the camp, neither of us had found the time.

I remained on the beach a few feet away from Solveig, who stood at the edge of the water facing the horizon, camouflaged against the night sky in her black leather tunic, her long dark hair loose. My heart ached for her.

'What's going to happen now?' she said, turning her head slightly so I could hear her over the crashing of the waves on the sand.

I slipped my hand into hers and squeezed her fingers in reassurance.

'We go home,' I said. 'We start again.'

In the darkness, I saw her nodding.

'Starting again sounds good,' she said. 'Baldred was the love of my life, and now he gets to drink and celebrate in Valhalla with my father and brother. I know he would want me to keep going. He'd want me to keep his princess safe too.'

I laughed as Solveig bumped my shoulder.

'I wasn't his princess; I was his friend.'

'Oh, that's not what he told me,' Solveig said with a laugh as she moved off down the beach. 'He said you were a real tyrant, always bossing him around and telling him what to do.'

She burst out laughing, and I marvelled at what an incredible sound it was. Understanding her need to make light of the moment, I joined in. 'If he hadn't been such a useless soldier, then maybe I wouldn't have had to boss him around as much.'

We both laughed as we walked, and it felt good. The boats drifted far out to sea and continued to burn brightly, and with them, I realised that Baldred's spirit would continue to burn brightly within all of us.

'Let's go home,' I said, threading my arm in Solveig's.

EPILOGUE

SIX MONTHS LATER

The sun was high in the sky over Hedeby as I sat on the jetty warming my face. I was enormous, my swollen belly the size of one of the pigs in the sty by the great hall. The warriors I fought beside in battle now laughed at me as I waddled when I walked. I was three when my mother was pregnant with Cynethryth and five when she had Ealhswith, and all I remembered from that time was how calm she'd been. Queen Eadgifu glowed at the best of times but even more so when she was with child.

I wondered far too often why I didn't look as beautiful and serene as my mother had, although Leif reassured me daily that I was the strongest and most lovely shield-maiden he had ever seen.

Eric and Leif were getting me some bread from the market traders to try to keep up with the constant hunger I'd been feeling for the past couple of days. It was nice to have everyone fussing over me, and young Eric had been such a help since we landed back in Hedeby and told him the news.

Ingrid had taken to tutoring me in all the gory details of what to expect when the baby came, and as the days crept by, I was confident that the arrival of our child was imminent.

'How in Freya's name do you get up once you've sat down?'

I blinked against the bright sun and smiled at the sound of her voice. Solveig had been sent on a raid by Jarl Aaric but had assured me she would be back in time to help me through the birth.

'Funny,' I said, trying to roll on my side and prove that I was still capable of standing when the need arose. 'It's not as easy as it looks, but I'm a fierce shield-maiden, and we can do anything.'

Solveig laughed and swept me into a warm embrace.

'It's good to see you, girl,' she said.

I was about to tell her how much joy I felt at seeing her too when sharp pains coursed through my body, knocking the air from my lungs. I bent over and clutched at my friend's arm.

'Looks like I arrived just in time,' Solveig said with a grin.

Within moments she had rallied a team to help me get to the great hall, where Ingrid burst into action, calling for the seer and the healers and banishing the men. I could hear Leif complaining outside the main doors but couldn't bring myself to care.

The pain was horrific, worse than any injury I'd received on the battlefield. All the times I'd stitched up various wounds paled into insignificance as my beautiful baby attempted to rip me apart from the inside out.

For hours I screamed and writhed in pain as I tried to push our child into the world. Solveig never left my side and clung to my hand like she was anchoring me to the very earth.

Finally, when I thought I couldn't stand the agony any longer, I gave one mighty push, and was rewarded by a high-pitched wail.

'It's a boy,' the healer said, leaning forward and laying a scream-ing bundle at my breast. Although he was covered in blood, I didn't think I'd ever seen anything so perfect in all my life.

'I did it,' I said between sobs, looking up at Solveig. 'I made a baby.'

She laughed and stroked the child's cheek. 'You did a wonderful job, Edith. He's beautiful.'

I heard Leif's voice getting louder beyond the black curtain as he pushed his way through the healers. Leif exploded into the room, his eyes flicking back and forth until he found me, and the look on his face melted my heart.

'We have a son,' I said as he knelt beside the cot and kissed my head.

We both wept with joy as we cradled our baby, and in the background, I was aware of Solveig ushering everyone out of the room.

'Welcome to the world, young Baldred,' Leif said softly.

Solveig stopped in her tracks and turned to look at us, her eyes glazing over. 'A wise choice,' she said. 'He'll be a mighty jarl one day.'

My friend pressed her hand to her heart and smiled. We all knew that this moment was only made possible because of our friend's sacrifice, and for that, we all thanked him in our prayers.

I gazed down at my son and was overwhelmed by the love I felt. Solveig was right; one day he would rule over these lands, and I hoped that they would be happy times full of peace and joy. He was going to do great things with his life, for he was the son of a Viking and the last princess of Northumbria.

ACKNOWLEDGMENTS

As always, thanks to Lee, Jamie, and Ella who offer me continuous support on my writing journey, and to my wonderful parents.

A huge thank you to the team at BHC Press for all the hard work you put into turning the inner workings of my mind into something special. Working with you guys is a true delight.

Thanks to Sooz for being the most patient, understanding, and dedicated editor a girl could wish for. You continue to keep me sane on this crazy journey.

To my incredible readers who turn the pages of my books—without you, I wouldn't be able to do what I do. Thank you for your support and engagement.

ABOUT THE AUTHOR

Shelley Wilson divides her writing time between motivational non-fiction for adults and the fantasy worlds of her young adult fiction.

Her non-fiction books combine motivation and self-help with a healthy dose of humour, and her YA novels combine myth, legend and fairy tales with a side order of demonic chaos.

Shelley's multi-award-winning motivational personal development blog has received several awards and has been named a Top 10 UK Personal Development Blog.

Shelley is an obsessive list maker who loves pizza, vampires, mythology, and history. She resides in Solihull, West Midlands, UK, where she lives with her three grown-up children and her mischievous black cat, Luna.

CPSIA information can be obtained
at www.ICGtesting.com
Printed in the USA
LVHW112257030522
717861LV00003B/81

9 781643 972480